Evelyn -
Enjoy.
JMManay

By E.C. Murray

A Long Way from Paris

The Tiny Books:

Life Kind of Sucks

and

Writers Unblocked:
Insights from Award Winning
Authors in and around Seattle

AN

UNFAMILIAR

GUEST

A Novel

By

E.C. MURRAY

Any resemblance to actual persons, living or dead, events, or locales is entirely coincidental. This is a work of fiction. Names, characters, places, and incidents are the product of the author's imagination.

An Unfamiliar Guest by E.C. Murray

Published in the United States by Writers Connection
January, 2020. Tacoma, WA. www.writersconnection.org

Table of Contents

AN

UNFAMILIAR

GUEST

By

E.C. MURRAY

First the acrid scent, then the blood. A crimson swamp under his legs, hips, chest—and finally she sees it: the gaping hole etched in the side of his head.

PART I.
March, 2014

1
Meaghan Farren

It should be easier, but it's not. I cram the last cardboard box into my Jetta and throw my whole body against the trunk until, finally, it latches shut. Racing up the dark staircase, I freeze momentarily— one final glance at that frayed green couch, the lamp with the tilted shade, and the thick oak molding that seduced me years ago. No, not even that once-elegant woodwork that reminds me of the Victorian I grew up in near Seattle redeems this mildewed, second-floor dive.

I grab a paper bag off the kitchen table, and call Chumley who's hiding behind the moldy sofa. She's reluctant to leave. She doesn't like her carrier, but I ply her with tickles under her chin until she purrs. Gently, I scoot her into her cage, dash back down the steps, and load her onto the backseat.

I taste the cool March air. A lone purple crocus forces itself through a thin patch of snow while overhead, streaks of early-morning sun trickle through the branches of a giant elm, reminding me that spring in New England comes with hope—hope we'll escape the dreadful, dark winter at last.

The car revs up at first try, and a nervous thrill bounces in my chest as our wretched duplex with its peeling paint disappears in my rearview mirror. I pass stately professors' homes with red doors and black shutters and evenly planted hellebores; drive down Main Street, it's shoe stores and dress shops and restaurants; pass the old railroad track with no trains rumbling by; and finally, I merge onto the freeway, Route 91. Northampton, Massachusetts, is behind me. Breathe.

I slam on the accelerator, fly over the hills, with Mount Tom to the right and to the left, a flat swath of gray cement, a mall like any other mall. At last I reach the Massachusetts Turnpike. I brake at the toll booth, drop my clinking coins, push a button, and retrieve my ticket.

"Thank you," I say.

I just said thank you to an empty toll booth. How's that for a good start.

"I'm okay," I repeat as I had practiced in the mirror for days, weeks, months. I switch on the radio, flipping between news of last month's Sochi Olympics to the oldies station playing "Leaving on a Jet Plane." Well, it's not exactly a jet plane for me. I surprise myself by laughing. I forgot I knew how. My car zips past woods and country homes, and finally I reach the Blandford Plaza, a rest area on the west end of the Mass Pike.

"In a minute, Chum." The sky is baby blue, a lovely spring day. Such a contrast to my churning stomach and the ugly taste of bile in my mouth.

Inside the rest stop, hungry travelers form lines at McDonald's, the donut shop, and the Original Pizza of Boston. Scents of hamburgers and coffee mingle as I push open the women's restroom door, gripping my paper bag, and dodge past bathroom stalls to my left, and six-foot mirrors to my right. Three women flick mascara onto their lashes, their noses inches from the mirror. Ducking into the handicap stall, I click the latch and slowly exhale, sagging against the cold metal door. A limp tissue seat-cover hangs halfway across the toilet.

Now. Now is the time. I close my eyes for a moment and punch in the number on the crumpled paper in my trembling hands. Smile, I coax myself, practicing as if Lorissa is standing in front of me. My fingers waver, but at last I press the final button: "Send."

No ring. After all my planning, my worries, my fears, is this the wrong number? No! Please, no! But, then it does ring. Once, twice, then again. The floor's geometric pattern of black and white tiles blurs before my eyes. I'm about to hang up when I hear "Hello."

"Hey. Is this Lorissa Orondo?" My voice sounds too sweet. Saccharine.

"It is."

"Hi!" I sound like a telemarketer. "It's Meaghan!"

No response.

A stall door creaks open on the far end of the restroom, then slams shut. "Meaghan Perkins." Still nothing. "Meaghan Farren. Meaghan Farren Perkins."

"Ah. What do you know?" Her icy voice slowly enunciates my maiden name. "Meaghan Farren."

I hear a girl's voice in the background: "Mom! We're going to be late!"

"That's my daughter. Almost late for a tournament. Nothing more important than soccer, right?" A slight laugh. Fakish. "Hey. I'll call you back tonight. Okay, Meaghan? On this number?"

On the ceiling a water stain seems to grow, a puffy orange cloud. "I'm coming out there," I say. "To Wilkes Island."

"Here? Washington State?"

"Mom! Come on!" I squeeze the crumpled paper in my hand. This won't work. I haven't seen Lorissa in twenty years, and if it hadn't been for that article in the college alumni magazine, I'd never have tracked her down. Was all that sleuthing a worthless waste of time?

"Brandon died," I blurt out. "My husband. He's dead."

"Ohhh." Lorissa pauses. "I'm so sorry."

"Mom! We'll forfeit!"

"Meaghan, I'm so sorry about your husband. Really. But. . . I'll call you back tonight."

I bow my head, rub my eyelids, sigh. "Sure." The click on the phone is barely audible, yet so final.

Lowering the baby changing table in the restroom stall, I extract a box of "Ink Black" hair dye from my bag. I slip on the enclosed gloves, stir the color in the stinking goo, then spread it over and under and through my locks, carefully wiping drips off my forehead. The fumes from the wretched smelling dye make my eyes water.

I set the timer on my phone and peek under the half-wall to see a pair of green Nikes traipse to the sinks. The minutes crawl as a hand dryer hums. The door to my stall rattles, snapping me out of my reverie. "Hey! You done in there?" A foot kicks the door.

"I'll be out in a sec!" I double-check my purse's hidden pouch: passport, cash, fake ID, just in case—all there. I open my phone, remove the SIM card, drop it in the toilet, and flush. No one will track me down by phone. I'll never know if Lorissa tried to call me back, but maybe it's better that way. The gall of phoning her after all this time.

"Hey!" The hoarse voice outside the door is pissed. With paper bag in tow, I draw my shoulders back and open the door, then skim past a doughy woman in her wheelchair.

"Ya know this is a handicap toilet, don't ya?" She spins, maneuvering her chair with surprising finesse, and I pretend to be indignant rather than mortified. I hurry to the sink to rinse out the dye, scratching my knuckles on the faucet. I lather until the rinse water is clear, wring my hair with my hands, and grab paper towels to wipe the sink, the faucet, the floor.

The odor of the hair dye nearly gags me as I check the mirror. Jet-black shoulder-length hair. This will have to do. I'll chop it off at the next rest stop. I should have done that first, but hey, I'm not thinking straight. I'm not thinking straight at all.

2
Lorissa Orondo

With binoculars pressed to his eyes, Graham follows a tugboat as it chugs by their Wilkes Island home, towing a huge freighter. He checks his phone and taps the Marine Traffic app. "Hondas coming from Hong Kong!" he tells Lorissa, excited to identify the ship.

"Really?" She sounds interested. She's supportive—but she knows that he knows that she cares nothing about freighters. "I'll go get the kids."

Poking her head in her teenage daughter's room, she calls, "Dinner! Where's your brother?" Mackenzie shrugs.

Lorissa pushes Connor's half-open door, catching sight of his tangle of clothes piled on the floor. "Connor?" At the end of the hall, she spots her son in her and Graham's bedroom, digging in her bureau. Connor spins around and crams his hand in his pocket. "What's up?"

"You're rummaging through my jewelry box?"

"Just looking for loose change. You sometimes have some on top."

Yeah. Sure.

"Looking for gas money."

The seventeen-year-old lost his driving privileges, so he doesn't need gas money. This is a battle Lorissa won't fight tonight. He shuffles past her, so close she almost chokes on the pot reeking from his clothes.

"Dinner's ready."

"Mmm," Graham says as the four gather at the dinner table. Lorissa tried to cook a decent meal to make up for all the frozen chicken pies her kids ate while she was working, singing in Seattle. "Tastes as good as it smells."

"So, Dad. Drones?" Fifteen-year-old Mackenzie dives into her curry. "That's what you're working on? Why you keep traveling?"

Graham's eyes light up. "We're looking at long-distance deliveries. They're the hottest thing for 2014—medicine into the mountains and remote deserts. Unfortunately—and here's the bummer." He turns to Lorissa. "I'll need to go back East again." Lorissa groans inwardly.

"But, Mackenzie, I'll be sure to be here for the state championship next month. Hey, we forgot to give a toast to Mackenzie—congrats for winning soccer quarterfinals!"

"The best defender on the team," Lorissa holds up her glass. Graham and Mackenzie and, finally Connor, clink glasses.

While Graham explains his work, Connor keeps his head down, silent. Graham peers up at Lorissa between bites, seeing she's not pleased that he has another work trip. Though her short term singing gigs mean a two-hour commute to Seattle each way, she doesn't mind the drive, but she *does* mind being away from home so much. Sure, Mackenzie and Connor seem old enough, but between chauffeuring Mackenzie to and from soccer, and all the trouble Connor gets into, it would be great if

Graham weren't in Singapore, San Francisco, Boston, or wherever. A first-world problem, she chides herself. The more money he makes, the more he's an absentee father.

"There's this great start-up in Boston with these grad students from MIT. Amazon wants me to see what they're doing. Maybe contract with them."

"Cool!" Mackenzie's the only one who shares his enthusiasm.

"So, Connor," Graham asks. "How was your day?"

Connor claws his rice with his fork, his fingers long and thin. "Fine."

Graham purses his lips. To live with Connor is to tiptoe on eggshells. Okay, then. Graham squints, his gears churning. He might be a computer wizard, but communicate with his son? Not that Lorissa fares any better. The family counselor suggested they ask open questions, not closed questions requiring just one-word answers. "So, what'd you do?"

"Nothing."

Pandora streams the Police singing "I'll Be Watching You." Forks and knives ring against the plates. Wine and milk is swallowed. A cough.

Family dinner. Great.

From across the street, Guru's barking interrupts their silence. "Joel said Guru dug up all Nicole's calla lily bulbs," Lorissa says. Nicole Whyrll, one of Lorissa's best friends, grows pink hydrangeas the size of grapefruits, perfect tiger lilies that last all summer, perfumed yellow jasmine—and they all surpass every other neighbor's flowers.

"Graham!" Lorissa slams down her fork. "I almost forgot. You'll never believe who called last night!"

"That lady who called before my tournament?"

"Yes! Graham, it was Meaghan. Meaghan Farren. Farren Perkins, now."

"Who is she?" MacKenzie leaned forward. "Dad, what's that funny look? How come we've never heard that name before?"

Graham coughs. "Someone from a long time ago. From Ohio Wesleyan. Went to college with your mom and me."

"Dad and I haven't seen her in, what?" Lorissa glances at Graham for confirmation. "Twenty years, right?"

"Twenty years? Not since college?" An eternity for a fifteen-year-old.

Across the street, Guru whines as Jim Corcoran drags him inside, away from the new hole he's dug.

"Meaghan's coming here," Lorissa says.

"Here? Washington State?" Graham looks baffled.

"I guess. Wilkes Island even."

"*Here?*" Their little island has just twenty-five hundred people, one post office, one store, mostly dirt roads. No streetlights, sidewalks, stoplights. People leave their keys in their cars and their houses unlocked and cross a rickety bridge to Yachts Village to get to school and work. "What on earth? *Why here?*"

"Her husband died."

"But. . ." Graham was rarely at a loss for words, but now he just shakes his head and pours another glass of wine.

Later that night in bed, Graham is reading *Wired*, but Lorissa is restless, rearranging her pillows, reshuffling them behind her back. Graham takes off his glasses and folds his magazine. "Meaghan coming here?"

Lorissa crosses her arms. "Well, what would you do, Graham?" She doesn't mean to sound so frustrated.

"If my best friend in the world cut me off, trashed my heart, no explanation given, and then called twenty years later? What would I do? I'd hang up!"

Lorissa puckers her mouth. "That's practically what I did."

"And I certainly wouldn't invite her in. To be my guest. If she showed up, I'd spit and say, 'No way. Get out!'"

"You would not!" Lorissa cracks a smile. "Besides, she's a widow. Her husband just died."

Graham's left eyebrow shoots up, as though saying, Oh, really? "I got that. Even so, I wouldn't let her in, Lorissa. You know I wouldn't. I was there. I saw. Sweetie, you were devastated. Why would you welcome her into our house?"

"I don't know that I will. But we really were such good friends once. I wish I could understand what happened." Lorissa rubs her nose, sniffing the Puget Sound salt air drifting through the curtains. "She sounded so different today. Weird. Not even familiar. Like a total stranger. I don't know."

"Maybe I won't open the door." Lorissa picks her cuticle. "I don't know. Or, maybe I'll be gracious like my Mom." Lorissa had inherited her mom's sense of propriety, the etiquette her mom learned at Northfield School for Girls and, later, at Vassar. Her mom, always cordial and polite, had tried to assimilate when she and Lorissa's dad, a Boeing engineer, moved from the East Coast to Seattle. But the white capped mountains looming at fifteen thousand feet, the mossy old growth forests, and the sparkling Puget Sound never captured her heart. Her mom had identified with Betty MacDonald of *The Egg and I* fame: once a debutante, always a debutante. Would her mom turn her back on an old friend whose husband had just died? Even if that friend had once been brutal to her?

Graham kisses her forehead. "You know I'll love you no matter what you do. But, just sayin'. Don't expect too much from that snake."

"Graham!" Lorissa throws a pillow at him, laughing. They turn off their bedside lights and snuggle, but her mind still spins. Sometimes the damage between friends is too great. Sometimes the pain creeps into crevices and buries too deeply. Sometimes there is no mending, no **healing**. Maybe the saints among us forgive. That's great that they do. But the rest of us? It's just too hard.

3
Meaghan Farren

I'd forgotten the charcoal gray of Washington skies, how rolling clouds cover any trace of sun, how the color of gunmetal spreads from the sky through the fog to Puget Sound. And now, the air, with its constant drizzle, is light as silk against my cheeks, smelling as alive as an ancient Douglas fir. I'm exhausted, having driven across the country from New England. I'd exchanged my Jetta in Ohio for a Subaru, crossed the frosty Midwest plains and the icy Rockies in a late-March storm. By the time I reached Snoqualmie Pass, the roads had cleared, and now I am here at Lorissa's doorstep.

Her house looks huge from the outside, set in a neighborhood of yards and gardens and fences. She's a block back from the sea and there's a large window facing the Puget Sound. I hear a seal calling from the south. Oh, this lucky woman.

I rehearse my line to the closed door. "So wonderful to see you." I remember Lorissa holding my hand at college, helping me make friends when I felt so shy. Lorissa had been so warm and welcoming. Always so sincere. And I was always such a creep. No, not always. Only when it mattered.

If her rural road had streetlights, they'd be on. Instead, a curtain of rain falls in the darkness as I flex my numb fingers, then ring the bell. I remain in the mist for one minute, two. A century.

At last a light pops on and the six-paneled door opens. With her brunette hair pulled back in a band, Lorissa looks as if not a year has passed, let alone two decades. She smiles, surprise in her eyes. "Yes?"

Does she really not recognize me? She's so pretty, so fit, in black tights, a Yachts Village High School sweatshirt, running shoes. High cheekbones, a delicate smile. So, so together. "May I help you?"

The last few years have been harsh for me—true. But have they aged me that much? I know spider webs extend from my eyes, twig lines spread from my lips around my small mouth, and waves are etched in my forehead. Oh, I almost forgot. This ridiculous chopped-off black hair. I look like a freak.

"Lorissa, it's me." My voice is barely a whisper. "Meaghan."

An infinite pause. "Meaghan. Of course."

Lorissa leans against the doorway. Will she welcome me in? I can see her brain whirling as she makes up her mind. I feel a chill slide down my spine. My hands shake. I break the silence.

"Lorissa. I'm staying at the Best Western in Yachts Village."

She nods. Her eyes glide up and down, from my hair to my boots. My mouth is parched and I pulse my hands, in and out, anxiously. Finally, she says, "There's a nice coffee shop near there. Rimbell Coffee. I could meet you tomorrow. Say, 10 a.m.?"

So, there's my answer. No, she's not inviting me in. She's not going to welcome me to her home. She probably has no interest in seeing me. "Sure."

Back at my motel, I flop on the bed. I'd felt so brave for six days on the road, but now all my emotions come crashing in. Did I really think Lorissa would invite me in? That she'd just pretend nothing happened? I feel so stupid.

I put Chumley in the bathroom, where she can be out of her carrier, and within minutes I fall into a deep sleep.

I get to the coffee shop here early, order a mocha and a bagel, then find an empty seat in the back. I pick up the newspaper left on the table and read. "Two dead in a massive mudslide north of Seattle." "Armed Russian forces take Crimean airbase from baton wielding Ukrainian soldiers."

A few minutes after ten, my second mocha now cold, Lorissa pulls out a squeaking chair and sits. We meet each other's eyes, twenty years of separation between us. I fold my newspaper.

"You look so different," she says.

Uh. . . yes. "You look so the same." We both laugh for half a second, and in that moment, we connect as if we've forgotten I'd hurt her so. We converse about the weather, her family—two teenagers, Connor and Mackenzie; her husband, Graham, whom I'd dated briefly in college two decades ago. "The kids go to high school here in Yachts Village since there aren't any schools where we live on Wilkes Island," she tells me.

"Actually, all we have on the island is a post office, a store, and, well, that's it."

She scratches her forehead as though wondering what to say next, how deeply to delve. "I'm so sorry about your husband. What happened?"

I'm surprised by the tears spilling down my cheeks. I suppose it doesn't matter whether they're tears of grief or tears of relief, but now a dam has burst. "A freak accident. Three months ago. One of those cold, icy days when the roads were slick, not just on back roads but even on the interstate. Our little Corolla fishtailed and landed under a semi. Brandon didn't stand a chance. Dead on the scene. A horrific freeway pileup on Route 91." I hold my coffee cup to hide my nervous, shaking hands. "A semi jackknifed." I peek up from my mug to glimpse her eyes. Do I sound convincing? Believable?

"I'm so sorry!" She sounds so sincere. I shift in my seat, wipe my eyes with the palm of my hand, self-conscious and uncomfortable. Changing the subject, Lorissa asks, "Kids?"

"No." Anxiously, I drill my teeth into the soft flesh of my inner lip until I'm afraid it might bleed. I watch the two women at the table next to us. Eighty years old, maybe? Silver hair and crinkled faces, laughing so naturally together as though they've been friends for thirty years. I'd once thought Lorissa and I would be like that. Now a grapefruit clogs my throat and the idea of opening up to this exfriend wrenches my stomach. I can't do it. I won't.

Yes. I must.

Lorissa pushes her chair back. "I've got to go to the restroom."

I think back to the afternoons rocking in my chair back in Northampton, with Chumley purring on my lap as I watched the minute hand circle the clock. *Maybe I should go where no one knows me at all. But I'd rather go where at least someone knows me, or knew me—far, far away, a place where no one would ever guess.*

I finish my coffee thinking, one day, I will redeem myself for the pain I caused Lorissa back in college. I won't ask for forgiveness—I don't deserve it, but I'll figure out a way to come through for her, to atone—as best I can. I will make it up to her. Somehow, someday, she'll be proud to call me her friend. But as I vow this to myself, I never imagine the guns or drugs or snarled relationships in her deceptively tranquil town.

The espresso machine whirrs loudly when Lorissa returns to our table, purse in hand, about to leave. "Meaghan, I can't stay. I have a million things I need to do today, but I wanted to say hi. Where are you going from here?

My voice shoots high. "I've been thinking of relocating. Here."

She crooks her neck in surprise. "Here? I don't get it. I thought you were visiting someone. Or passing through. Why on earth are you moving from—where did you say? —to this isolated little village in the Northwest?"

I measure my words carefully. "Well, you know I grew up in Port Townsend, only a couple of hours away. I guess I always expected I'd end up near Seattle. And since my dad passed away a few years ago. . ."

"Oh, Meaghan, I'm so sorry." Lorissa's genuine compassion surprises me. She puts her purse back on the table. "I remember your dad so well. He helped Mom put together my end table on move-in day at college. Took us out for milk shakes at the L & K restaurant. Remember that? He was your whole world. You worshipped him."

I had gushed about Dad, my only living relative, whom I loved more than anyone in the world. My eyes begin to cloud. "And now I've got no one—now that Brandon's gone." I chew on my thumbnail, a habit that's only gotten worse over the years.

"I'm so sorry, Meaghan." Lorissa stops, as though choosing her wording carefully. "But I don't get it. Why here, Meaghan?" She presses me. "Why in this remote town? Near Graham and me, of all people?"

I'm not going to tell her that I don't have a single friend in the universe. I won't make myself even more pathetic. "Well, after I read the article about Graham in the Ohio Wesleyan alumni magazine, I Googled Wilkes Island and neighboring Yachts Village, and it's just so. . .I don't know. Quaint? Remote, but not that far from Seattle."

"Not that near, either! Sometimes my commute is two hours each way." Lorissa rests her elbows on the table, still digesting that I, Meaghan, will be back in her life. And now her turn for questions.

"So, you drove all the way across the country by yourself?"

"Well, with Chumley." Any talk of Chumley makes me smile. My cat. My wonderful, adorable cat who stuck with me through thick and thin, since—since the accident." I'm stuttering.

Honestly, what *am* I expecting from Lorissa after all this time? My throat tightens. She clearly doesn't want to waste time with small talk. She lifts her chin, and says with harshness, "Meaghan, what happened back then? Why were you so awful to me? One second a friend, a best, best friend, and the next I'm banished. A pariah. An outcast. No warning. No explanation. Trashed."

My pulse races, muscles tense, but I can't say a thing. I smell the coffee, so rich and fresh. "My best friend," she continues, her voice sharper, "the one who I shared all my secrets with, the one I told about what happened with Ashley in high school, the one I told about my Kurt Cobain grunge years—she wouldn't turn on me, would she?

"Imagine if the closest, closest friend stared past you as though you didn't exist. She didn't answer when you spoke to her. Brushed by you in the hall as though you were invisible. Do you know how that kind of betrayal feels?" She catches her breath. "Like you're shrinking into oblivion and you have to touch yourself to figure out if you are truly alive. But you know you are alive because you feel a cold chill whenever that ex-

friend enters the room. The temperature plummets. Goose
pimples cover your arms and legs.

Lorissa catches her breath. "And then you see her, that
college roommate who was once bonded to your heart, that
confidante, the friend who you trusted more than anyone—she's
walking down the hall, leaving the room you shared, carrying her
pillow and dragging a suitcase, moving out. You hear her
suitcase scratching along the rug, and then she disappears around
the corner, and you enter your room and it is empty, a dull scent
of her tangerine candle, and a white institutional mattress on a
metal cot that just yesterday was a bed with a downy green
comforter and three fluffy pillows and even a well-worn little
kangaroo with hardly any fur, the stuffing resewn over and over,
one eye hanging down."

I listen to Lorissa, nerves vibrating, feeling like I'll be
sick. My stomach churns, empty, hollow.

"You know what the emotion is called? It has a name.
It's called *bereft*." As her voice rises louder, I lower my head. "I
locked myself in my room for two days, leaving only to use the
bathroom, although you wouldn't know anything about that."

Every word she says is true. That's what I did to her.
That was me. I feel shame in every pore. I cringe. I wish she
would stop. I wish I could scream "Liar!" But I can't. It's all true.

"I called my mom and told her I wanted to fly home,"
she continues bitterly. "And then in an odd twist of fate, when
the taxi arrived, I saw you with those other girls, laughing, and
you glanced at me, just an instant, and turned back to your new

friends. But in that moment, I saw you. *I saw you*. You knew what you'd done. You knew what I felt. And you didn't care one bit! And now you have the nerve to show up here?"

I don't answer at first. She is so angry I expect flames from her eyes. "Meaghan, what happened? What the hell happened in college?" Her jaw is hard, tight. "What are you doing here?"

I try to swallow, but I can't. A rock is stuck in my mouth, my throat, my chest. I cough.

It's time. I bite my lip, expecting to taste blood. Or bile. Something. Something to put off the moment. But no. The time is now.

"Remember that my dad was my only family, the most important person in the world to me? And when I was eighteen, he was the only person in the world I could trust?" I am whispering.

"Of course, I remember. You said that over and over in college."

"And that I'd do anything in the world to protect him?"

"I got that, Meaghan. You must have said that a million times." She sounds so impatient.

"Something happened when I was four." I squeeze my eyes together. "It dictated the rest of my life." I feel wooden. Can't move or speak. But it's time to plunge ahead. "When I was four years old, I was petite for my age but so, so proud of being a 'big' girl. One night, for the first time ever, I was going to get my own glass of milk in the middle of the night." Thirty-four

years have passed, and this is the first time I've said these words
out loud. I take a deep breath and go on.

I tell her about padding down the broad wooden
staircase, my hand sliding on the railing in the dark, stepping
lightly on the Oriental rug, once bright red, now worn and dirty.
I ran my hand over the top of the velvet couch, felt the rip near
the seam, and flicked on the kitchen light where the refrigerator
hummed so loudly I wanted to block my ears. I pulled open the
large white door and stood on my tippy toes to reach the milk. A
few minutes later, full glass in hand, I clicked off the light and
headed back to bed.

"That's when I heard the noise outside," I tell her.
"Those boots were nearly a block away, but on our quiet street I
could hear them, recognize the stomping."

I stop speaking, reliving the scene. "I froze behind the
couch and before I heard his voice, I smelled that awful stink. I
didn't know then what it was, but he was drunk. He banged
open the front door, screaming 'Trudy! Trudy! Where are you?'
Angrier than usual. Furious!" I close my eyes for a moment as I
tell Lorissa about crouching behind the sofa, my hands shaking
with my glass of milk, shaking until I spilled it.

"Then I heard my mom coming down the stairs, and she
and my dad hollered at each other while the cold, sticky milk
trickled down my legs. My mom and dad yelled even louder,
shouting words I'd never heard but knew somehow were bad,
bad words, and my mom screamed them back, and then. . ." My

heart is thumping so hard as I speak, I'm afraid it will explode. Still, I've started; I need to finish.

"And then I heard a thud. My daddy hit my mom like he'd done so many times before—but somehow, I knew this time something was different. I didn't dare peek from behind the sofa, and then I heard steps—Mom climbing back up the stairs, trying to run, trying to run away, and then the crash, the horrible crash that even today I still hear in my sleep."

I stop, watch a pair of deer cross the road, their heads high. They begin munching on a flowering peach tree. "I remember the screams, the screeches, my mom shrieking, shouting, and crying—then the pounding, the *thump, thump, thump*, each *thump* a different step as my mom tumbled downstairs.

"Then quiet, stillness, silence, maybe two minutes, and next I heard a howl, like a wolf in the Olympic Mountains, a wolf howling." I remember wrapping my hands over my ears, not feeling like a big girl anymore, so scared, so frightened, hiding, crouching, curling inward, whimpering, pressing my hands as hard as I can against my ears, crushing my eyes closed.

"I waited and waited and waited behind that couch, hearing sirens and voices, smelling that mildew odor from the rug, feeling the sticky milk that had dribbled down my legs, and an ant, two ants, three, crawled up my legs until finally someone picked me up and carried me—a stranger, someone in a blue uniform, a policeman. And it was over. Finally, over."

I'm exhausted. I thought I'd never utter those words. Never in my life. Lorissa remains silent as she listens, as though she doesn't realize she's been holding her breath. I tell her about being left at a stranger's house, strangers who treated me horribly, unbearably, like Cinderella, making me clean toilets and wash the floors, even though I hadn't turned five. "I wished I had an aunt, an uncle, a cousin, a grandma, but I had none of those, no family at all, and I wanted to go home, and I wanted to be with my mom and dad, and finally, at last my dad knocked on their door and picked me up and drove me home.

"He acted so different after that. So kind. No more stinky smell. No more yelling. He stayed home every night instead of going out like he used to when my mom was alive. And yes, I missed my mommy so, so much, but at least I had my daddy, my only person in the world, and I wouldn't let anyone take him away. Or guess our secret. Our secret that might take my daddy to jail and away from me forever."

I can't raise my eyes, but I imagine Lorissa scratching her forehead, taking this all in. "So, they arrested your dad and then let him go?"

"This is what I've put together as I've gotten older. Back then people didn't use the words 'domestic violence.' The sheriff was a friend of my dad's, a drinking buddy. He must have thrown Dad in a cell till he dried out and then given him a stiff warning, knowing otherwise I'd end up like an orphan. Those Wild West towns out on the peninsula. That must have been what happened." I squirm in my chair, and push myself to finish.

"When I was nine, in fourth grade, a schoolgirl invited me to my first sleepover. I gathered my sleeping bag and pajamas, put my toothbrush, toothpaste, and washcloth in a bag.

"'Don't forget your pillow,' my dad said. And little Roo. Roo was my worn and torn stuffed kangaroo. Just before I opened the door to leave, my daddy asked me to sit down on the couch, and he pulled up a stool and sat right in front of me, his eyes more intent than I'd ever seen. I even felt a little afraid. He put his hands on my knees. I'd never seen him so serious. 'Sweetie, we have a secret, you and I, don't we?' I remember putting my thumb in my mouth, even though I hadn't sucked it for years.

"'Yes, Daddy.' My voice must have been a little shaky. I was scared.

"'Sweetie, you must never, ever, *ever* tell our secret.' I sucked my thumb harder, smelling coffee from his cup on the table. I hugged Roo closer, feeling her soft ear that needed sewing, that might fall off. 'Yes, Daddy.'

"'Because you never want to go back to that mean lady where you had to stay that time.' He didn't need to say more than that. I knew exactly what he meant. His pupils were tiny, dark pricks of black focused clear and sharp on my eyes. I bet I didn't blink. I know he didn't. His words brought up my hidden fear, my terror. 'I don't want to be separated from you ever again, Sweetheart. Do you?'

"I dropped Roo and threw my hands around his neck and started sobbing. 'No! No!' He hugged me so tight I knew I was safe and secure, but the message was clear. He never had to mention it again."

Lorissa stares, giving me her full attention. I plod on. "And so, Lorissa, when you told me about Ashley, in high school, I was bursting to tell you about my dad killing my mom. I nearly did. I started to. And then a reflex kicked in. You know how some people snap rubber bands on their wrists as their own little reminder *not* to do something or go somewhere? It was kind of like that. A door slammed inside of me. Slammed colder and harder than you can imagine. I didn't just pretend I didn't see you or hear you. You were dead to me."

We are both silent. I need to pinch myself to figure how I feel. Relieved? Yes, a little bit.

"My dad has been dead six years, and this is the first time I've ever said this out loud. To anyone, Lorissa. You are, quite honestly, the closest friend I ever had *and* the person I've been most cruel to, more than anyone else in my life."

The coffee grinder churns again. Those eighty-year-old women with their white hair and tennis shoes hug good bye to each other. Lorissa finally speaks. "And so, when I asked something about your dad, you totally freaked because you thought if I guessed your dad killed your mom—which I can't imagine how I would—you thought I'd tell somebody, and he would have to go to prison?"

"No, no. *I almost told you. I was afraid I'd tell you my secret.* That's what scared me. That's why I slammed the door on our friendship."

I collect my thoughts. "Honestly, I've been trying to figure out how to make it up to you. How I can make things right. I just don't know."

I smell the scent of blueberry scones, just out of the oven. Lorissa says nothing. That's her answer. She'll never forgive me. I swallow. What else can I say? My mind is blank. Pretend like we've just met? That we have no history at all? Our coffee cups are empty. Lorissa's eyes flash to the side, as though she's thinking, absorbing all I've said. Finally, she turns to me. I feel no sense of closure, no idea what's going on inside her head. Is she processing all I said? It's so hard to tell. Clearly, she needs more time. She changes the topic, her voice somewhat warmer.

"Well," she says at last, as though ignoring all I've said. "There might be some houses for rent, but there's only one apartment complex on all of Wilkes Island, just eight units, right behind the Wilkes Island Store. You know we're pretty rustic, right? Lots of dirt roads. Mailboxes are all across the street. In winter, we can lose power for a week at a time. Here in Yachts Village is where we do all the grocery shopping and, well, everything, and it has only ten thousand people."

A tall, lanky teenager in jeans and a grey sweatshirt approaches the table. Lorissa jumps. "Connor!" Her face loses its color. "What are you doing here?"

"I was on my way to the skateboard park and saw your car. I need ten bucks." His neck is bent, and I see little of his face under the hood of his sweatshirt.

"Connor, this is my old friend Meaghan. Meaghan, my son."

The boy, who looks about seventeen, grunts and nods at me, and in that nanosecond, I see clear blue eyes, shining and sharp, but he quickly turns back to his mom. She starts to ask something, but instead searches her wallet. Lorissa hands him a ten-dollar bill, he mumbles something, and slings his backpack over his shoulder, disappearing as quickly as he arrived.

4

Nicole Whyrrl

Nicole unlocks the Harvard Street Pharmacy, her baby, the last of the family pharmacies in Yachts Village. The small brass bell above the door rings as she enters and flips on the lights. The outside world, black and wet at five a.m. vanishes behind her, as she faces half empty shelves of lavender soap and greeting cards and Yachts Village tee shirts. She ambles to the back, past the Prescriptions Filled Here sign, through the swinging door to the multipurpose storage room–office, where she hangs up her damp coat, shakes out her thick red hair, and slips on her white pharmacist jacket. In the bathroom just off the storeroom-office, she stares in the mirror. Not bad for thirty-nine. She pushes up her eyebrows, runs extra strokes of liner under her eyes, and adds more scarlet lipstick, rubbing her lips together. Extending her leg and pointing her toes, she checks: no runs in her stockings, no marks on her $400 heels.

The bell above the pharmacy's front door rings. "Hellooo." A deep George Clooney voice. Sexy. His dark hair tumbles across his forehead, and dressed in khakis and a blue button-down shirt, her new assistant has that hot Nordstrom's model look. "Hey," he says.

A moment passes and she feels that flutter in her tummy she hasn't felt since—oh, forever. "Easy commute?"

He smiles slightly, barely parting his lips, and nods, which brings out the dimple in his chin. "So glad I moved from Tacoma to Wilkes Island. Yeah, real easy, and no bridge tolls."

She catches her breath. Okay, then. "How about finishing that pricing you started yesterday. We have a new pallet of aspirin for the shelves." She checks out his tight butt as he swivels around and steps towards the back room. Sweet. "Oh, Scott," Nicole calls after him. "You have a copy of your technician license? I need to post it. Be legal and all that."

"Oh, sure." He steps back toward her, standing close, too close if it were anyone else. She can almost feel a day's worth of stubble on his cheeks. He pulls some neatly folded papers out of his pocket. "Here you go." She opens them and reads. Reads again. "Ah—it's great to see you got good grades and all that, but your license isn't here."

"What?" Scott seems genuinely surprised, edging even closer so their elbows touch. "Let me see." She catches his light musk, just faint enough to be alluring. He chuckles, deep and throaty, and a tingle flies up and down Nicole's neck. There's a magnetic pull between them, side to side, leg to leg, arm to arm. "Oh, man," he says. "Sorry about that. I must have grabbed the wrong papers. Want me to run home and get them?"

Nicole feels her face flush. What's that all about? She's the one in control here. But she could stay next to him for a long, long time. Even closer. Yes, even closer. "Tomorrow," she says, trying to sound firm, the boss that she is. "Bring them in tomorrow."

"Sure!" He breaks the spell. "Okay, then." "Inventory it is." He saunters toward the pallets as Nicole heaves a heavy sigh.

5
Lorissa Orondo

Lorissa hovers in her scalding shower with the temperature so hot the pipes creak and groan. She's so sick of her daughter's soccer. She can barely admit that to herself, much less anyone else. Heresy! Why is going to the state tournament such a huge thing? Who comes up with these ideas? But it's Mackenzie's passion, and she's a fantastic goalie. The team's been playing since September, working so hard—Lorissa would never admit her true feelings.

And Connor! Oh, her son. Lorissa squeezes the mango body soap into her palms and breathes in the soothing scent, then rubs her arms, turning her face to the showerhead. And her job! So many frustrations. She has so little work that when she does get a gig, it's important to her—really important. This current contract is for only six weeks. Surely her family can survive with her singing in Seattle three evenings a week. Right? But it doesn't seem so. And Meaghan Farren? Showing up after twenty years!

Lorissa lays her hands on the faucet, relishing every moment under the steaming shower. She reluctantly turns it off, ready to emerge from her private sanctuary, only to be jarred by the blaring landline. She wraps herself in her towel and runs to get it.

A half hour later Lorissa stands in the high school office with her jaw clenched, drops from her damp hair trickling down her jacket. "May I help you?" asks the woman behind the desk, her boobs hanging like pendulums, wearing silver-framed glasses on a chain around her neck. No warmth in her smirk.

"Where's Connor?" Lorissa asks. How many times has she been through this?

"You're here to pick up Connor?"

"You know I am." Lorissa is still reeling from the conversation she'd had with the principal, that pompous jerk. She'd pictured him with his slightly frayed collar, swiveling in his chair behind his desk. What had he said on the phone? "Your son got into a fight and we found marijuana in his locker. The boy's belligerent and disrespectful." He'd snorted. "Your son is suspended for a week."

"Great. That will help him get an education, Mr. Deane." Lorissa couldn't believe she'd been so flippant. Her mom would have curdled at her rudeness, but this is her son.

"Where's Connor?" she repeats to the receptionist. Connor comes out of a side office where, apparently, he's had a one-to-one talk with the principal. Gluing his eyes to his shoes and stuffing his hands in his jean pockets, Connor lopes past Lorissa out to the parking lot and waits by the car. Lorissa bristles as she follows through the school's broad glass doors, ready to shoot her quills. Once she's driven out of the school parking lot, she yells. "Connor!"

"Mom! It wasn't my fault! Jacob Lawson—you know what a jerk he can be—he kept calling me a stupid dip just because I lost my assignment."

"Your assignment?"

"You know that group project we're doing? And I had to punch him out, and just 'cuz he's on the football team and I'm a low-life loser, I got in trouble and he didn't!"

Lorissa squeezes the steering wheel. Where to begin? Connor shouldn't be fighting, but she can't stand that whole Lawson family. They're arrogant slime-balls, every one of them. On the one hand, Connor can't keep getting into fights. On the other, she doesn't want her son thinking he's a low-life loser. Just as her old therapist advised, she takes a deep breath. Thinks before she speaks. *"Damn it, Connor!"*

That advice rarely works. "I don't care," she screams, "what that idiot Jacob Lawson did. You can't just go pounding someone because he says something stupid. You're always losing stuff! I can't keep coming to pick you up in the middle of the day. You know what a big deal finishing this project is. Lucky I had today off."

"Oh yeah, you've made that clear," Connor says. "Microsoft made you sign a confidentiality contract so you can't say what video game you're singing on and all that. I don't really give a crap, Mom!"

Lorissa screeches the car over to the side of the road and points to the door. "That's it!" she screams. "Walk!" He stares straight ahead for a moment, then bolts out of the car and slams the door so hard she's surprised it doesn't fall off the hinges.

Lorissa watches him walk away, wanting to call him back, but instead throws her hands to face and moments later, the sobs begin. Waterfalls flush from eyes, her nose runs, she has to gasp for air. She cries loud and hard, a year's worth of fury and sadness and helplessness all pouring out until she is an empty vessel.

Is she just furious at Connor because nothing seems to be getting better? Or pissed at Graham for working out of town again? Or shocked at Meaghan showing up out of the blue? Maybe it's that perimenopause everyone is talking about. Or perhaps her karma for being such a horror to her mom when she was growing up. *I'm losing it*, she thinks. *I'm absolutely losing it.* She switches on the ignition and slowly drives toward home.

6
Meaghan Farren

Two days after arriving in town, I sign a six-month lease for an apartment behind the Wilkes Island store, then head back across the short bridge to the Goodwill in Yachts Village. So much to pick from! My first thrill is a rocking chair I can paint—firm back, soft cushion, solid pine.

I surprise myself at how much fun I'm having shopping at the Goodwill. Starting from scratch feels remarkably good. Freeing. Is this happiness I feel? It's been so long. I think of Brandon and immediately a surge of panic derails me. Can I really pull this off?

But then I find a metal bed frame. I could build a headboard. Next, a funky round wooden table that folds, all scratched, but I can cover it with a flowered tablecloth. I buy it all, and more. I push the rocking chair in my roomy Subaru, shove in the bed frame, and twist and turn the pots and pans and lamps, until finally my car is full.

Driving back across the Wilkes Island bridge, I check out the striking grandeur of Mount Rainier to the southeast, and I feel, what? Joy? More than I have in months. *Who am I kidding?* In years. Just before I reach the end of the Wilkes Island bridge I

notice a second, tiny island, tiny, close to shore. There's a quaint lighthouse. So romantic.

I back my car up to my apartment building's outdoor stairs, grab as many bags as possible, and hustle up. I twist the key left, then right, and the door flies open to my empty apartment and the smell of window cleaner. Back at the car, I wiggle out the rocker and heft it overhead, taking one careful step at a time.

"May I help?" I'm so startled I nearly drop the chair. When was the last time anyone asked if they could help me? His eyes are magnetic, a force field, and I can't look away. I laugh nervously. No, I won't let myself get to know this guy. He's too, too hot. But a little help moving furniture? Sure.

"Just a sec." Jiggling the chair this way and that, I twist through my front door and carry the rocker to the sliding-glass door at the far end of the living room. Then I inspect the man in my doorway—am I being cautious or admiring? Both, actually. His smile brings a dimple to his chin, and his green eyes shine bright as headlights, as if he's excited to see me. And that smile. It's a big old grin, white teeth, perfect for a toothpaste commercial. No, no, no. I won't get involved.

"Hi! I'm Scott."

"Thanks for the offer, Scott." We bop down the stairs, finesse the table out of the Subaru, and with his back to the stairs, we lug it up, turning first the legs, then the top, and finally it slides through the doorway. Without any appliances or utensils or canisters in the kitchen, the nicks in the Formica counter and the permanent bend in the metal window blinds seem more pronounced.

Chumley appears from the bedroom, purring, and lifts her head and neck high, swishing her tail around my leg. Then, in a surprise move, she does the same to Scott. "She doesn't usually greet strangers this easily."

"She's a good judge of character."

"That she is." I'm sure I'm blushing.

"Your apartment is a mirror image of mine. I live right there." He points to the other side of the landing.

"Ahh." I feel speechless. I feel tingles up and down my spine, tingles that I'm determined to ignore. After three more trips, we've unloaded the car. "Thanks so much," I say, thinking I should invite him in for a beer or tea or at least a glass of water, but I don't. This place is all mine, my own fiefdom, and I want it to remain that way. "Thanks," I repeat, with genuine appreciation, but still I want him out, and I do my best to nudge him back through the door without being blatantly rude. "Thanks again." And at last the door is shut.

When he leaves, I lift Chumley, petting under her chin till her purr becomes a low roar. "Look around," I whisper to her. Newly painted white walls, threadbare green carpet, a tiny bedroom closet large enough for my few clothes, although I doubt if it would work for anyone else. I'll need boards and a mattress for the bed frame, but the chairs and table fit perfectly in my miniature kitchen, and for me this little rental is a dream home, just because it's mine. Truly mine.

I chuckle, thinking of Lorissa trying to live here. Where would she put her Cuisinart or Mixmaster or Keurig coffee machine? All those hoity-toity things I imagine that she could never live without, things that I have never owned.

I should start scrubbing the new table, but instead I edge my new rocking chair smack in front of the sliding-glass doors that open up to my unsteady, tiny deck. This will be my meditation spot. If it hadn't been for my meditation practice, I'm not sure I would ever have survived my ordeal in Northampton. This is perfect.

Eventually, the gray sky darkens and a few stars prick through the velvet night. A rabbit hops in the field behind the apartment building, then into the deep forest of firs and hemlocks that smell so fresh, even from my chair. Boughs sway ever so slightly and I hear an owl hoot, hidden high in the trees. I ignore the muted voices from the television seeping through the neighbor's wall, imagining what's to come in my sparkling new life on this perfect little island, hoping that tragedy won't follow me here.

7

Lorissa Orondo

"Much homework tonight?" Lorissa asks Mackenzie as they drive home from soccer practice.

"I need to write a report about the damage bulkheads cause," she says. "Did you know how horrible these cement bulkheads are for Puget Sound? Or for any bodies of water?"

Lorissa doesn't know, so Mackenzie elaborates in great detail as they pull into the Wilkes Island store parking lot. "Hold that thought, Mack. I need to run in and get some milk for dinner."

Lorissa rushes into the store and heads straight for the dairy cooler when she hears a familiar voice. "Hey, Lorissa."

Meaghan! Lorissa hasn't seen or called her since their meeting at the coffee shop weeks ago. Meaghan's cheeks are still gaunt with that awful, scraggily cut hair. Lorissa feels guilty. She should have at least called Meaghan to see if she'd actually moved to Wilkes Island.

"Meaghan! How are you?!"

Meaghan confirms that yes, indeed, she moved into the apartments behind the store. A chilly breeze shoots out from the cooler as Lorissa pulls out a jug of milk. "Right now," Meaghan says, "I'm putting up signs on the bulletin board for my bookkeeping business."

"You're a bookkeeper?"

"I was a CPA back in Northampton."

"You never said that!"

"Well," Meaghan hesitates. Lorissa realizes she'd been in and out of that coffee place so fast, she hadn't given Meaghan a chance to say much. "That's what I did after college."

"You were an accounting major?" Lorissa asks.

"No. Math. But what can a math major do? I waitressed for a year, then went to grad school at Northeastern."

"In Boston?"

Meaghan nods. They both move aside as a woman opens the door to get a block of cheese. "I earned my masters, began working at a high-powered CPA firm in Cambridge, and then I met Brandon."

"Ah." Lorissa did the arithmetic. Graduated college, got her masters, married, then husband died and she showed up here. Twenty years.

"Well, congratulations, Meaghan. That's an accomplishment!"

"Getting my CPA?" Meaghan sounded a little indignant, as though Lorissa assumed she'd been a helpless housewife just making dinner and going to the garden club.

"I mean, you were always smart. We just hadn't talked about it," Lorissa says as they walk together toward the counter. "So, how's business?"

"Good. I've got my first customer, anyway. I think I'll be able to earn enough to build a nest egg and save quite a bit."

"Great!" Lorissa hands the clerk a five-dollar bill. Then, without thinking, she says, "Hey, my neighbors Joel and Nicole Whyrll are having a neighborhood barbecue next week. Want to come?"

Meaghan stutters "Ahh, sure." She's as surprised as Lorissa at the invitation.

A week later Lorissa steps up to Nicole's cedar deck for the neighborhood's first barbecue of the season: picnic tables with orange tablecloths, tulips in mason jars tied with raffia for centerpieces, pineapple-shaped lights hanging from the posts. Lorissa loves the scent of the pink clematis climbing the trellis. It already feels like summer, though it's early May and school isn't out for four more weeks.

"We're all set," Nicole says. "Put your spinach salad and chardonnay in the fridge for now. The flank steak's marinating." She wipes her hands on a yellow dish towel. "The Corcorans are bringing a new hummus dish and Zoe Massey said she was trying a new shrimp salad from the latest *Costco*."

"That will be a hit. Recipes from *Costco* magazine are surprisingly yummy and," Lorissa whispers, "easy."

"Only one disaster," Nicole says. "Torrie dumped a roll of toilet paper in our other bathrooms, clogging them both, so now the only working toilet is in the master."

"Oh, well. That's what a four-year-old does. We can live with that." Lorissa surveys the plates, silverware, glasses all neatly arranged. "It's just feels so good to be getting together." She heads to the kitchen with her salad and wine.

"Jasmine!" The kitchen shines, spotless but for a cutting board with sliced limes next to bottles of gin and tonic. "I've missed you!"

When Lorissa had first moved to the neighborhood, she, Nicole, and Jasmine walked together every Sunday. They'd talked about everything: Lorissa's parenting problems, Jasmine's dating issues, Nicole's work. They'd counseled each other, all with a good dose of laughter. They knew they lived a good life. "A crisis on Wilkes Island is the Volvo getting a flat tire" one of them had once said. But changes over the past few years—troubles with Connor, the birth of Torrie, Jasmine's new law practice—meant they'd hardly seen each other.

"I'm thinking of moving back to Seattle," Jasmine says. "I mean, I love it here and all, and my law practice has grown in leaps and bounds. . ."

"No! You can't leave the neighborhood. We're the 'walking trio,' right?" The refrigerator hums as Lorissa stuffs her wine bottle between the milk and another white wine.

"You've got to be kidding," Jasmine smirks. "You know I'd never be friends with Nicole if it weren't for you. I wouldn't trust her as far as I could throw her." Her eyes scan the door. After all, they're standing in Nicole's kitchen. "There's something about Nicole that gets me revved up. I get near her and I start grinding my teeth. I'm telling you, Lorissa, there's something wrong with that woman." Jasmine moves toward the door. "I just feel like I'm talking to a mask."

Lorissa had always tried to ignore how much Nicole irked

Jasmine. "Well, you're here now."

Jasmine pats Lorissa's shoulder. "That's because I'm a good neighbor, my dear," she says. "And I love you."

Now alone in the kitchen, Lori sucks on a slice of sour lime, crinkling her nose. Does Jasmine want to go back to Seattle because Yachts Village, and Wilkes Island in particular, is so lily-white? People can be so polite and utterly nasty at the same time. Plus, it's a hard place to be single.

Still, Jasmine has never been quite so frank about her feelings for Nicole. Lorissa understands. Nicole flips out periodically, but Joel always protects her, keeps her highs and lows in check. After all, she has the Harvard Street Pharmacy to run.

But Lorissa has her own secrets that she's confided in Nicole. Not just running away as a kid, getting into the goth and grunge scenes as a teenager, but the episode that shames Lorissa the most. The only two people she's told are Nicole—and Meaghan, back in college.

A car horn rouses Lorissa from her reverie. She sprints down the steps to meet her sister and husband. "Hey, Sis! You look pretty hot in that red Maserati." Lorissa hugs Ashley and kisses Graham.

"You wouldn't believe Ashley's housemates." Graham closes Ashley's door. "Everyone in the group home gave her all sorts of grief because she got to ride in my snazzy car." The three stroll under Nicole's arbor covered with sweet wisteria.

"Mackenzie's coming," Lorissa says. "And Connor swore he'd be here." Her look to Graham says *as if we can ever count on anything Connor says.*

"Darcy wants to ride in Graham's red convertible so much," says Ashley. "I told her she can, *if* she does my laundry."

"Really? You're bribing your housemate with my car?" Graham eggs her on.

"Yes, but she'll never do it." Ash holds the handrail to steady herself up the steps to the deck. "She's too lazy." Her sky-blue eyes flash behind her tortoise shell glasses.

"Ashley! Graham!" Nicole greets them. "You're one of the first ones here. Now it's a party."

Joel fiddles with the music, setting small speakers on a table near the grill, and turns on an old Foreigner tune. "Too loud!" Nicole shouts.

In no time more neighbors arrive, then cluster with drinks and appetizers in hand. So much to catch up on after the winter hibernation: What grade is Jason in? Is Maddie going to Washington State for college? How do you get rid of those nasty moles? How about those Mariners? Then, in hushed tones, when are the Corcoran's going to do something about that Guru and his digging?

Eighties music segues into nineties. Graham and Joel, friends since the Orondos had moved to the neighborhood years ago, lean on the railing holding Seven Seas brews. Joel laughs while Graham flails a hand, recounting some old fishing expedition he's told and retold over the years.

A blue Subaru drives by, then turns and parks. "Oh, that's the girl I went to college with in Ohio," Lorissa says.

"Oh, yeah," said Nicole. "I remember the story of how she dumped you." She jabs her elbow into Lorissa's side.

"Shh!" Lorissa says with a half grin.

"Why did you invite her anyway? I mean, really?"

Lorissa shakes her head. "I honestly don't know." She does know, though. When Lorissa ran into Meaghan at the Wilkes Island store, Meaghan had seemed so lonely and lost that Lorissa couldn't help herself. Before she knew it, the words had slipped out. "Our neighbors are having a barbecue. . ." Afterward, Lorissa had felt like banging her head. *What am I doing? I need to remember I hate that woman.*

8

Meaghan Farren

Oh, no. Everyone's watching from the deck while I circle to park. What was I thinking, accepting an invitation with all these total strangers? Well, I have to start meeting people if this is going to be my new home. I climb out of my car, clasp the bottle of wine in one hand and the Greek salad in the other, and slam the door shut with my foot. Lorissa meets me before I reach the stone path. "Let me help you," she says.

There's a crowd of men and women on the deck. What is this? Everyone's dressed in jeans, tee shirts, and sweatshirts, and here I am in my Lilly Pulitzer pink shift and heels. I'm so overdressed! My anxiety ratchets up another notch.

I smell something cooking—hot dogs burning? In the backyard, children chase each other and play on the swing set. "Here," Lorissa says, clearing a place for my bowl between the cheesy bread and baked artichokes—and then, to my surprise, she gives me a lackluster, duty-filled half hug. "Graham," she calls, "look who's here." Graham! There's a familiar face I haven't seen in two decades.

"Meaghan. It's been a long time." He steps back. "A few gray hairs ago, for me anyway. You're looking well."

"You're full of crap, as always," I say. We dated for one measly month in college, but that's enough for me to still feel comfortable teasing him. He'd seemed heartbroken when I'd broken up with him, but really, we'd never clicked. Not on a romantic level. Not at all. "This, you mean?" I ask, holding up clumps of my shorn black hair. "Not exactly what you'd call beautiful."

Graham laughs in his polite, stiff manner. "You've moved here? To Wilkes Island?"

"I have."

Lorissa and Graham stare at me. Suddenly I feel weighted by sadness. Once, these were good friends. Best friends. "The apartments behind the store allow cats, and lucky for me, they had a vacancy. It smells a little like mildew, but with a vanilla candle and a little elbow grease, it's not bad."

"I'm so sorry about your husband." Graham says. I avert my eyes, examine my feet. Graham swigs his beer. "Did Lorissa tell you I'm going out to Boston for work?"

"No!" A spark of panic explodes in my chest. *Get a grip, Meaghan!* "No, she didn't." I pretend to be calm.

"Isn't that where you used to live? Massachusetts?" Bono is singing in the background.

"Yes, but," I add quickly, "but not near Boston. I wasn't anywhere near Boston."

"Northampton, wasn't it?" Lorissa pipes in. "Isn't that where you moved from?"

"Joel! What are you doing?" A red-faced woman screams inches from a man's face. The burned hot dogs smell like a full-fledged fire. He's holding the grilling fork in his hand, but turns from her, merely rolling the ruined hot dogs off the grill into the wastebasket.

"Charcoal, anyone?" The crowd laughs at his jest, and the party goes on. Wow! If that had been Brandon. . .No. I'm not going there!

I turn back to Graham and Lorissa. "Uh, now, where were we?" Do I sound as jumpy as I feel?

"Well, welcome," Graham says, raising his glass as though to toast and eyeing Lorissa as though. . .what?

Lorissa takes my arm and guides me to Ashley, who's lounging in a white Adirondack chair eating a brownie, a paper napkin on her lap. "You remember my sister, Ash?"

I reach out my hand. "Yes, of course. Hi, Ashley."

Ashley finishes her bite, chocolate crumbs dribbling on her blouse, and pushes her headband high on her head. She shakes her finger at me. "You were mean to my sister. I know you. You were mean to my Lorissa."

"Oh, Ash." Lorissa takes her sister's hand.

"Meanie," Ashley says with a scowl.

I pull back my hand and try to slip my hair behind my ear, but there isn't enough after that brutal haircut I'd given myself in the highway restroom. "You're right, Ashley. And now," I look directly at Lorissa, "now I'm so sorry for it."

Lorissa doesn't answer. The awkward silence is interrupted by a little girl's voice. "Lorissa!" She wiggles out of Joel's arms and bounds up to Lorissa, who twirls her partway around, then stops before she smacks a neighbor who's yakking about batteries for electric fences.

"Don't you look lovely, Torrie!" Lorissa says to the child, who giggles, then scrambles down. Then, Lorissa introduces me to the couple who argued about the burned hot dogs, but apparently made peace. "Nicole and Joel Whyrll—our host and hostess. And this is my old friend Meaghan."

We all say "Hi," at once.

"And this is Scott Crowley," Joel pats my neighbor on the back. "Nicole's new assistant."

I feel slightly lightheaded as I stare dumbfounded at my neighbor.

"I believe we've met," Scott says, shaking my hand with that magnetic grin of his.

"Really?" Lorissa turns to me. "Meaghan, I didn't know you knew anyone around here."

I force a smile. "Actually, Scott and I just met. He's my neighbor at the Wilkes Island apartments."

"Oh, funny!" Joel says. He might have said more, but Torrie yanks on his Yachts Village tee shirt.

"Swings, Daddy. Please!"

"Gotta go!" he says, taking his daughter's hand.

"Oh, Meaghan, there's Jasmine. You've got to meet our third amigo." Lorissa waves good-bye and says "Nice to meet you Scott," and I nod nervously at him, then follow her through the crowd.

"So," Lorissa whispers to me, "was that my imagination or did I feel some electricity between you and that Scott?"

"No, no, no." I'm vehement. "He just helped me move a couple of pieces of furniture." Still, I peek over my shoulder and see Scott and Nicole leaning on the deck rail, their faces glowing, a flash in their eyes, smiles that look altogether dangerous.

9

Nicole Whyrll

The barbecue is in full swing when Nicole knocks on the door to the master bathroom. "Just a minute," says a garbled voice.

"Hello?" Nicole asks.

"Just a minute!"

Nicole put her ear against the door, trying to overhear. Crying? She raises her hand to knock again. "Okay," says the voice, followed by a sniff.

"Mackenzie? Mackenzie, is that you?" Nicole hears Lorissa's daughter clear her throat.

"Ye. . .es," she sputters.

"It's me. Nicole." They both wait for the other to speak. Finally, Nicole says, "Can I come in, Mack?" A minute passes. Then the door opens slowly, Nicole slips in, and Mackenzie, who is standing behind the door, shuts it quickly.

Nicole hunches on the side of the tub. "Mackenzie, what's wrong? It can't be that bad, can it?" At that Mackenzie's tears gush. "Come on, honey. It's me, Nicky." Mackenzie sniffs. "It couldn't be worse than anything I've done." That brings a slight smile to the girl's face.

"I just hate being so fat. I hate it!"

Nicole remembers her conversations with Mackenzie's mom. "It's not the weight," Lorissa had said. "It's that every time she grows into a larger size, she gets grumpier and grumpier and shuts the door between us a little more. Now she never talks to me. And she's the good one!"

"Oh, Lorissa, you can be so dramatic," Nicole had said.

But now, sitting with Mackenzie, listening to her cry, she understands Lorissa's worries a little more. Everything is hard when you're a sophomore in high school, but even worse when you feel fat and ugly.

"Mackenzie. Did something just happen? You really do look good, you know. And boy, I've heard about you on that soccer field."

Mackenzie's round cheeks frame her petite nose. Her dark eyes shine with a luster that reminds Nicole of fine china. Mom said one of her little quips," says Mackenzie. "All she has to do is scowl and say, 'Do you really need another cupcake?' Jeez. It's a barbecue. Are two cupcakes too much at a barbecue?"

The laughter of the party below filters in through the window. A knock on the door. "Use the other bathroom," Nicole says in her easy-to-come-by authoritative voice. It would be awhile before whoever it is figures out this is the only working bathroom.

"Mackenzie, sometimes being a mom is super hard, because we love our children so much. We want what we think is best for them, and sometimes our words just come out all wrong." Is Mackenzie following her? "That's why it's so hard to be a kid and also why it's hard to be a mom," she adds. "Do you know that sometimes we moms kick ourselves after some of the things we've said to our kids? Your mom knows you're hurting, but she doesn't know how to help."

"That's for sure!"

"Is there some boy you really like?" At fifteen, there's usually a boy. Mackenzie stares through the window at the silhouettes of branches dancing in the trees. "There is, isn't there?" Nicole guesses. "Who is he? What's his name?"

Mackenzie bites her nail and whispers, "Yeahhhh." She draws it out. "Rhys. A friend of Connor's. But he won't even look at me."

"I see." Rhys. She's heard about him for years. The one Lorissa blames for all Connor's problems. But at this moment, seeing Mackenzie's tears, Nicole is on her side, not her mom's.

"And, well," Mackenzie's lip trembles, "Rhys is not allowed in our house."

"So that's why you were crying?"

"Not really. I hate it when my mom says that kind of stuff, and, well, maybe that's how Rhys sees me too."

"Oh, sweetie. No! I bet he thinks you're hot. You just need to convince yourself. How about trying this? Look at yourself in the mirror and say 'I'm beautiful' every day. And say it like you mean it!" She wonders if Mackenzie is actually listening. "And this is what I do. I carry apples and flavored water everywhere. That way, when I get hungry, I always have something good to eat. If you're hungry, always eat. I bet in a month Rhys will start calling you. You'll be saying, 'Back off, Rhys! I need some space!'" Mackenzie chuckles.

That's about as much as Nicole can do for now. "Okay," she says, "wash your eyes off with cold water so nobody can tell you've been crying, then get out of here! I need to use the bathroom!"

After Mackenzie leaves, Nicole thinks, Not bad. Maybe I've just done some good for the world. She sighs. Well, I haven't brought peace to the Middle East, but if anyone knows what it feels like to be left out in her teenage years, it's me. She's never forgotten how her dad had shamed her, always coming in drunk to her school plays. How she had never had enough money for clothes and scoured the St. Vincent de Paul for fashionable clothes that fit.

As Nicole washes her hands, she notices a drawer under her sink open just a smidgen. She pulls it out, and lifts the towels, shaking them out, one after another after another. Gone! She frantically rubs her fingers on the bottom of the drawer, then slams it shut. They're gone!

10

Meaghan Farren

A week after the party, when my cupboards are nearly bare, I drive the twenty minutes it takes to get to the grocery store in Yachts Village. I stick the bags of apples, lettuce, bread, cheese, and eggs in the car, then meander next door to my favorite coffee shop, with its barn-wood slabs and wrought-iron railing, aged walls and artwork. My eyes scan women on laptops, men in conversation, couples reading the news on their iPads—and then, *him*!

It's been a month since Scott Crowley helped me move, a week since the barbecue. All this time I've watched him through the window. Not "stalked:" I never hid behind the curtains, but we share the same outdoor staircase to our apartments, so I see him leaving every morning when I'm doing the dishes. He hops down the stairs, zooming out of the parking lot early. Occasionally in the evenings there's a whiff of ginger or coconut. Perhaps he's a good cook. I never was. And what kind of cook was Brandon? His idea of cooking was buying a precooked meal from Stop and Shop and heating it in the microwave.

All this time I've avoided Scott, but now in this coffee shop, I decide, enough with the self-restraint. I mean, aren't coincidences cosmic and all that? He makes my whole body quiver, just the sight of him, and while part of me wants to shut off those feelings.

He's in the back corner with a guy in a pressed shirt who has neatly trimmed hair, a short goatee, and a briefcase. I'm reluctant to greet him, but not reluctant enough, because almost involuntarily my feet wander over to their table.

"Hi!" My voice is chipper, as if I'm a teenager running into the football star. I feel ridiculous. Scott's eyes beam. Do I see him jump?

"Meaghan. Hi." I shuffle my feet. "This is my. . .my friend Mitch."

"Hi." Mitch extends his hand, then quickly shoves some papers from the table into his briefcase. "Nice to meet you."

"I didn't mean to interrupt." I'm embarrassed.

"We were done." Mitch, despite his professional appearance, doesn't seem bothered by my intrusion, and within moments, he says good-bye and is out the door.

"I'm so sorry."

"Don't be. We finished our business."

Finished with what? I wonder. But if I pry, he'll pry back, and I won't have any of that.

"Would you like a latte? Mocha? Tea?" He strolls with me over to the counter.

"You don't have to." I realize that this could have started the old argument over who pays: *"But I want to." "But no, really." "But."* None of that happens. He lets it go and I order myself a double tall nonfat latte. Three points for him: good-looking, kind, and now respectful. I've got to stay away.   He orders another drip coffee for himself, and we find a tall bistro table. Oh, no. Now I'll have to make small talk. It's been forever. I hate this part. Going from stranger to acquaintance, maybe from acquaintance to friend. But we find we have so much in common: Yeah, I love mystery books. Oh? Like Mike Lawson and A. J. Banner's. Yes! Even those super early authors. Wilkie Collins. Really? The *Woman in White* is my favorite.

Eighties bands? I love Heart and Journey and Foreigner. But Jim Croce? Why is he suddenly famous again? So overplayed. Like Marc Cohen. I know!

Then cats. He loves them, too. I tell him about Chumley and how I've started volunteering at the Humane Society in Tacoma. "Chumley just showed up at my door back in Massachusetts. She arrived as a mangy stray and now she's my favorite *being* in the world." I catch my breath. I don't want to go below the surface, but I've opened a door into myself and now Scott wants to crawl through: Chumley, Northampton, do I regret leaving Massachusetts? My hair stands up on the back of my neck, but still, I tell him about Brandon's accident. He senses my reluctance and backs off. No more questions. I'm liking him even more. Danger!

My turn. I ask about his past, but he digresses, re-channels, redirects. I get nothing. Still, I'm falling for that dimple, the gentle tilt of his head, his flashing eyes. *Must get away. My instinct was right.* I'm so contained in my own thoughts I don't hear his last words. "What?" I ask.

He pushes back from the table. "I said, 'Hey, it's a gorgeous day. That rare thing called *the sun* is out. Want to go to this cool park I found?"

And what do I say? "Sure!" Oh, brother. I can't trust the words that come out of my mouth.

"I need to make a quick stop," he says. "Left my jacket at work."

I climb the high step of his Ram truck, as big as a turbo jet, and we drive the few blocks to the Harvard Street Pharmacy. "You met my boss, Nicole, at the barbecue, right?" I nod. I've been out of the dating world a long while, but when a man spends more time with his eyes on me than the road, it's a clue. I tingle as if my chakras are blinking like Christmas lights.

Scott opens the pharmacy door, setting off a little bell that tinkles overhead. A rich scent greets us from lavender soap, alone on a shelf which, according to the small signs, was once filled with face creams and lip gloss and expensive shampoo.

"Nicole," he calls out, and then says to me, "The office–storage room is in the back." He pushes the swinging door, reminiscent of an Old West saloon, and it opens to a cement floor and bare drywall. Not much of an office. Nicole, behind a large pine desk, swivels her chair. To her left, pallets with cartons of aspirin and hemorrhoid ointments and Pampers. On her desk, a stack of papers on one side, a laptop on the other.

And how she's dressed! Red stilettos, short black skirt, her white pharmacy jacket open to reveal a white silk blouse, and oh, whoa! I can see a red lace bra as easily as I see that rock of a ring on her finger. I never thought of myself as prudish—I *have* been around the block—but, my! Booma-boomas! Her skin is pale and smooth, powdery, soft looking—thick mascara, fine-tuned eyeliner, and—are they? Yep. False eyelashes. With a pen in her mouth, like she's sucking on it, like it's—well, you know. What an aura of sensuality, sexuality, seduction.

"Well, hello, Scott," she says in one of those deep sexy voices, her smile vanishing when she notices me. She stretches her back higher, as though changing gears. "Oh, hi, Meaghan. Nice to see you again."

I nod. "Thanks for having me at your barbecue."

"Sure. You two are neighbors? Small world, right?" Nicole makes me feel creepy, like she's a spider weaving her web. I just want to get out.

"Left my coat last night." Scott grabs his fleece jacket from a hook. "See you Monday." The little bell rings again as he hustles me out.

I shut the truck door and snap my seat belt. "What was that about?"

"What do you mean?"

"As in, what's going on between you two?" Now that's pretty ballsy of me to ask. What happened to not prying into his world? But the words fell out, and now it's in his court. He starts the engine, so loud you could hear it all the way to Wilkes Island.

"It's complicated. Let's leave it at that."

11
Meaghan Farren

Scott glances at me with a wry smile that's hard to read. "She's attractive," I say, stating the obvious. She flaunts her sexuality more than Marilyn Monroe. *Yeah*, she's attractive.

"Yep." And now there's that grin on his face. I remember how they looked at each other at the barbecue and I'm convinced there's more to this whole pharmacy story, but I don't know if I'll ever hear it.

We drive up a forested road, then downward to catch a glimpse of Puget Sound beyond the trees. He pulls into a dirt and gravel parking lot. Maybe tar and asphalt aren't as big a thing out West as they are on the East Coast.

"Sunrise Beach Park," he says. "I've been here a couple of times. It's tiny, pretty, and mostly deserted. Usually only one other car—that Toyota. And that bicycle. We never see anyone, though."

We? I don't ask. It's none of my business who "we" is, but I can't help but wonder. I seal my lips. That's the thing about Scott: so many subjects off-limits—anything to do with his past, for example. What a mysterious air, almost exotic. And yet, I guess, I'm the same way.

We stroll across the parking lot, down the lumpy field lined on each side with blackberry bushes, to a stony path that leads to a tiny rocky beach with driftwood and a damp, weathered log to sit on. The first thing I notice is how clean the air smells, with the serene sound of waves rolling off the Sound and the scents of the fir forest on either side of the beach.

"That's Vashon." He points to the fir-covered island directly across from us to the east, a few houses visible through the trees. Salt spray coats my face, and I feel a touch of the spiritual. I'm being cleansed, transported by the natural beauty. Scott's arm and leg touch mine, but just barely, like the stroke of a gentle feather.

I sigh, as I often do these days. I'm in a new world with a new lease on life. How did I get to be so lucky? I feel connected to Scott. An invisible twine binds us together, although I can't say why. Up the hill two boys, teenagers, emerge from the bushes. They're close enough I can smell pot. A good place to get high, I suppose. I can't imagine a more peaceful spot.

I wave, recognizing Lorissa's son. "Hey, Connor." Since all I've ever heard from him is a grunt, I'm surprised to see the two boys saunter our way. "Have you met Connor, Lorissa's son?" I ask Scott as the boys head towards us.

"Lorissa, the friend of Nicole?"

"Right. I moved here because of her," I say.

"Oh. So, you're close?"

I rub my forehead. Close? Well, we once were, eons ago at college. "Sort of," I say. I can equivocate as much as the next person.

When the boys reach us, Connor says "Hey," although I'm not sure he remembers me from the coffee shop and the barbecue.

"I'm Meaghan, your mom's friend from Ohio Wesleyan."

"Oh, yeah." He does have a voice. He introduces his Friend, Rhys, a square fellow with a pudgy stomach, his lower shirt button undone just above his jeans. *Swarthy.* That's the word that comes to mind. I introduce Scott, and we all nod in acknowledgment. Connor turns his phone down toward the stony beach and snaps a photo of a hermit crab scurrying under a rock. The boys smell like they've smoked a field full of pot. Still, I get a good vibe from Connor.

Not sure how he gets along with his parents, though. No surprise. How many kids at seventeen blame their parents for everything, rain and all?

"Hey, check it out." Scott points to a bald eagle. Both Connor and Rhys snap photos with their phones as the majestic bird dips its white head and flaps three-foot black wings as if in slow motion, circling above the water, graceful, as though time is standing still, and then suddenly dives like a bomber, splashing into the water. He ascends and flies toward Vashon with a salmon the size of a baguette in his talons.

"Oh, man," says Rhys, his flannel shirt rolled up to show his hairy arms and strange curling tats around his biceps. "I got some great shots."

"Me too!" says Connor. Scott and I check out the photos on both their phones.

"You guys could have those framed."

"Yeah. It's iPhone 3, but it still takes good pics." The eagle was spellbinding, and my mouth hangs open. This majestic moment seems to unite the four of us, like witnesses, bonded somehow to the bird, the water, the cloudless blue sky overhead. I imagine these boys are rebels—I have no way of knowing, of course—but still, they remind me of the old James Dean movies, rebellious kids with a good heart. I'm tempted to say "Shouldn't you boys be in school?" After all, it's eleven in the morning. But of course, I don't.

"Catch yer later." They head up the hill and disappear into the parking lot, while Scott and I listen to the waves ripple against the shore.

12
Meaghan Farren

It's as though I'm in high school, rocking in my chair by the sliding-glass doors, waiting for *the boy* to call—but really, I'm waiting for my friend, my old friend, once my dearest friend. I haven't seen Lorissa since the barbecue. Now that it's nearing the end of May, my faint hope—that Lorissa will forgive me, accept me—is fading. I tickle Chumley under her chin, setting off a purr that sounds like an old Buick rumbling to life, and I smell the neighbor cooking burgers.

I nudge Chumley off my lap, pick up my keys, and hop into my car, heading to Lorissa's neighborhood on the south side of the island. I pass mammoth trees, firs twice as tall as the houses, and reduce my speed, putter along the dirt road, my foot barely touching the accelerator. The forest opens to the four-block neighborhood, little houses at the beginning of the block, then larger and more ostentatious as I approach the Sound and views of Mount Rainier.

I turn onto Lorissa's road, passing a one-story ranch house with fenced yards and six-foot rhododendrons. Next to it is an olive-green house with beige trim, rows of lavender by the front door, a manicured lawn with a swing set on the side. An older teen jumps into one of the cars in front of the three-car garage and drives off.

I flash to being about that age, eighteen, my first day at Ohio Wesleyan, when I met Lorissa. Her mom was so sophisticated, my dad so blue collar. I wasn't ashamed of my dad, though. Not at all. I loved him completely from the time I was five. I was devoted to him. All my life I had tried to hide how poor we were. People didn't guess, even though Dad worked at the mill, because we lived in a huge old Victorian that my mom had grown up in and then, inherited from my grandparents. We used the same ancient, outdated furniture and appliances that she had as a child. It may have been a beautiful house once, but some slats in the banister rails had cracked, light fixtures were broken, and the hardwood floor was black and scratched. It looked like a broken-down museum inside, so I never invited friends over. Since I didn't actually have any friends, that wasn't a problem.

I snap out of my reverie and notice I'm close to Lorissa's gray house. The tall, green shrubbery, the huge windows, the second-story deck. I slow past her driveway. If she only knew how much I'd missed her over the years. That I'd never had a friend like her before or since. That I'd do anything I could to make it up to her. In the twenty years since college, I've learned that friends— true, heart-to-heart friends—are not easy to come by, and if you have one, you should do all you can to smooth over the rifts, to make amends for your faults, to forgive the screw-ups.

Two blocks past her house, the street bends east, a sharp ninety degrees. I stop at the turn and gaze at the woods ahead of me and to my left, the magnificent Mount Rainier, as white as a holy shrine, and then, Puget Sound, a greenish gray with a current swiftly carrying a stray log. I realize this is the high bank, southern tip of Wilkes Island.

Up ahead I see the backs of three women, one with an auburn ponytail flapping back and forth, one dressed in shiny pink shorts and a pink baseball hat over her red hair, and a black woman, swinging weights in her hands as she power-walks. They're moving at a fast clip. I slow the car, my heart beating a little faster.

As I approach, I roll down my window, inhaling before I speak. I want to sound bright and happy, but I'm not sure I can pull it off. "Hey, Lorissa," I call, leaning my head towards her.

"Meaghan!" She stops, a bit out of breath. "What are you doing here?"

"Oh, just driving around. Such a nice day." The other two women wave and speed ahead.

"Nice to see you!" Lorissa points up ahead. "Sorry. I've got to get going or Nicole and Jasmine will be around the block. No one waits for anyone on a power walk, I guess. Hey. Good to see you!" And with that, she sprints ahead to catch up with her friends.

I feel my eyes begin to water, but I'll refuse to cry here—here in Lorissa's perfect little neighborhood, here with her perfect little friends. I do my thing—latch my teeth on my bottom lip and squeeze, just enough hurt on the outside to stop the hurt on the inside—and drive onward, waving to Lorissa and her disgustingly happy, pretty, privileged friends. I've lived here more than two months and she hasn't called once. Message received. She wants nothing to do with me. I wipe my nose with my sleeve.

The charms on my bracelet chime as I drive over the gravel into my apartment parking lot. I wonder if Lorissa remembers us buying our matching charm bracelets on a chilly Ohio afternoon, a foolish purchase when we were both so broke. I've kept my bracelet with its tiny, silver Eiffel Tower and sewing machine and musical note, so precious to me all these years.

Back at my apartment, I make some lemon-ginger tea, and sit in my "spot," my rocking chair by the sliding-glass doors. I close my eyes to meditate, and within moments I drift off. Twenty minutes later, Chumley leaps onto my lap.

What can I possibly do to make it up to Lorissa? I've told her I'm sorry. I've told her why I behaved so horribly, why I was such a total demon. Clichés run through my head: Friends don't grow on trees. You never know what you've got 'til it's gone. I remember that quote by Charlotte Eriksson, "Hurting people you love is the heaviest kind of regret."

The knock on the door startles me, and I hop from my chair, shoving Chumley to the side. "Oops. Sorry, Chum."

It's Scott. Oh, so hot! "Hey, Meaghan." His voice is soft, warm, a gentle murmuring.

"Scott."

"I just finished these old Rex Stout mysteries. Thought you might like them." While I see Scott all the time through my window, we've only spoken a few times. He hands me three slightly worn books, one with a corner of the cover ripped off.

"Thanks," and just then the phone in my pocket trills. I check the number. "I'm so sorry. I've been waiting for this call." I don't mean to shut the door in his face, but that's exactly what I do.

"Meaghan. Lorissa here."

I clear my throat. "Hey."

"Hey, good to see you today. I was wondering, would you like to go for a walk sometime? That's my social time. You know? Like in the olden days when Lucy Ricardo would meet with Ethel over coffee? Well, we take walks."

I can't imagine living anything like Lucy and Ethel—a home, a friend, a husband who laughs and jokes. But I consider her words, her reaching out. "Sure."

13
Meaghan Farren

Two days later I ring Lorissa's bell, and she sticks her head out the second-story kitchen window. "Come on up. Graham's on Skype."

I find Lorissa at the dining room table across from her laptop, where Graham's face fills the computer screen. "You're looking good," he says to his wife.

"Right. Nothing like taking a shower every four days to keep a woman beautiful." He laughs.

I peek over Lorissa's shoulder. "Hey, Graham," I say, before plunging into the deep, leather couch. I pick up *Sunset* magazine and begin leafing through photos of "cabins"—that is, luxury homes in the woods, on lakes around the West. "Cabins."

As if.

"I'll get the kids," Lorissa says. She hollers from the top of the stairs. "Dad's on Skype. All the way from Massachusetts." Massachusetts? My antennae go up as I continue to flip the pages, slowly, quietly, eavesdropping every word.

When Lorissa returns to her laptop, Graham tells her that work is going well. "But you'll never believe this. You know my boss from Boston? He has a country house in Easthampton, of all places. I'm there right now."

"Easthampton?" Lorissa turns to me. "Hey, Meaghan. Didn't you say that's where you're from? Easthampton? That's where Graham is right now. Weird, right?"

I close my eyes and ignore the shiver on my neck. "No," I squeak. "I lived in. Northampton. They're different." I don't add, "But right next to each other."

"Yeah, but here's what's odd," Graham continues. "There's a real estate sign with 'B. Perkins' on it. Isn't that Meaghan's husband's—I mean, Meaghan's dead husband's name?" Lorissa turns to me, questioning, but I shrug my shoulders, pretending to study a magazine recipe for grilled shrimp with garlic. Still, I stiffen. My armpits are moist. I will ignore Lorissa and Graham. I will ignore them. *I will ignore them.* I realize I'm holding my breath.

The kids hop up the steps and speak with their dad while Lorissa throws him a kiss and tells me she's going to change her clothes for our walk. Minutes later, Connor and Mackenzie say bye to their dad, and Mackenzie scoots down the stairs, leaving me alone with Connor. Uncomfortably, with Connor.

"That park is nice, right?" I ask.

"Sunrise Beach?" Connor opens the fridge, grabs some mango juice, and drinks it straight from the bottle. "Yeah. It's cool." I expect him to take off downstairs, but he rests-against the counter. "So, you hanging out with that guy that works for Nicole?"

Seems like a strange question. A kid talking to me like an adult, as if it's any of his business. I don't mind, though. I like Connor. I respect his candor, being so blunt, forward. "Not really," I say. "I really don't know, actually." An odd answer, but true. I don't know what's going on with Scott and me. I laugh a little, directing my eyes toward Connor, and his doesn't waver. "He's my neighbor and I'm just getting to know him. It's been awhile since I've been on the dating circuit."

Now I'm treating him like an adult. What is it? Connor seems so closed off to his mom, but for whatever reason, I like the kid. "Why do you ask?"

He puts the juice back in the fridge, hangs on the door for a minute staring into it, apparently decides there's nothing good in the refrigerator, and closes the door. "I dunno. I've just seen him there a lot."

"Oh?" I ask.

"He works for our neighbor, Nicole, right?" Connor's eyes now burn into mine.

"The pharmacist? Yeah."

"Huh," he says and jaunts down the stairs, passing Lorissa on her way up.

"Oh, hey, Connor. Good talk with Dad?"

That supercilious grunt. A door shuts before Lorissa finishes her sentence. I laugh to myself. I guess I should be honored Connor deigned to have a conversation with me. "It would be nice to hear one complete sentence." She fills her water bottle at the kitchen tap, tightening the lid.

"Well, Lorissa," I say, sounding philosophical in my most unqualified manner, "weren't you like that when you were growing up?" I'd like to be supportive, but one thing I learned early in life: *don't tell parents how to raise their kids*. It doesn't help the kids, and it ruins the friendship. And, of course, I'd found out in college that Lorissa was, as a teenager, so much worse than Connor. And I remember what had happened, too, and I'll always keep that secret.

14
Nicole Whyrrl

"Please, Dr. Whyrll. Please," says the scrawny boy wearing a dirty Mariners tee shirt that's ripped at the collar. "My grammy got sicker. She's in bed all day. The doctor said this was all that would help her." The boy tries to give Nicole a prescription in his shaking hand. Nicole sweeps out from behind the dispensary counter and shakes her finger, her bracelets ringing and diamond ring flashing. Scott watches from the back-shelf corner where he's arranging cold and flu medicines. Nicole's emerald eyes flare.

"Now, Damian," she says. Damian folds his hands behind his back, averting his eyes. "We've been through this," she says, her nose inches from his face. "I've given your gramma all the medicine I can give for free! Don't you come back here!"

Tears silently flood Damian's cheeks and a muffled cry escapes his quivering lips. He stares at his big toe popping through the hole in his ragged sneakers. Scott stops his work to eye the crestfallen boy. "Go!" says Nicole, pointing her long red nails toward the front door.

"What am I supposed to do? What am I supposed to do for my Grammy?"

"I don't know, Damian. Can't you see?" Nicole takes a deep breath in exasperation. "My shelves aren't exactly full, are they? I can't give away anything more. Go!"

Nicole charges back to the storeroom, flops into her chair, and slips a small pill from her breast pocket into her mouth. The swinging door creaks on its hinges. She listens to the boy's sniffles change to throbbing cries as Scott follows Nicole into the back room, glaring at her while she covers her ears to block the boy's wailing.

"What was that?" he asks. "What are you doing?" He lunges toward the door, back into the pharmacy, but Nicole grabs his arm.

"He's just that white trash begging for his gramma."

"Whaaat?" Scott has worked for Nicole for several weeks, and in that time, they've gotten close. Emotionally, physically—too close. Close enough for him to say what's on his mind.

"Nicole!" Scott says, his hand on the door. "Couldn't you have helped the kid? He's crying for his sick grandma." Scott's nostrils tighten. "We can call Fishline or the Red Cross or Catholic Community Services. He's only eight years old."

"Twelve," Nicole says, slamming her chair back against the wall. "He's twelve."

"Well, he looks eight. Probably 'cuz he hasn't had a decent meal." Nicole tries to stop Scott, and he snaps his arm away from her grasp. She stands by the doorway, observing as Scott marches out of the supply room and kneels on the store's cement floor, eye level with the boy, then winces. Old football injury, Nicole remembers him saying. Digging through one pocket, then another, Scott finds a candy mint. "Would you like a mint, Damian. That's your name, right? Damian?"

He nods. "Thanks, mister."

"So, your Grammy's really sick?" Nicole observes Scott, watching that Cary Grant dimple that drew her to him in the first place.

"Really sick," the boy answers. He nods his head up and down. "I don't know what do." He sniffs.

"Well, maybe I can help," Scott says to the boy. "It's kind of scary, isn't it? Having your gramma so sick?"

Ten minutes later Scott barges back through the storeroom door, his face scarlet. "Great job, Nicole!"

Nicole stops slicing open cartons filled with tampon boxes. He rips open a carton of Neosporin, squeezes the counting gun, and starts adding inventory. "Nicole, don't you feel bad, at least a little, for the boy?"

"Yes!" Nicole can't help screaming. "Yes! Okay." She tries to calm herself. "Yes, I feel bad. Besides…" but she stops herself. Her eyes narrow.

"You treated the kid like dirt!" Scott is spitting. "What's wrong with you?!"

"Hey! You can't talk to me like that. I'm your boss." In a flash, without thinking, she flings her hand back, snaps her wrist, and releases the box cutter so hard it lands in the carton inches from Scott's ear.

Scott touches his ear, then checks his hand for blood. "What the?" He pulls the cutter from the carton behind him. "Nicole. Two inches to the left, and you could have killed me!"

As Nicole slides into her chair, her red skirt hikes high up her sexy, muscular thigh, but Scott barely notices. He opens the back door, ignoring her as she yells, "Don't you dare walk out that door." The door slams shut. Silence.

Nicole feels her jaw harden as her fury rages. She picks up the box cutter and tosses it with full strength against the carton. Hell, she'd been the dart queen in the bars in Bellingham when she was in college. Did Scott really think she'd hurt him? Idiot!

She returns to her desk and lifts the top bill on the pile for insurance reimbursements. The pile shrinks every day. This pharmacy is slipping through her fingers like all the other small family pharmacies failing in America. She should never have hired Scott—certainly not full time, not before checking references or even his license. She knows she made a mistake, but can't help herself around that wry grin, those eyes that laugh at the world around him, that tight butt.

Once she'd hired Scott, work became fun again. She loves her job like she did when she first bought the pharmacy. She and Scott—they connect in a way that's different from how she and Joel do. Sure, she still loves Joel, at least she thinks she does, but Scott! Scott is something different altogether.

A half hour later, a whish of wind through the backdoor ruffles Nicole's papers. Scott comes in and goes straight to the pallets where he picks up the counter, clicking to count the boxes of diapers. Nicole swivels her chair back and forth. He moves on to the pallet of tampons, his body stiff, his eyes on his job. Click, click, click.

"Okay, Scott," she says, a little too loudly. "Yes. Yes, I was hard on the kid. Sorry. Okay? I'm sorry!" Trying to sound like a sensuous Jennifer Lawrence, she slips out of her chair and attempts to circle her arms around his chest, but he brushes her away.

"Forgive me?" she pleads, her pharmacy jacket falling open to her silk blouse, the V reaching to her cleavage. Scott's eyes strip her from her pearl necklace to her plunging round breasts, tight skirt, and pointed stilettos. "Scott, if we're going to be working together, we need to get over this...this hump."

She waits. "Look," she continues. "We need to talk. The park? A different environment where we can talk rationally."

Finally, he explodes. "You almost killed me! What's there to talk about?"

"Please! Let me explain. The park after work. Okay?" He appears to think about it. Nicole taps her nails against her desk impatiently, then catches herself and stops. "Alright," he says at last.

Nicole phones Joel to say she'll be late, and at 6:30 flips the window's "Open" sign to "Closed." With Scott following in his Ram truck, she drives around the bay, over the wooded hills to Sunrise Beach Park. Nicole loves the scent of the fresh cedar trees that border the field leading down to the beach.

"So, Nicole," Scott snaps. "What's this all about?" They've been here many times, but never like this, in anger and rage. Nicole is determined to bring back the loving feelings. As they lumber down the hill toward the water, an eagle glides by, its wing spread wide as it soars over the Sound, hunting for prey in the water below. Clouds pepper the pale purple sky.

The breeze invigorates them, and he seems to soften. They stare at the sparkling of lights of Tacoma and Vashon Island across Puget Sound.

"I don't know," she says, her voice faint. "I just kind of flip out sometimes." As she reaches for his arm, he pulls away. "I had a bit of a hard life, and every blue moon I snap."

"Nicole," Scott steps backward. "Who hasn't had a hard life? You nearly killed me. You got that? Nearly killed me."

"I know it seems that way, but really, Scott, I was a dart champ."

He doesn't seem convinced. "Let me guess. Your dad beat your mom."

Nicole nods.

"And you were ashamed and embarrassed and swore you'd never be like them, and you'd get as far away from them as you could."

"Okay!" Nicole feels herself starting to lose it again. "You get it. It's a story that's been told in every backwoods in America. But damn it, I made it! I worked my way through school, I bought the Harvard Street Pharmacy, and now I'm afraid I'm losing it. Don't you notice the shelves are half full? I'll be lucky if we hold out until the end of the year!"

"And that's a reason to almost kill me?" Even though his words sound accusing, she feels him warming toward her. Their bodies drift closer.

Nicole speaks in earnest. "I am really sorry about that, Scott. I really am. I don't know, I just…"

"You just saw yourself in that little poor boy, but you…you never begged for anything."

Now Nicole bursts out laughing. "You're saying it's just Psychology 101?"

"I'm saying that box cutter nearly killed me."

Nicole puts her arms around his waist, and this time Scott hesitates only a moment, then hugs her back. She tips her head back and feels his lips on hers, his tongue in her mouth. *Ahh. Just where we belong.*

15
Meaghan Farren

"Ready?" Lorissa snatches her five-pound weights from the kitchen shelf, and we begin to walk down the middle of her dirt road, where not a single car goes by. My stomach is in knots. I'm not sure how to act, how to behave, but Lorissa seems so casual. The neighbor's dog barks a hello with his furry thick tail flopping. "Guru Corcoran," she nods toward him. "His invisible-fence batteries must be working today. He's usually all over the neighborhood, digging, bringing toys, gloves, even hand tools, and carrying them back to his yard." Today he doesn't stray from the Corcoran's lawn.

"I was so glad you called," I say, feeling it was a lot easier to make conversation with Scott, a stranger, than with Lorissa. "So, when did you move here?" I ask tentatively.

"When I left Ohio Wesleyan at the end of freshman year, I came back to Washington State to be close to my sister, Ashley, and my mom. They helped me so much after. . .well, you know." She could have said *After you betrayed me at college. Devastated me. Ruined me.* I feel like a snake is slithering down my spine. I've tried so hard to block out that part of my life.

Lorissa tells me she finished up college at the University of Washington and, on her mom's insistence, moved to New York to follow her dreams. "Maybe because she never did. I mean, Mom had such aspirations, so many hopes. Anyway, she said, 'Go to New York. Give it a try!'" Lorissa's eyes glaze, lost in reflection for a moment. "So that's why I applied to Juilliard."

"You went to Juilliard? That's fantastic! That was your dream, even way back when we were fresh. . ." I stop myself. No. No college talk. "And you ended up here?" I ask. Once the words tumble out of my mouth, I regret it. "I mean. . ."

"Oh, I know what you mean. After all those years, and expense, at the best music school in the country, maybe the world, what am I doing with my singing? On Wilkes Island in Washington *State*? Not even DC?"

I grit my teeth. Well, yeah. That's exactly what I meant. From New York, she says, she studied music and theater at Juilliard, then summer stock out in the Berkshires, where she reconnected with Graham. "It was *A Midsummer's Night's Dream*, which is—well, you know, such a fun play. Serendipity running into Graham? Fate? Something. Ironic, though, right?

"He still loved singing and acting, but at the time was in grad school for computer science at NYU. This fling in the Berkshires was his grand finale before he poured all his energy into software development."

"And you guys moved from New York to this little island?" I try not to sound too flabbergasted.

"Dated, married, had our kids, and then, yeah, when Mackenzie turned one, we came back home to the Northwest."

How much should I pry? How much should I keep my mouth shut? I'm stalling, of course. There's an elephant in the room—exactly how I hurt her, and yet I'm so curious about her singing. "Do you miss New York?"

Lorissa looks past me up the deserted road. "Well, yeah. You know: the greatest art community in the world. Singers, painters, writers. Galleries and concerts and readings. I loved that. And the food! The best Chinese delivered to the door." She sighs. "You know you can't even get a pizza delivered to Wilkes Island? Only to the boat launch!" Lorissa chuckles. "And New York! You just say the words and it feels exciting."

She finally exhales, as though returning from a trance. "But this—little Yachts Village and littler Wilkes Island—this feels good for me, for Graham, for the kids." A bird in a fir tree coos as we walk by. "There's a give and take to everything, right? Still, Graham and I moved back here because Mom and Ashley lived just north of here in Port Orchard, until Mom passed away two years ago."

"Lorissa, I'm so sorry. Your mom was so. . .so elegant." I can still see Lorissa's mom on moving day the first year of college, her auburn hair neatly pulled up in a bun Katherine Hepburn style, pressed wool pants, leather loafers. Was she wearing a silk blouse and pearls? Probably, even on college move-in day. Stunning.

"Thanks." Lorissa draws me out of my memories. "She was, wasn't she? I may have grown up here in the boonies of Washington State, but I inherited at least a bit from my mom. Maybe you remember that after she and my dad divorced when I was eleven, Mom considered moving back East. Anyway, you know what happened," Lorissa stammers.

Yes, I know exactly why her mom stayed here. My stomach knots, thinking about it. "Simple twists of fate can carry us in directions we least expect," I say.

Lorissa swings her hand weights and I'm having trouble keeping up. "But you're singing?" I ask with excitement. "Singing is what you wanted, right?"

"Oh, I'm still singing. Yes. I'm singing on—wait for it—video games. Yep." It's as though I hear her thoughts: *Can you believe it?* "Of course, there's a one- or two-hour commute, depending on traffic, and the gigs are only six to eight weeks at a time." She's speaking faster and faster, building herself up into a frenzy.

"Here's the thing," she says. "I enjoy the singing. Sure. I like being with people from my 'tribe.' Singers. Okay? But you know, even with this, I get screwed. I did a super famous video game—all of Connor's friends play it—and it paid a decent amount. But at the time, I had to sign five pages—*five pages*—of nondisclosures, et cetera, et cetera, legal papers basically giving away my rights. And now the video game is a movie. And my voice is on it. And I don't get a cent. Not one cent!"

Her face is scarlet, on fire. She's enraged. I try to think of an intelligent, educated response. "Well, that sucks."

To my surprise, Lorissa grins with a spontaneous puff of a laugh, and once again we have a tiny moment of being the close friends we once were. "I guess I needed to get that off my chest. But you know me." She pauses for a moment, as though reflecting on those words. I do know her, I think. Even after no communication in twenty years. "Singing is my passion. My release. My—oh, I don't know. It's just in my soul and I need to do it." Lorissa is close to crying and I'd give her a hug if I felt an ounce more comfortable.

"So," says Lorissa. "That's my story." She forces a smile.

"How's Ash doing without your mom?" I ask. On college

move-in day, I hadn't realized at first that Lorissa's sister had Down syndrome. She was chatty and friendly and huggy, and boy, did she love her big sister.

"She's doing well." Lorissa lightens up for the first time all morning, always the devoted sister. "She likes her roommates and the staff at her group home."

I hear songs from a nuthatch and a chickadee. There must be all sorts of nests in the trees. "Puget Sound is rougher over there"—she points through the woods at the corner of the street— "but that's where the seals hang out on the rocks and whales pass in spring."

What a paradise!

"So," I don't want to push it, be intrusive, but I'm so curious, "what's going on with Connor?"

Lorissa continues several steps before she answers. "I'm crossing my fingers about him. Over the years, I've said 'Boys will be boys,' glossing things over. He's got ADHD, for one thing. Kicked out of public high school, but now he's at the alternative school and still fights with other kids and reeks of pot every day. Back in middle school, he started a fire with that delinquent friend of his, Rhys."

Lorissa is talking to me! She's telling me what's really going on, below the surface of this perfect life of hers! "He gets in so much trouble, ever since middle school," she continues, "and we finally started him on ADHD meds.

"Jasmine—my neighbor who's a lawyer for kids at Grayson Center, the juvenile detention center—anyway, she convinced me about the meds, and Graham has a friend who said the same thing. His son improved, I mean. Meds aren't for everyone, and Graham and I always thought we should be able to handle Connor. Who wants to put their kid on drugs? But honestly, we've tried everything else for years."

A doe and her fawn cross the street, from one neighbor's yard to another, as though we weren't ten feet away. "Between that and his new counselor, I think maybe Connor's turned the corner. We took away his car privileges after his last screwup, and now he's riding his bike all over."

"I saw him and Rhys at the park the other day."

"Oh? He didn't—well, of course, he wouldn't mention it. I wish I could keep that creep Rhys away from him."

Then I guess I won't mention that they reeked of pot.

"So, you met Rhys? God, I hate that kid. If it weren't for him, Connor would never have gotten into so many fights at school. Never would have gotten kicked out over and over. He was a good kid before Rhys." She's spitting, literally spitting as she walks.

Now, I'm running trying to keep up. She wipes her mouth and slows down, changing the subject. "That's Jasmine's house," she points. Bunches of daisies flourish along the edge of the road next to her mailbox.

"Connor and Rhys were taking photos of an eagle," I say, trying to spin the boys in a positive light. Why? I don't know. I naturally root for the underdog, the one in trouble, the runt of the litter.

"Mmm. Maybe that will keep them out of trouble." Lorissa sounds like a curmudgeonly old man. Somehow, I doubt if a camera phone is going to keep anyone out of trouble.

"Actually," Lorissa continues, "I'm worried about how much Mackenzie asks Connor about Rhys. 'Was Rhys in school today?' 'I saw Rhys got a new car.' 'Do you know what Rhys's doing this weekend?'"

"Mackenzie's fifteen?"

Lorissa nods. "Thank God for the never-ending soccer to keep her busy."

"Never-ending?"

She picks up her pace again, and now she's a full five strides ahead, but then she abruptly stops. "Okay. Here you go. I sometimes turn up my shower till it is scalding, till the pipes groan, and you know what I'd think? I'd wish Mackenzie's soccer team would lose. These guys act like soccer is as important as running water, and since I'm the one who 'doesn't work'—*ha*! —I do all the carpooling. And Graham's working out of town again." She doesn't take a breath. "I mean, it's great he loves his work and all, but I love my work, too, and I miss it. I miss it a lot."

I'm trying to be compassionate, listening to Lorissa, but, honestly, is this all she has to complain about? Okay, I've got to improve my empathy skills, I'm first to admit it. But here's the important thing: she's telling me how she really feels, so maybe, just maybe, we can reconnect. I'm not sure where I stand, but as long as she's talking, I'll listen.

The sun shoves its way through the clouds, and I draw my sunglasses from my pocket and wipe them off with my tee shirt, surprised they're not more scratched.

"Hey, I do have good news," she says. "I've got a contract for this coming fall, starting in October."

"Congratulations! A new singing contract?"

"For a sequel to some video game that's a huge seller that Connor always talks about. I'm so excited. I won't work all summer, and when it starts, I'll need to drive to Seattle every day for a while, which is a pain, but I can deal with it. Apparently, this game is a big deal. Still confidential, of course."

"Cool."

Lorissa sighs. "If Connor's medicine kicks in and that new counselor helps, Connor can drive Mackenzie to some of her practices. It won't matter so much that Graham is traveling all the time." She rolls her eyes and groans. "And I mean *all* the time."

I actually do understand how much Lorissa's work means to her. Her kids should take more responsibility, I think, but who am I to say.

"It pays well, too," she says. "Well, not enough for mortgage, cars, soccer. But maybe a weekend retreat. A trip to

Hawaii. Golden beaches, turquoise waves, Mai-tais. I'd love to
be steamy hot, reading a beach book under a sun umbrella,
diving in the waves to cool off." It's as though she's already
drifted to the tropics. "I can't wait to see my old singing friends.
This is a strict contract, though. Can't miss a single session, or
I'm out."

"Not one?"

"Not one day. They stipulate that in bold letters. '*Not one
absence.*' Nerve-racking, actually. What if the car stalls? An
accident on I-5? I'll leave, like, *three* hours early." She laughs. "I
guess it's crazy how excited I am."

We hustle around the neighborhood, past ten-foot-high
rhododendrons. "Check out Nicole's garden." Lorissa points to
hydrangeas blue as sapphires. "Always wins number one on the
Wilkes Island Garden Tour."

"I saw your friend Nicole again. She runs her own
pharmacy?" I'm particularly curious about her, now that I've
seen Scott a few times. He's getting under my skin, and I can't
help but wonder about his working in such tight quarters with
that woman. I mean,

I can still see that lacy red bra. Really? It would be one
thing at a Victoria's Secret fashion show, but at a pharmacy?
That you own? And then stilettoes to match? Who wears
stilettoes to work? I've thought about it more than I'd care to
admit. Surely, she comes on to him.

"Nicole's husband, Joel," says Lorissa, "is a house
husband, that lucky girl. He's great. Does everything around the

house. I mean, everything. Nicole and I used to talk every single day before she had her baby, but it's been awhile. I'm godmother to their daughter, Torrie, who's four now." Nicole's lawn is immaculate, so green, trees ringed with primroses.

"We're still close, even though she does break into rants on occasion." Lorissa describes nights she and Graham used to go out with Joel and Nicole to movies, comedy clubs, and concerts. Then, after Nicole and Joel had Torrie, they all stayed home Sunday nights playing games. "Joel's the smartest one in the neighborhood. No matter what we played—Yahtzee, Scrabble, yes, even Hearts— he always won."

I don't get it. "So, what's Joel doing with someone like Nicole?"

Lorissa rolls her eyes. "Come on, Meaghan. What do you think?"

"Trophy wife?"

"The guy grew up dirt-poor out on the Key Peninsula, in a trailer. Then his mom lived in a cabin somewhere. Lake Cushman up in the mountains, maybe?"

I chuckled. "Got it."

"Joel ended up with a full ride to the University of Washington. From there to Microsoft, then Intel. He's the brains, and she's the beauty, and he holds on to her like duct tape. She can do no wrong in his eyes."

I want to talk about Scott, tell Lorissa that my heart flits every time I see his truck drive into the apartment parking lot. When Scott and I talk, he stares so deeply into my eyes, I feel lightheaded. I'm falling big-time.

"There will be zillions of blackberries here in a month or two," Lorissa says, looking at the roadside bushes. "So, you saw Nicole at the pharmacy?"

"I saw her a while ago when I was with Scott. Scott, my neighbor. Actually, I've been seeing him a fair amount lately." Next thing I know, I'm pouring out all the feelings that I've held back. It's like Lorissa and I are back in the dorm room, sitting with our legs crossed on the lumpy mattresses, our backs propped against the yellow-painted cinder-block wall, confessing our crushes while Allman Brothers tunes play in the background.

"Soooo." Lorissa drags out her question. "You ready to take it to the next level with Scott? Or have you?"

Will I ever be ready? Will I ever get over what happened with Brandon? On one hand, I'm anxious about getting too close to anyone—Lorissa *or* Scott. On the other, I've made it this far. When it comes right down to it, I'm a survivor: a strong, hearty survivor. So why do I forget that sometimes? Forget my own strength?

"A couple of dates, that's all," I say. Ha! That's all? The truth is, I go gaga just thinking about him. "We saw an indie film at the Grand in Tacoma. He held my hand—we didn't kiss—but I felt a volt. I think I hesitated a second, but then. . ." Does Lorissa understand? How gentle he felt, holding my arm when we left the movie, the intensity of his eyes, my stomach swirling. I truly felt dizzy, as though I'd keel right over. "It was the best I've felt since...I'd hate to guess."

"Sounds hot and heavy." There's a note of flirtation in Lorissa's voice.

"If by 'hot and heavy' you mean sex—no, it's not that. Not at all." I blink my eyes, itching from pollen.

"Oh?"

Is that cynicism in her voice? Why does that simple question bug me so much? He's so attentive to me, like I'm the most beautiful, magnificent woman he's ever seen. But why hasn't he put the moves on me? I flash once again on those red stilettoes and shudder, blocking out the image.

"We even checked out the LeMay car museum."

"Cars?" Lorissa looks flabbergasted. "Since when are you interested in cars?"

"Oh, I'm not, I can assure you. Well, I *wasn't*." I tell her about him asking me if I wanted to go, and of course I'd said no. "I had no interest, but somehow on one of those typical drizzly days he fast-talked me into it: 'Hey! Do you want to see a DeLorean?' My face must have been blank because he said, 'You know! Like in *Back to the Future?* The movie?'

"So, we saw the museum, which is housed in something like a fancy Quonset hut. I was bored at first, looking at car after car, but then there was an old Ford like my dad's station wagon that he inherited from my grandparents. Memories came flooding back: Lake Crescent in the Olympics, hiking, canoeing, camping. Ocean Shores, playing on the sand and in the waves. Up to Victoria, tea at the Empress Hotel.

"Scott was so excited by the DeLorean cars. He shouted like a ten-year-old, 'Just like giant yellow birds, right?' The doors that swing out and up like they're going to fly. All with supercool seats and gears."

Lorissa and I walk by yet another rhododendron with giant blossoms a foot above my head. "I got a kick out of the museum. Can you believe it? The 1906 Cadillac. The 1921 Model T. Who would have thought?" I tell her that when Scott and I left, somehow we just happened to be holding hands, and we thought we'd get some coffee, but then my voice trails off as I remember more than I'm going to say.

The sun had burst through, the sky was that perfect azure we rarely see in the great Northwest. Truly a perfect afternoon. Soon we were laughing, joking, and honestly, I felt high, like my heart was a kite floating away. At Starbucks, I'd twirled my foamy latte with a straw and told him, "You're so suave and debonair, with your hot looks and all. I don't know if I should be spending this much time with you. I might just regret it." He'd reached across the table and touched my hand. "I'm more than just a pretty face. Believe me."

As Lorissa and I mull our own thoughts, our power walk becomes a slower stroll, thank goodness, and I cast my eyes to Puget Sound, just to the west, clear green water sparkling without whitecaps. "Lorissa, I might be falling for him. That's what I'm worried about."

She smiles and touches my arm. "That's wonderful, isn't it?"

I hope so. We reach her house and climb the stairs to the kitchen. She pours us glasses of water and clinks in some ice cubes. We kick back on the couch, feet on the coffee table, quiet for several minutes, taking in the view of Mount Rainier, an enormous, majestic triangle with edges of blue: glaciers melting. I breathe, slowly, deeply.

Love. Yes, love. No matter how much I want to deny it, love is creeping into my heart.

"It's odd," I say, "living right next door to him. After our museum date, we both climbed out of his truck and up the staircase, and then his kiss was more like a peck and he disappeared into his apartment as quick as lightning in a summer storm."

"He didn't make any moves?"

"No," I say, wondering how I feel about that. At first, I'd thought, *He's waiting, holding back*, but now I wonder. Shouldn't he have tried a little harder?

I get up and place my empty glass on the counter. "Lorissa, thanks *so* much for calling. For taking this walk today." If she only knew how much it means to me that we got together. I drive off, my eyes damp. *I'll make it up to her*, I vow to myself. I will. There's little as precious as friends in college, when we're first away from home, sharing ourselves, figuring out life, meeting boyfriends, missing family. As I start to unlock my apartment door, I hear my landline ringing. I'm not sure why I bothered to get one—it seems like a waste since I use my cell all the time. Habit, I suppose.

I jiggle my key—it's such a fussy lock—and finally I burst through the door, hoping it's a new client for my fledgling bookkeeping business. "Hello?"

I hear nothing. "Hello?" I say louder. My hand shakes, tightening around the receiver, while I brace myself against the counter.

Breathe. Just breathe, I say to myself. I slam down the phone and sit, sweat dripping between my breasts. My hands won't stop trembling. I thought I'd left terror behind, but here it is again.

16
Nicole Whyrrl

Nicole picks at her cuticles while Willie Nelson croons on the juke box. "Another G & T?" The bartender has puffy red lips; maybe a college girl who didn't cut it and returned home to figure out her life. Sexy and sharp.

"Thanks. Not tonight. I've got to hustle home." But Nicole remains, listening to the *snap* behind her as pool cues connect with balls, sinking in the corners at the Pilchuck Tavern. Her plans with Scott fell through again, like the past four—yes, she is counting—the past four times, and since Joel is used to her coming home late, what the hell. A stop at the Pilchuck won't hurt.

Nicole checks her red nail polish. It's chipped, which bugs her. Like she really has time for a manicure. She opens her wallet and slips a small pill in her mouth. She stares at the beer bottles across the bar and studies her reflection in the mirror. Her chin falls just a touch lower than it did a year ago, deeper lines circle her eyes, and her neck! The telltale signs. Getting old sucks.

"You seem like you're in another world." The voice, disrupting her from the bubble of her thoughts, unnerves her. The man on the stool next to her smiles with snow-white teeth. Though his Brooks Brothers shirt is a bit wrinkled, his hair is styled. A polished sort of guy. She doesn't know if she actually likes it.

"Yes," she answers. "A million miles away." She reaches her long fingers into the bowl of beer nuts and chews slowly, crunching ever so quietly. "And you?"

"Yep," he says. "I'm from a million miles away." She laughs, feeling her breast tingle underneath her sweater.

The man calls to the bartender. "How about another? Three limes." He slams his glass on the bar and swivels to Nicole. "I'm Al," he says, extending his hand for a shake. No callouses.

"You're not from around here. I can tell from your hands you've never chopped wood in your life, which is kindergarten stuff in the great Northwest."

He chuckles with a deep, throaty laugh. "I like you," he says.

Nicole tries to size him up. "What brings you here, Mr. Al?"

Al waves to the bartender. "And another for this gorgeous woman," a flash of that cheetah smile. "I'm looking for the missus."

Nicole rubs her finger along the line of her cheekbone. This guy is a throwback to some other era. Idiot. He pulls out his phone and scrolls through his photos. "This is my one and only."

Nicole regards the phone, then brings it up closely to examine. The hair is long and blonde, the makeup different—but...She holds it closer. Sure enough. Meaghan. Lorissa's friend. But who is this "Al"? If Meaghan *wanted* to be found, she wouldn't have chopped off her hair, dyed it, given herself a new look, would she?

"Nope, haven't seen her." Al gazes at Nicole for several minutes, as though he knows she's lying. She returns to her drink and swallows. The spilled beer in the tavern stinks, but the dark lighting, the sound of Brad Paisley warbling in the background, the pool players shooting over in the corner offer a strange sort of soothing comfort.

"What's your story?" Al asks.

Is it the gin, the music, or that lulling, husky voice that gets her to open up? He's a stranger she'll never see again. What the hell. She tells Al about Scott, his dark eyes, her melting feelings, his air of mystery. She finds herself carried away like a schoolgirl thinking about a prince. She even tells Al about all the meetings after work at the park, and the times— she can't believe she is telling him this, but she reminds herself she'll never see him again—the times at the motel up in Port Orchard. And then, in an "oh, by the way" fashion, she adds, "Oh yeah. I'm married. Have a kid."

Al listens, eyes focused, so attentive, making Nicole feel like she is the only one in the world. She waits for the pickup line. None comes.

"Later," he says.

"Sure."

And he is gone. Nicole brings her glass to her lips, drinks until it's empty, and ruminates about Scott. His sweet buns, his half smile, his enigmatic air. He has a story, that's for sure. Nicole could get used to him. She imagines running away with him to Fiji or Tahiti. Just thinking about him makes her feel warm. But these past few nights he didn't meet her at the park. He's probably hanging out more with Graham and other guys. She's paranoid. That's all. It's just beers with the boys.

17
Lorissa Orondo

"Please. Be nice, Connor." Lorissa brakes at the stoplight and glances at her son, seeing only his nose under the hoodie of his sweatshirt. Every conversation with him is confrontational, and sometimes she just feels like *Screw it*. Today she won't walk on eggshells. She'll say what she wants and won't let her son hold her hostage.

Back in middle school, when he had started smoking and skipping classes, she and Graham had brought him to the psychiatrist recommended by his pediatrician. He'd introduced them to the terms "attention deficit disorder" and "hyperactivity." Both parents had done Google searches for articles, checked out library books, studied up. "Okay," they'd each said. "We can handle this." But the psychiatrist had insisted that Connor needed medicine. They'd paid for one missed appointment, then canceled the rest.

"No way. No way is our son going on *drugs*. And certainly not for the rest of his life." Graham had been so adamant, he'd reminded Lorissa of cartoon characters with smoke flying out their ears. "Now that we know what's wrong, we'll get him a tutor. Tutors. However, many it takes.

"We'll make this right."

Graham had always succeeded. A star soccer player in high school. When he'd decided he wanted to sing, he attended Ohio Wesleyan, where both his parents taught. Next, moderate success in New York, a small role in an off-Broadway play, and when he'd decided he wanted to make money, he'd excelled at NYU's computer science program. After one summer in the Berkshires, he reunited with Lorissa, married, had two kids, and moved out West. Then at Amazon, he'd zoomed up the corporate ladder. He didn't get why his son had so many problems.

"After all," he'd said to Lorissa, "he's our son. He just needs to apply himself. If he weren't so lazy!"

Lorissa had bristled. "It's not laziness," she said. "He's got a condition that you and I don't have." But she also didn't like the idea of Connor on meds. She had her own diagnosis: influence from his new friend, Rhys. Up through elementary school, she had known all the kids in his classes because she volunteered so much at the school. But in middle school, it had changed. Then she'd heard, "Rhys this. . ." and "Rhys that. . ."— Rhys, a boy she knew little about.

For two years she'd gritted her teeth. Then, the fire. Both of them suspended from school for setting a fire in the boy's bathroom. She and Graham had met with the principal, then drove Connor home in a harsh silence. They had handed him a list of chores and restricted him from leaving the home after school for two months.

"But Mom! It was an accident, really!"
"And Rhys is not allowed in our house. Ever. No buts, Connor. That's final. I've never even met his parents. He runs wild, and you're not going to be kicked out of middle school again!"

She knows that in reality, she has no control over who Connor sees, especially now that he is in high school. The boys still hang together, from the rare tidbits she gleans from Mackenzie. After his last encounter with Principal Deane, Connor had been expelled once again, and Lorissa had finally said to Graham, "We've got to do something different."

When Lorissa had proposed the new counselor, his third in as many years, Connor had been willing, especially after her bribe: she'd cut his restriction—being grounded—in half.

Now Lorissa keeps the engine running in front of the counselor's office. "This guy's name is Jonathan Fleury. ADHD is his specialty."

"I know, I know," Connor says. "You've told me a million times." She could feel the tiniest ounce of hope in his voice. She wants to say, Connor, I know you've been miserable. But really, maybe with the meds, maybe this Jonathan might help. Maybe if you stayed away from that awful Rhys. Maybe things might get better.

Connor flicks his hood back and opens his car door, jumping up the stairs two at a time. Lorissa sighs and says a little prayer, wondering how on earth they would ever get through the next year of high school if something didn't change.

"See you in an hour. I hope it goes well," Lori calls. "Love you." Those last words were really just a whisper to herself, since Connor had bounded into the office, more anxious to get away from her than reluctant to see a new counselor.

18
Meaghan Farren

A Jimmy Buffet concert, a hike up Mount Si, a local performance of *The Music Man*—the summer flies by. Scott and I rent kayaks, hike to hot springs in the Olympic Mountains, have dinner on top of the Space Needle, explore the Nisqually Delta. Now, as the days get shorter and maple leaves turn from green to red, I realize we could have done nothing, nothing at all, and I'd still be smitten.

I think back to the first time he took me out to lunch at a sandwich place in rural Port Orchard. His eyes bored into me as he drove, and it scared me, made me afraid he'd drive off the street. And that energy, encompassing me like he'd wrapped me in his cocoon, safe and warm and delicious. That's love, isn't it? That feeling when I can barely breathe, all I feel are tingles, and I just want to be with him, us together. If that isn't love, then whatever it is, I want it.

But physically? Nada. He keeps a distance, like I'm precious, but maybe too precious. *No*, I think. *Tonight, will be different*. I'll make sure of that. Tonight will be our night.

I'm like a schoolgirl, figuring out what to wear. Casual but beautiful. Tight jeans and a cashmere sweater I bought at the consignment store, unbuttoned a little too low. My mom's heart necklace that my dad gave me when I turned eighteen. My charm bracelet that matches Lorissa's from college. This will do. Simple yet attractive. Desirable.

"Hey." Scott welcomes me at the door to his apartment, his eyes clear, shiny in the light of the candles. "Come on in." Dozens of tea lights are set throughout his small kitchen, the living-dining area . . . and, I wonder, the bedroom? I recognize a pink and blue blown-glass bowl I saw last week at the Goodwill— and that seascape oil painting on his wall? Yes, that was at the Goodwill, too. So why is he starting all over again, just like I am, at his age? He must be around thirty-eight to forty.

He beckons me to a card table he's covered with a white cotton tablecloth and pulls out my chair, a small fold-up, in a gallant gesture. Simple elegance. Very simple, a fun sort of chic. When he touches my hand, I meet his eyes, then glance to the art on the wall, drawn to him, yet wary. I hope he can't hear my heart pounding. I've lost it, I realize. I'm head over heels.

We've never had dinner at one of our apartments before. Code for, this is the first time we've had a "date" where a bed lies empty in the next room. I lift my wine glass, the charms on my bracelet ringing. His ocean-green eyes never leave my face. I see his lips spread to— a kiss? No, a smile. A gentle, kind—or is that an ironic, smile? I try to read his face.

"I don't know how long it's been since I've felt this way around a woman," he says, and I tremble. He laughs, heartily, as if embarrassed. I am smitten. I'm over the cliff. I've forgotten Lorissa, Nicole, —even Brandon. It's only Scott and me. Just the two of us. He reaches for my face, holds it with both hands, comes so close I smell spearmint on his breath, and he pulls my mouth inches from his. "I," he says, and instead of finishing his sentence, he puts his mouth on mine, swirls his tongue, and I am transported, we are in another world, another universe. I am in love.

He falls back in his chair and his arms drop to his side. I try to breathe, but can I? I don't remember where I am. And then he asks, "Shrimp fettuccine?" dishing out pasta and placing it ever so carefully on my plate.

I laugh. "Mmm. Sounds delicious."

"My only dish," he says. I talk about Chumley, how she caught a mouse yesterday, about the new stray kitten at the Humane Society whose fur was half burned off, and the tiny runt of a chihuahua who was adopted by the sweetest little girl with—perhaps she had autism. I wave my fork as I talk and watch his eyes, wondering if he's heard anything I've said. He's attentive, his eyes never wavering, and yet he seems elsewhere, as if there's something on his mind. Suddenly I say, "You didn't hear a word I said."

The glow of the candle highlights the lines carved on his face. His hasn't been an easy life, I think. I refold my napkin, wondering how to crack his shell. I want to hear his story. I hum along to Eric Clapton singing "Layla" on Pandora. "I haven't felt this happy in a long time, either," I say, feeling naked, vulnerable.

He clears his throat. "Meaghan, I want to tell you about myself." He sounds so earnest. "I was in foster care."

I chew a bite. It must be frozen shrimp, but it tastes so delicious. I'm listening...*you were in foster care, and...*He says no more. Wait. Did I miss something? "You were in foster care?"

"Yes."

Help me out here, I think. Thousands of kids are in foster care.

"And, well, I was flung around a lot. A lot of different homes, if you know what I mean."

"I'm so sorry."

"No, no, I wasn't looking for you to be sorry. It's just that by the time I reached eighteen and they threw me out of the system, I didn't know much. Didn't know much about how to survive." I wondered if he'd been beaten. Or worse. Sexually abused.

"There was this elderly woman. Her name was Mrs. Lucas. And, well."

My ears perk up. I don't realize that the October rain has ceased, that the luminescent moon has slid from behind the clouds, that stars are pricking the sky like tiny pins. I don't know that the Big Dipper has spread over Wilkes Bay or that whitecaps have shrunk to quiet rolls under the bridge. I don't know that a man has vaulted the apartment building stairs two at a time. This world is Scott's and mine.

"Meaghan!" A fist bangs on the door. Once, twice, *bang, bang, bang!*

I jump from my chair, spilling wine on my new sweater. "Goddamn you, Meaghan! Open up!" I press hard against the wall. The voice hollers louder, a man pummeling the apartment door across the stairwell, pounding on *my* door.

"Meaghan," Scott asks, "what's going on?" My mouth freezes in an O, my eyes stretch wide open as I try to blend into the wall, standing flat against it, quivering. Scott stands next to me, tries to put his arms around me. "Darling, darling"—words I've never heard from him.

"Quiet," I snap, sounding rough, raw, angry. Instinct takes over.

"Goddamn you, Meaghan!" The man roars outside as Scott and I huddle together. "I'm going to kill you!"

"I'll tell him to get the hell away." Scott starts for his door, and I grab his arm.

"No! Don't go out there!" I can tell by his look of surprise that he is shocked to meet this other side of me—grim, determined, yet terrified. "No!"

We hear another set of steps. "May I help you, sir?" The manager. I hear the words "complaint," "police," "Meaghan Perkins? There's no one here by that name," and then the footsteps tramp down the stairs. A motor thunders; tires shriek out of the parking lot, fade away until finally we feel the silence.

Scott flips on the lights, the romantic mood shattered. The candles flutter in the breeze that slips through the cracks of the apartment's thin door. "Meaghan. What's going on?"

Though I'm still shaking, I can feel my pulse steady, my breath return. I pour out my wine and refill my glass with water, then return to the living room. "Who was that?" Scott persists. I swallow a gulp of water, take a breath.

"Brandon. My husband."

19

Meaghan Farren

"Brandon? Wait! You said your husband was dead."

"I did." I am no longer the delicate flower I was moments ago. "I did say that." I sip my water, cross my legs, face the inevitable. Secrets can stay secrets only so long. Scott lifts his chin, rigid, as if to say he'll wait as long as he needs to, to hear what's going on. He looks like he'll wait till Christmas if need be.

"When I met Brandon," I begin, "he swept me off my feet. Dashing. Truly a Prince Charming, treating me with flowers, little notes, diamonds on my birthday. Tiny diamonds, of course." I smell our creamy uneaten fettucine. "That lasted awhile. Quite a while, actually; eleven, twelve years. And then it started."

I take a deep breath as I try to explain the contempt; the demeaning, hateful diatribes; the slaps that turned into slugs, kicks that turned into vicious stomps. Seventeen years of marriage, and of that, the last four years were a siege of horror. Of torture. Of terror. Then secrets, plans, escape. Lies. Right up to my arrival at Lorissa's doorstep. Pandora's music has ended. The only sound is a drip from the kitchen faucet.

To think I thought I'd pulled this off. That I'd ever be safe. Still naïve after all these years.

"He beat you for four years?" he asks. I hear—is that sadness in his voice? Compassion? My re-hardened heart is touched.

Silly me. I thought he'd never find me on this island, three thousand miles away, the other side of the country. I mumble to myself, "Silly me."

"Come here." He wraps his arm around me, and I snuggle into him. I hear the limbs of the cedar trees outside, like an orchestra, knocking against the window. A baby cries from an apartment on the first floor. He kisses my forehead. "You're actually married."

What? So that's your takeaway from all this blunt, brutal honesty of mine? "If you call it that. If getting beaten to a pulp is called a marriage, sure, I'm married."

The last tea light has extinguished itself. "I don't know why I said that," Scott says. "Stupid." He shakes his head. "I'm so sorry, Meaghan." He sounds sincere. I want to believe him. Somehow, I feel safe in his arms, even knowing that monster Brandon is out there, somewhere, waiting to pounce once again. For one small moment I feel like I am safe. Then he asks, "So how do you think he found you?"

I shake my head. "I don't know. I left in March, about seven months ago." Now all my emotions unleash—the desperation, the gut-wrenching hopelessness, the loss of all I have worked for, my plan to hide from him forever. It's all for nothing. Nothing.

It's the fruitlessness, the failure, that deflates me, drains me to emptiness. I have no place to go, nothing I can do. I am Brandon's captive once again, and he's come to kill me. He will, too. I'm sure of it. It's as if blood is being siphoned right out of my body, from the top of my head to my toes. I am a vacant shell. "I don't know."

I reach behind my neck, scoop up my grown-out hair, and twist it into a bun. "You know, Graham traveled for work to Easthampton, Massachusetts, several months ago. That's near where I used to live. He said he'd spotted one of Brandon's real estate signs at the house next door to where he was staying."

"Did Graham speak with Brandon?"

"I can't imagine he did. He saw a real estate sign with the name B. Perkins on it, that's all I know." I focus on the painting above the table—a sea with grays and blues whirling with whitecapped waves. A sliver of moonlight shines on one small boat sailing aimlessly. We sit in silence for seconds, minutes. The rising wind howls outside the window.

"Come on," he says. "We're going to do something about this."

"No, Scott. Wait!" I rub my temple. "Where are you going?"

"We're going to Lorissa and Graham's. We're going to fix this. Find out what happened, then fix this."

"You don't understand!" I'm clinging to his hands.

"Understand what?" His voice is harsh, maybe harsher than he wants it to be.

"Lorissa and I. . ."

"What?" His raincoat is on. He's standing by the door, hand on the doorknob. "What?"

"Lorissa and I. We. . .we had a falling out in college and it's all my fault. I was awful. If you're thinking of turning to Lorissa and Graham now, I can't. I just can't. Underneath her polite veneer, she hates me. Hates me."

He spreads his arms around me, engulfing me, tight, tighter. He kisses the top of my head. "Trust me, Meaghan." He steps back, lifts my chin. His fingers so soft. A tear skates down my cheek. "Okay?"

"Okay," I whisper, but of course nothing is okay. I'm tired, so tired. If he wants to try with Lorissa and Graham, I will not resist. I have only relied on one person in my whole life, and that was my dad, and he is gone. "Okay," I say again.

20

Nicole Whyrrl

Poised on what has become her usual barstool at the Pilchuck Tavern, Nicole orders her gin and tonic, checks her face in the bar's mirror, wondering if any new wrinkles popped up overnight around her eyes, her mouth, her forehead. Beauty is everything, and she isn't going to lose hers without a fight. The dark, stinky tavern has replaced her confidantes, Lorissa and Jasmine, her former walking buddies.

She doesn't want to admit to herself that she's waiting for anyone. In truth, she wants to see him. Desperately. The last three times she's been here, he landed on the barstool next to her, so attentive—yes, fully engaged, the stranger with the clean-shaven face, the polo shirt and pressed Levi's, who listened to her talk about Joel, about Scott, about her most private feelings.

Al. The stranger who'd shown Nicole a photo of his wife, who'd said that he missed his wife, the wife who'd broken his heart, who he loved to the moon and back. This sleek man who had a shiny veneer that screamed "a little too slick, a little too polished," the man who'd never asked for her number. Just showed up again and again, all those times that Nicole had told Joel she'd have to work late when in reality she wanted to meet Scott. And when Scott hadn't been able to get together for one reason or another, she found her refuge in this womb-like tavern.

And then she'd learned the truth. Lorissa had spilled the beans. That scumbag Meaghan had a boyfriend, and that boyfriend's name was Scott. Scott Crowley. Lorissa had said it so casually, so lightly, and Nicole had pulled off her best acting skills to seem indifferent. Whatever. But inside, her chest hammered: Meaghan's new boyfriend was Scott Crowley. Her Scott. The two-timing Scott Crowley.

"The usual," Al says to the bartender, the girl with the ring on her pierced puffy red lips. "Hey, how's that puppy of yours?" He edges his stool closer to Nicole, scratching it along the cement floor.

"Real cute." The bartender eyes him flirtatiously, glad for the attention, probably hoping it will translate into a big tip, which it usually did.

"And get the lady a refill," he says, nodding toward Nicole. Nicole swirls her glass, clinking the ice cubes in her otherwise empty glass.

"So, what's on your mind today, little lady?"

Nicole lifts her chin to face him, then takes the lime from her drink and sucks on it until her face puckers. "Little lady? Give it up."

"Whaaat? Bad day?" He leans back, arms outstretched, elbows straight, clean hands resting on the bar. "You're good. You know that, Nicole? Too bad that asshole boyfriend of yours don't appreciate you. And too bad that husband of yours is too dumb to know what he's got." Nicole doesn't bother to protest. She sips her drink, barely hearing Keith Urban sing "Break on

Me." The smells of beer and wine and gin all fuse together, making her slightly nauseated.

"Whoa, lady," Al says. "Something's worse than usual. What's going on?"

Is it the dull lights, the gin and tonic, or the "poor me" country music that loosens Nicole's feelings? She's furious, crushed . . . murderous.

"Okay." She lifts her drink to her lips. "I told Scott I'd leave my husband and even leave my daughter to be with him. And you know what he said?"

'Let's run away tonight?'"

Damn it. How did she ever get herself into this mess?

21

Meaghan Farren

Scott and I shiver on the Orondos' porch in the dark and rain—so reminiscent of that night I arrived here a mere six months ago. Wind lashes our hair, our coats. "It's past eleven. Almost midnight. They're probably in bed." I nearly trip on the uncarved pumpkin at my feet. Scott doesn't care how late it is or whether or not we wake them. He is determined, with a mission, like a marine ready for battle. He rings the bell again. Bangs on the door. I feel myself shrinking inside my Gore-Tex jacket. The porch light pops on, and Lorissa opens the door slowly and squints.

"Meaghan? What are you doing here? Do you know what time it is?" Her eyes narrow, her voice sharp, accusing.

"We need to talk," Scott says. "Now." Lorissa cocks her head, puzzled. "You need to get Graham," he says. "Now."

"It's the middle of the night. Graham needs to get up at four a.m. to go to Seattle. What is this?"

As Scott and Lorissa argue, I feel squished in the middle, speechless, numb.

"Get him," orders Scott. He's not giving up, that's for sure.

I watch Lorissa's eyes change from fury to distaste to curiosity.

"Alright." She's pissed. Of course, she is. "Come in. Have a seat in my office."

I imagine Lorissa prodding Graham out of a deep sleep, Graham resisting, Lorissa insisting. Fifteen minutes later, the four of us convene in Lorissa's office. "What's this all about?" Graham asks, standing in the doorway in his plaid flannel bathrobe.

"Graham, you met Scott at Nicole's barbecue," I remind him. "He's my neighbor. My friend."

Graham nods. Enough for preliminaries. I glance around Lorissa's office, note bills spread across her desk. Is this her life? Paying bills at eleven o'clock while Graham sleeps?

Graham looks groggy, as though roused from a deep REM sleep. I cut to the chase. "Did you meet B. Perkins in Massachusetts when you flew back there for that business trip?"

"What?" He shakes his head, surprised. "Well, no!"

I wait. "*Well, no*?" There's more. I know there's more.

The desk lamp casts a burnished glow on the bookcases, the soccer awards, the russet leather armchair where Graham now sits behind Lorissa's desk, his fingers steepled as though he's thinking before he speaks.

"Please, sit down," Lorissa interrupts. "Can I get you guys anything? A glass of wine? Juice? Coffee?" No one answers as she leaves the room.

"Not really," Graham adds.

"Not really?" Scott is on the offensive.

"Why is this any business of yours? Why are you coming into my house, waking me up?"

I spring from my chair, my courage returned. "Graham, what did you say? What did you say to him?"

Graham presses his lips together, clearly confused. I'm inches from his face. I try to mow him down with my eyes. "Did you tell him where I live? Did you?"

"Of course not!"

"Graham, you've got to tell me. He banged on my apartment door tonight. Tonight! He said he's going to kill me."

Graham's mouth hangs open. "Tell me," I say. "Tell me everything."

"Meaghan, calm down." I clench my fists, readying for a fight. No one tells me to calm down. Not since I left Brandon. "Meaghan," Graham says, backing up. "You told us your husband was dead. We believed you. Of course, I wondered about the realtor sign with the name 'B. Perkins' in Easthampton, right next to where you said you were from—but hey, Perkins is a common name, especially back East. Still, Lorissa and I wondered. So, *is* that real estate guy your husband? You lied the whole time about his being dead?"

"Lie?" I bury my face in my hands, then look up, bleak. "I lied because he's cunning and vicious and would kill me if he found me." Now I start to shout. "I knew he'd track me down. Somehow. Three thousand miles across America on a remote island, and he finds me!" I squeeze my fists so tightly my nails cut into my palms. "Actually," my voice changes and I feel— what is it? Gumption? "I finally thought I was safe. I relaxed. But I was wrong. I need to know what happened, Graham."

His face is blank, but I can see he's thinking, remembering.

"Graham, please, what happened?!"

His lips tighten, as he begins to realize how serious this is. "Okay. After my meeting in Boston, my host invited me to his summer home in western Mass. They have a gorgeous country house. . ."

"Graham!"

"Well, next door a house was listed for sale by a B. Perkins. On Sunday, the day we left, a guy who said he's Perkins came over with an open house flyer just as I was sticking my suitcase in my rental car."

"And?"

"I said, 'Thanks.' That's it."

"You didn't mention my name? Say you knew me?"

"Why would I? I barely spoke to the guy."

"And you didn't say where you live, either?"

"No, no, no." But his voice sounds a bit less confident. "Why would I do that? We exchanged two sentences about real estate, and then I drove back to Boston to catch my plane. That's all."

Lorissa returns, balancing a tray of coffee cups, a carafe, a pitcher of milk, and a plate of grapes. She pours everyone but Graham a cup. Four in the morning will come soon enough without coffee.

I'm seething. Something must have happened. Something more.

Scott turns to me. "Meaghan, there's no one else who knows where you are?"

"No one! I didn't tell anyone in Northampton that I was leaving. I literally snuck out of town. I cut and dyed my hair, traded in my Jetta for the Subaru on the road, and started using my maiden name so he couldn't trace me."

I groan. "Brandon didn't die—I left him because I couldn't take the beatings anymore. Now he's found me here on Wilkes Island. He wants to kill me." Lorissa's jaw drops.

"I guess it was silly to expect dying my hair would make any difference. I just couldn't think straight. I was running for my life." Scott pulls on his earlobe, as if his mind is whirling. "Graham, can you think of anything? Any clue you might have given unknowingly?"

Graham shuts his eyes, trying to recollect. "You know, I may have worn my Ohio Wesleyan sweatshirt." He squeezes his lips together in thought. "Maybe if Brandon wanted to ask anything about me, follow up with his client's neighbor, my boss, about the visitor with an OWU sweatshirt, follow such a hair-thin lead."

"Did you tell your boss about an old friend from back East visiting you at home?" Scott asks, poised on the edge of his chair. My very life teeters in the balance and Scott is going to bat for me. I am so relieved.

"No. Nothing."

"Brandon's smart," I say. "Wicked smart." Such an understatement.

"Maybe Brandon put one and two together," Graham says. "Ohio Wesleyan: checked alumni online; sees you and I went to school together; asks my boss about me later. Wasn't there something in the yearbook about you and me?"

"You mean like us dating that first month of freshman year?"

"What?" Scott looks aghast. "You two dated?"

Oh, jeez. I didn't expect that. "Yes. Graham and I dated. It was nothing, meaningless. Just the first month of college."

"That's how I met Graham," Lorissa adds.

"It was no big thing, Scott." This topic bores me.

"Really." Graham nods. Scott lets it go. I move back on track. "Brandon is obsessive," I say. "And I can tell you, I'm sure he's been obsessing on finding me since the day I left. And now he's found me." I exhale all the air from the room. My energy is zapped. I'm defeated. I speak so quietly I don't know if anyone can hear. "I should've known I could never be free. There's no place I can go."

Lorissa hugs me. "We've got to get you out of here." She wants to help. I'm so, so grateful, and yet how can she want to help me, after all I put her through?

My strong façade melts. "Where? There's no place. He'll track me down wherever. I'm all the way across the country, as far as I can go and he's found me." Lorissa opens her mouth, then shuts it. Platitudes. The only words she can say will be platitudes and clichés, and I'd rather have silence. "Because where can I go? Here I am, on a rustic island, three thousand miles from home, and Brandon still found me."

Graham reaches for my hand. "Do you honestly think he's going to kill you?"

"Graham! Do you think I'm making this up? Do you want to see my last hospital record?" I remember all the times I'd thought I might leave; the times Brandon had convinced me that the beatings were all my fault. I deserved it.

"The last time I ended up in the hospital, he smashed me against the wall, shattered the windows, kicked me as hard as a rodeo bull, breaking my fingers that were protecting my stomach. I tried to turn so he would kick my back, my legs, anything but my tummy. But it was as if he knew. He aimed dead center and, yes, I was pregnant. And I miscarried!" I stop. All eyes are on me.

Sometimes it's hard to hold onto my anger when I want to shrivel up and die. "He killed my baby and now I can't have anymore." By now my voice is a mere whisper in the dim light.

"Oh, yeah. I could get a restraining order. Do you know how many women are killed by a man, even with a restraining order?" I'm back to shouting now, sure to wake up Connor and Mackenzie if they're not already awake. "No one can keep me safe. Don't you get it?" I hear ticking, the grandfather clock from the hall. I take a tissue from the box on the desk and wipe my nose. A toilet flushes upstairs.

Scott touches my shoulder. "Lorissa's right, though. We've got to get you out of here."

I attempt a smile. "Where? There's nowhere I can go."

Graham paces back and forth, back and forth. I take a grape and peel it. A trains whistles across the Sound. The walls of Lorissa's office are closing in on me. What can I do? Where, where can I go?

No one speaks. Finally, Lorissa says, "Meaghan, we will figure this out. We will. But it's one in the morning. None of us are thinking straight. The guest bedroom has fresh sheets. Spend the night here. We'll all sleep on it and come up with something in the morning.

I feel so exhausted, I can't argue. Before I ask, Scott says, "I'll take care of Chumley." I walk him to the front door and hug him tightly. I don't want to let him go. This is not the way the night was supposed to be. He opens the front and walks out into the rain. "Thank you," I whisper as his truck drove away.

I sleep until eleven. When I crawl out of bed in Lorissa's pajamas I have a moment of serenity before I remember why I'm here. Before I remember Brandon.

I climb the stairs to the kitchen, slowly pour myself a cup of coffee, and plop onto the couch, gazing at the mist in the picture windows. A fog horn blows off the Sound. A sweet, story book sound. This is no story book. I feel paralyzed. I can barely lift my cup to my mouth.

The front door bangs open and Lorissa, followed by Graham, run up the steps. "We've got it!" Graham exclaims. "Corey!" He throws his hands in the air, his voice growing louder, excited. "Yes, Corey."

"That's our answer, Meaghan," Lorissa says.

I wait expectantly. "What are you talking about?"

"Corey is Graham's nephew," she explains. "He's an astronomer for some laboratory in Texas, I think. But now he isn't working in the lab—he has an even better assignment."

"You still don't get it!" I flail in frustration. "Brandon will track me down. If he can find me here, of course he'll find me in Texas." I'm deflated. "He probably has cousins in Texas for all I know."

"No," says Graham. "Corey doesn't work in Texas."

I freeze. "Doesn't work in Texas?" I squeeze my eyes, wondering.

"That's just where his lab is headquartered."

"Then where. . .?" I'm baffled now.

"La Serena," Lorissa says.

"As in Mexico?" I begin to feel a speck of hope.

"Better." She smiles for the first time. "South America. Corey is in La Serena, Chile."

PART II.
October 15, 2014

22

Meaghan Farren

Lorissa's voice is so clear, I hardly believe she's a hemisphere away. "Meaghan, you made it!" Her tone is warm, friendly.

"It's strange going from fall to spring in a day," I say. "La Serena turns out to be a deserted tourist town. I just wanted to let you know I arrived." There'll always be a crack in our friendship, but the wound has healed more than I had hoped. "Tomorrow I'll call Corey. Thanks, Lorissa." The words come from the deepest part of my heart. "So much. Graham, too."

"Sure, Meaghan."

It had happened so fast. Graham had phoned his nephew Corey, who'd said yes, he and his girlfriend had an extra room. Scott said he'd pack up my apartment. There wasn't much, most of it could go back to the Goodwill, and the Orondos had said I could store the few boxes that mattered in their garage. Scott said he'd take care of Chumley, claiming to be nervous about such a huge responsibility. He knows how much I love my cat. Lorissa found this small motel in La Serena online—one of the few open during the off-season.

Now, after my long flight to Santiago, then shorter flight to La Serena, I feel wiped out, but so relieved. I cross the street from my motel to catch the sunset—blue and pink and orange clouds meshing over the Pacific Ocean. I stand next to a closed café where, inside, chairs are stacked upside down on tables, just like in all the other cafés strung along this silent four-lane road. The shops remind me of ones on Cape Cod that sell trinkets and ice cream and sweatshirts, but these are tightly buttoned and shuttered, prepared for any storm. I step from the sidewalk onto the moist white beach, carrying my socks and shoes so the sand slips between my toes as I approach the shoreline. A wave recedes, leaving rivulets and eddies that curl up the beach, then roll back down, into the vast sea. The sky darkens, adding a gray tint to the lavender that stretches out before me.

I cross the road again, the night sky now black. A single car passes, its wheels gliding through puddles, splashing remnants of the afternoon's rain. And then the street is silent once more. I unlock my motel-room door, crawl under the covers, and sleep for ten hours straight.

The next morning, golden streaks of sun stream through my windows. I'm rejuvenated. I fluff my pillow, thinking about Scott—how strong he was at Lorissa and Graham's. So decisive— pounding on their door—and now he's caring for Chumley until Brandon gives up and disappears. Scott has crept under my skin, in a good way. I imagine him here with me, under the hot sun on the white beach.

No! I've got to snap out of it. Call Graham's nephew. Graham said Corey and his girlfriend offered their extra room for weeks, maybe months. They have friends who might hire me to cook and or even manage their household finances. I might restart my booking business on line from here. And as long as my savings from my business on Wilkes Island holds out, I'll be okay.

An hour later, I amble past the front desk and wave to the small man behind the counter, his dark hair neatly combed, a straight part on the side. "*Hola*," I say. Around the block, I spot a self-service laundry–Internet café among the two-story blue and green adobe buildings. What a perfect pairing—wash your clothes while you email. I step inside for a coffee and sign on to a computer.

I begin an email to Scott. "Hey, Scott and Chumley, I'm here safe and sound. Sorry to have dragged you into this." The row of clothes dryers whirs, while a gaggle of long-haired millennials in jeans and tee shirts chatter in Spanish.

I never expected Scott would stir so many feelings. Clothes churn and twist in the washing machines, spewing the scent of detergent, and I feel like I'm watching my stomach tossing in confusion. Is this love? I think it is. "Thank you," I type to Scott. "Your support means everything."

And this is where I halt, my hands lingering above the keyboard. "And I also want to say, I miss you more than I expected." My fingers dangle. Delete. "And I also want to say, I miss you." Again, my fingers stop. Then, finally, "Send." I stretch my arms, feeling satisfied. I pick up my phone and text Corey. No answer. Call him. No answer. Send him an e-mail. It's only Friday.

But then it's Saturday and still no response from Corey. I pay for another night at the motel, then return to the beach. Waves swoosh, breaking before they roll onto shore. To my left across the bay, a peninsula crests at a hill where, high on top, an enormous cross presides over the 360-degree view. *How big is that cross?* I wonder. The height of a two-story building at least. The damp air tickles my cheeks; the smell of salty ocean and the eeriness of the empty tourist town merge into a feeling of peace. The cross, so magnificent, so overpowering, gives me hope about my new life here in Chile, free from Brandon again.

Sunday, another day without an answer from Corey. Now I'm getting anxious. My life here depends on this thirty-something astronomer. Corey, Graham had explained to me, had started off in New York, tried his hand at acting, attended— where was it? Cornell? —and ended up in Houston, employed at the Space Center. Now he's an astronomer working at Cerro Tololo Inter-American Observatory up in the Andes Mountains outside La Serena. Corey is probably just away for the weekend, I reassure myself. He'll be back by tonight, right?

23

Nicole Whyrrl

They hang like Christmas ornaments, the hydrangea blossoms once sapphire-blue, now dead, the color of dung. Nicole clips her brown flowers, dropping them into a plastic bucket. She kicks at the weeds with her black leather heels. Her garden, her pride and joy when pink cosmos and dahlias and lilies bloomed all summer long, was the most spectacular garden in the neighborhood. Now it looks like hell.

She tosses her bucket of weeds into the compost pile and returns to the kitchen, where she lifts her phone from her back pocket and dials. Taps her fingers on the counter while it rings. "Police, this is Nicole Whyrll, owner of the Harvard Street Pharmacy." A crow flies across the yard, nearly hitting her window, cawing in its malicious voice. "I'd like to report a theft of a controlled substance." "Yes. Roxicodone." She listens to the questions. "Two thousand." She switches her phone to speaker and sets it on the counter while she drops a Keurig packet into her coffee machine. "No, I have no suspicions. None whatsoever." She pulls the lever to start the coffee brewing. "No, I have no idea," she repeats. "Although," and now she pauses. "I do have an assistant who's been working for me for several months," she says. "He seems like a good enough guy. A hard worker. Seriously hard worker. I mean, I hate to say anything bad about him."

She watches Jim Corcoran's enormous dog yank on his leash, eyeing a squirrel he wants to chase. Between Guru's digging and barking, Nicole wonders why the Corcorans haven't dropped him off in the middle of the woods.

"His name? Scott. Scott Crowley." She sips her coffee. "Well, he *has* been acting a little weird lately." She listens. "I have all his personal information in the files back at the pharmacy." She glances at the clock: 4:30 p.m. "Yes, with his application." Joel will be home soon from Torrie's preschool gymnastics class.

"Yes, officer. I can come down to the station. Yes, in the morning." Nicole hangs up, wraps one arm around her stomach, and finishes her coffee. The stars will align.

"Mommy, Mommy!"

Torrie leaps into her mom's arms. "Guess what? I did a cartwheel! All by myself. Miss Nancy said it was the best cartwheel ever! I should be on the gymnastics team! I should be in the Olympics!" Joel lags behind Torrie and disappears up the staircase.

"The Olympics," says Nicole. "Why not? Someone's got to do it, right? Why not my angel?" Torrie hugs her mom, nuzzling her head into the crook of Nicole's neck. It's been a long time since her mom has called her "angel."

24

Nicole Whyrrl

The tip of Wilkes Island is too remote for any food delivery, so residents must drive to the boat launch next to the bridge to get Domino's pizza. As Nicole drives down Wilkes Island Boulevard, passing the fire station on the right and then the cemetery on the left, her mind swings back to last night's conversation at the Pilchuck Tavern.

The familiar face next to Nicole had smiled, that ugly, annoying grin. Nicole had opened her wallet, slipped a pill from her coin purse, and swallowed it, no longer caring if Al noticed.

Actually, she didn't care about anything.

"Let me see if I've got this right," he'd begun with that wicked, sly smile. "What that stupid idiot Scott said—or, rather, what he meant—was, he didn't want to run away with you because he's hung up on his neighbor lady, that friend of Lorissa's, that lady I've got a picture of on my phone. Well, well, well." Al was a slime ball, a polished slime ball, but he was her only confidant, the only one she could tell about the mess she was in.

He'd crossed his arms and leaned back on his stool. "So, you've known where she is all along." Nicole had felt rabid, like a feral coyote ready to pounce. At first, she'd figured if Meaghan hadn't wanted to be found, she wasn't going to blow her cover, but if that witch was screwing Scott, her man on the side? All bets were off. Al hadn't acted surprised when Nicole said she knew Meaghan. Maybe he'd tracked her down weeks ago.

"Let me get the picture," he'd said. "You told Scott you'd run off with him, leave your family, your pharmacy, and he said no because he's hot on some other lady?" Nicole had stared straight, sipped her drink, rattled her ice cubes. "You're not going to let him get away with that, are you?" Al's voice leached slime. "What are you going to do about it, sweet Nicole?"

Raucous laughter spread through the tavern, the snap of darts missing the dartboard, the reek of drunkards. "What do you mean by that?" she'd asked him.

"Whatever you want me to mean." The light had caught Al's eyes, cold as blue ice. "Maybe you want some revenge?"

"Revenge? What?" Nicole glimpsed a shadow from his pocket, the lines, the curves. She'd tapped her manicured nail on the bar. "Gun? Is that a gun?" Her words had slurred.

"I might have an extra."

"An extra!" Nicole had nearly spit out her drink. She tried to whisper, but instead her words came out as more of a shout. "What are you?"

"Hey, maybe we can take care of that lady problem together?"

"What the hell are you saying?" She'd glanced up to see the bartender coming back toward their end of the bar, but a woman in a cowboy hat at the far end waved. The bartender lifted a clean glass and pulled the Michelob tap, handing her a beer.

Al had scratched under his chin as though thinking of a plan. "You could scare that boyfriend of yours, then come to the rescue. That would get him."

Nicole had cocked her head. "What are you saying?" She didn't want to do anything that would jeopardize the Harvard Street Pharmacy. Not lose all she had worked so hard for. All those years Mr. Ferrier pawed at her until he finally got too old and she had bought him out. She owned the Harvard Street Pharmacy now, and yes, maybe it was failing, what with all the big-box stores moving in with pharmacies—Target, Safeway, Albertson's—but damn it, it was her baby as much as Torrie was. She'd grown up as trash and would not ever, ever slip back into that life. "What are you suggesting?"

"Tell the cops he's ripping off the Harvard Street Pharmacy. Set him up, then save him. He'll be crawling to you."

"With a gun?"

"You know. To protect yourself."

Nicole had slammed her glass on the counter. That didn't even make sense. *A gun? No way.* She'd swayed to the ladies' room, her thinking on overdrive. *Well, maybe. Maybe.* She'd added lipstick and pinched her cheeks, but when she'd emerged from the bar, the stool next to hers, where Al had been sitting, was empty.

25

Meaghan Farren

Finally, on Sunday evening Corey's girlfriend answers the phone. Within an hour a tall girl with curly, short hair meets me at my motel. She, too, is an astronomer, she explains, working at another observatory, Cerro Mamalluca. She drives a curving road, snaking up a hill and punches a code to open the wrought-iron gate, entering the community of expats. "This area is Elqui Valley," she says. "Quite the international hub for astronomers with its clear, black night sky."

Corey, peppy, cheerful, and apologetic, hugs me like an old friend. "Meaghan, so glad you made it! Sorry we missed your calls!" He is about a head taller than I am with brown glasses and sandy hair that is slightly mussed. He reminds me of a happy border collie—loose, gentle, sweet. "Consider this your home as long as you need."

The living room has a red couch covered with red, orange, and purple pillows. Two wrought-iron lamps light the room. The art on the wall reminds me of children's finger paintings, but I suppose it's exotic and gallery-worthy—just beyond my meager understanding. A teapot on the table is steaming with the scent of lemon. Oh, such a cozy home. My relief at being away from Brandon only deepens. How lucky I am! But I'm also superstitious—always waiting for the other shoe to drop.

"We were visiting friends farther up in the mountains over

the weekend. There's not much cell service once you get far from La Serena," Corey says as he leads me to a small bedroom at the back of the house: white walls, a white comforter, dazzling neon green pillows. My own bedroom, but I'll share the bathroom with him and Anastasia. Ahh, the kindness of strangers. "And you're welcome to use our computer," Corey says, "if you need to send e-mails or whatever." After all the years Brandon had abused me, I had forgotten how generous some people could be.

The next day their friend and neighbor introduces herself and asks if I'd like to work for her family, doing laundry and basic cleaning. I can't wait to get started. I email Scott: *This will work out!* Maybe he and Chumley can visit. I'd love that.

I take a bubbly, hot bath, so grateful for these kind strangers. Afterward, I polish my nails a flaming red, treating myself to celebrate my good fortune. I'm hunched next to the bathtub on the cool porcelain floor when the phone rings. I ignore it, fantasizing about my future with Scott, although a voice in my head warns me: Don't get ahead of yourself.

26

Lorissa Orondo

Connor has been improving these last few months. He has! Since beginning counseling with Jon Fleury, he's shown up at meals without all those condescending monosyllables. He rides his bicycle everywhere, even though we lifted his restrictions on driving months ago. He carries on conversations—actual conversations—about the weather, the Seahawks, the neighbor's dog. Laughs now and then at Lorissa's stupid, witless jokes. His eyes gleam with a spark—albeit minuscule. Last June, he passed his grade—barely, yes—but here he is a senior, getting some Bs. She can't believe that now, once again, she's in this insufferable principal's office. What happened?

Rhys. Every time the school boots out Connor, every time Connor is busted smoking dope, every time he gets drunk and is dumped off at his house by one of his friends, there is one common denominator: Rhys. Rhys must have egged him on— just when Connor was getting better!

Yes, Lorissa felt exhausted these past few days because of her commute—two hours to Seattle in heavy traffic, but only an hour back when fewer cars fill the road. Exhausted, but a *good* exhausted. Music means so much to her; her singing keeps her somewhat sane. She didn't work through the summer, and now she's having fun singing for the latest, hot video game, even though she's anxious about the part of her contract that says she can't miss a single day. Miss one day, and she is out. This little gig means so much.

And then this morning, just after she opened the garage door, before she could even get in the car, she received that infuriating phone call: Connor in another fight just like the last time. Now she waits impatiently as Principal Deane drones on and on about acceptable conduct. The sound of the wall clock, tick, tick, tick. Damn it! She'll be late.

She silently fumes as she and Connor march out of the school. "Okay, Connor." She tries to hold her temper, tries to control her voice because she knows every straggler in the high school parking lot can hear her. "Why did you do it? Rhys egged you on, right? Connor, if I lose this job, I'll be so pissed."

"Mom! Rhys wasn't even in school today. Don't blame everything on him."

"Connor, I thought you had turned the corner. You, you, you. . ." Lorissa glances around, sees a boy staring, his face dotted with tufts of an uneven beard. What is his name? Someone she hasn't seen since preschool. "I should have said something when I realized the bracelet was missing. You thought I didn't know, but after I caught you rifling through my jewelry box last spring, I checked. You stole my bracelet, didn't you? You've been screwing up all along, haven't you? Have you even been going to your counselor appointments? Get in the car!"

"No!"

"*What?*"

"No, Ma. I'm not getting in the car. Why should I? You don't believe anything I say. I rode my bike to school, and I'm going to ride around before I go home. So, screw you!"

"*What* did you say to me?" Connor turns his back to her and heads to the bike rack. She kicks her tire. *Ow!* She hasn't been this mad since. . .since the last time he was suspended.

"Ma, I'll get back your stupid bracelet!"

She and Graham had moved to this godforsaken island at the end of the earth for what? To raise this precious darling who is belligerent, who doesn't appreciate a thing? And now Lorissa is falling apart at the seams. Graham is always gone, traveling for work, Mackenzie always has her bedroom door shut, and now this. If she loses her job—the one fiber of sanity in her life—because of Connor. . .She squeaks her fob, unlocking her car. Maybe I should just run away, she thinks. Just leave them all. Join some choral group and sing around the world.

She has to be in Seattle in an hour and a half. She checks Google Maps on her phone. An accident on I-5! A semi rollover. Still, she has to try. Her tears feel sticky, rolling down her cheeks, first a trickle, then a flood. She drives from the high school to Route 16, reaches the entrance to Interstate 5, and traffic is at a dead stop. She checks Google Maps again and switches on the traffic radio station. The backup is hours long. Two trucks and a car. There's no way she can make it to Seattle. Not even close. Forty-five minutes later, she gets to the next exit, turns around, and swings into the nearest parking lot.

Her stomach aches—a big ugly weight pulling her down. She bangs her head back against the headrest. She knows she has a good life. An easy life. She should be grateful. But her life is ripping like an old cotton sheet, piece by ragged piece. Maybe her coping skills just aren't that good. She has so much more than most people: two cars, a house with a view, vacations to the Oregon coast. And now she'll go back to the way it was before: half her days worried about her son; half her days furious. *I need to sing on this video game. I need it.*

And now I can't. I've lost my job.

Oh, Graham is a great husband. He really is. She couldn't be happier for her husband—except that he is never around. Travel, travel, travel. So excited about his work. But this time her inner self is torn at the seams, and even the best husband can't fix her. Nor the best friend.

Friend? A small light sparks in her mind. *A friend. Nicole.* She'll talk with Nicole. Sure, she hasn't spoken with her in months, but that's why their friendship is so important. They can go long stretches without speaking, but then when they catch up, they're back where they left off. Nicole has that quirky, crazy side where she'll blow up out of nowhere, but that's also why she is such a close friend. Because of her imperfections. She knows Lorissa's past, her shame. Lorissa needs that right now. An imperfect friend who will understand the feeling of wanting to run away to the farthest corner of the earth. Who'll understand how much a career might mean to a woman, even if she puts her family first, which Lorissa definitely does.

If only Lorissa felt as validated being a wife and mother as she does with her singing jobs, but somehow, she doesn't. Her career balances her out. After all, when Lorissa sang on her first computer game, the choir master had complimented her voice. Lori chuckled at the time. No one ever said, "You've done a wonderful job cleaning the toilet."

Yes, Nicole will understand. Lorissa feels a little better as she flips on her windshield wipers—it's raining, but lightly—and she steers her car back to Yachts Village, back toward the Harvard Street Pharmacy.

"Nicole?" Lorissa opens the door, the little bell ringing above her head. "You back there?" The florescent lights sound like a horde of bees, an eerie sound in the otherwise silent room. She heads toward the storage room–office where Nicole spends most of her time filling out insurance forms. Lorissa sniffs. "Nicole!" Lorissa feels an awful sense of foreboding.

"Nicole!" Tapping open the storeroom door, she halts and her feet freeze to the ground. Her heart pulses. She blinks, not believing. First, the acrid scent, then the blood. A crimson swamp under his legs, his hips, his chest—and finally she sees it: the gaping hole etched in the side of his head. The blood seeps from a body, a body she recognizes, Scott Crowley sprawled in a sea of red.

Lorissa looks up past Scott, across the desk, to Nicole, leaning back in her chair, stiff, limp wrists dangling from her arms. Her eyes open. Vacant. Her chest rising and falling. Alive. In shock.

A jolt of electricity shoots up Lorissa's spine. She pulls out her cell phone and dials 9-1-1. "There's a body here! Yes. Harvard Street Pharmacy." She swallows. "I don't know." Her heart feels like a runaway train, but a calming instinct takes over, and she listens intently to the woman on the other end of the phone who says that help is on the way and that Lorissa should check his pulse—she squats next to Scott's body and lifts his wrist. "Yes! Yes," she says. "A thread."

"Where is the blood coming from?"

"Everywhere! I mean, I can't tell! It's his head! There's a hole in his head!" Within moments, she hears sirens—she's so glad that in tiny Yachts Village both the EMTs and the police are only blocks away.

Sirens scream outside the pharmacy, then medics burst in, equipment in hand. Lorissa steps back as a medic who appears to be twelve years old bends over, does a cursory exam. "He needs to go to Harborview. We need a helicopter," he shouts.

Lorissa is nearly paralyzed. Harborview. In Seattle. The only place to handle a head gushing out blood.

"Defibrillator," a different medic says. A pair of men and women cradle Scott's body, place oxygen over his face, an IV in his vein, check his blood pressure. Suddenly the room is a hive of activity: Scott, unconscious on a gurney, police officers roping off the scene with yellow tape. Outside the pharmacy, gawkers are held at bay by more police. Lorissa steps back to survey the scene. Now she sees a gun swimming in the blood next to where Scott's body had lain.

Nicole still hasn't moved, although Lorissa can see that her eye lids flicker. A breeze across Lorissa's face draws her eyes to the open door behind Nicole. Nicole mumbles something incoherent.

"Let me in! Let me in!" A police officer blocks Joel, but he barges past. "She's my wife. I've got to see her! Let me see my wife."

"Stay out of the blood. We can't have this scene contaminated."

Joel rushes to Nicole, who's still in shock. "Sweetheart!" He drapes his arms around her head. Lorissa hears people gathered outside the front of the drugstore, probably making up stories, starting rumors that will spread like the flu around town. This tiny town has had only one shooting in a decade, and now people are scrambling for details: "He's alive." "He's dead." "A boy did it." "Her friend did it." "A man came in."

A deafening roar descends: the helicopter; a flurry of men and women run in. Lorissa searches for any movement in Scott's eyes, fingers, chest. She sees none. They haul out the gurney, a battalion of ants carrying off their victim.

An officer closes the front door, where police measure, analyze, and murmur among themselves. Lorissa realizes she, too, is somewhat in shock. She'd been dazed and on autopilot when she'd phoned, followed the 9-1-1 operator's directions, watched the medics shuttle Scott away. Now the horror of the scene strikes her. So much ghastly dark blood on the floor, on the walls, splattered on the side of Nicole's desk. Lorissa has seen gory TV shows, but they haven't desensitized her to the shocking scene in this room.

Nicole's white face reminds Lorissa of a Halloween ghost. Joel shakes her shoulders, rousing her. "Nicole! Baby! Snap out of it!" Finally, she comes to, hugging Joel, tears flowing.

"Oh, Joel. It was awful," she gasps. "I thought I was going to be killed!"

"Who, sweetie? Who did this?"

Lorissa glances at the two officers who, like her, watch from a respectable distance. One woman, suddenly aware of her presence, says, "Ma'am, we're going to need to ask you some questions."

"Sure."

"Let's step into the other room," she says, motioning to the pharmacy on the other side of the storeroom door.

"Okay, just a sec." Lorissa turns to Joel, who holds both of Nicole's hands in his. Nicole's eyes are glassy, unfocused, like she's in another world. "Joel, is there anything I can do? Where's Torrie?"

"Oh, Lorissa," he says, coming over and hugging her. Lorissa feels his arms shaking. "Yes. I just dropped Torrie off at Jasmine's law office—so close, you know—and if you can. . ."

"I'll answer this policewoman's questions, then I'll bring Torrie back to our house. She can spend the night if she needs to. I'll just go get her pajamas, stuffed bear, and toothbrush."

"You've got a key to our house?" Joel's face is as pale as Nicole's.

"Of course." She's had one for years. She nods to Joel, hopefully reassuringly, sees no response from Nicole, then turns to the officer. "Okay, to answer your questions. Yes, I'm the one who dialed 9-1-1." They walk into the main section of the pharmacy and shut the door to the storeroom behind them.

"Were you here when it happened?" the officer asks Lorissa.

"No."

"Why were you crying?"

What a question! "I was upset. I know Scott and Nicole. Of course, I was upset. Besides, I was already dealing with something before I came in." God, that was a million years ago. To think she'd been sitting there in that parking lot when Scott— the love of Meaghan's life—was shot in her best friend's pharmacy. Lorissa realizes how petty she'd been acting. She shakes her head in disgust with herself. "Anyway, I came in to talk to Nicole, that's her, the pharmacist, and…"

"What were you dealing with? Before?"

"Oh, don't even ask. It all seems so insignificant now. My son. My son, Connor, was suspended again from school, and I was pissed off at him, and then that made me too late to get to work, I lost my job, and…well. This isn't relevant."

"Any information can help." The officer's unsympathetic tone rattles Lorissa.

"Well, it's not like my son had anything to do with this," Lorissa says in a high-pitched voice, laughing nervously, but then checks the policewoman's eyes. No laughter there. None whatsoever.

27

Meaghan Farren

Corey knocks on the bathroom door, surprising me. "That's your phone ringing."

"Oh! Thanks!" I tighten the top to the nail polish bottle, blow on my nails, then race to my bedroom and answer the phone. I hear only sobs.

"Meaghan." I can barely make out her words.

"Lorissa?"

The sobs, the wails, go on for minutes. I wait, wishing I could hug her. "What happened, Lorissa?" Her voice sounds like she's gasping for air. "Lorissa, breathe. It's okay." I speak as calmly as I can. "I'll just wait till you can talk." I wonder about the possibilities. Connor in trouble again? Graham? Was Graham in an accident? Did their house burn down? It's something bad.

"Meaghan. It's Scott."

"Scott?" I pause a moment, wondering. "What about Scott?"

"He was shot."

"Scott? Shot?" *No*, I think. There must be some mistake.

"I found him. Found him laid out on the floor. Blood." Her cough is a cry. "Lots of blood. From his head."

Before she can say more, the phone slips from my hand, crashes onto the mosaic floor and I slide down the adobe wall, scratching my back and landing hard, my legs outstretched like a broken doll's.

"Meaghan. Are you there?" Lorissa's voice is faint, calling out from the phone lying on the floor. "Meaghan!" I lift the phone and hold it to my ear, but my hand feels numb; I'm not sure I can grasp it for long. It's as if I've been struck by lightning and there's nothing left. I am empty, floating in a dream. I'll wake up on Wilkes Island, sitting at Scott's little table with my glass of wine, seeing the charms on my bracelet shine in the candlelight.

Words finally trickle from my mouth. "What happened? What happened to Scott?"

"He was shot at the pharmacy." Lorissa sounds like she's in a tunnel—far, far away. "In the back room of the Harvard Street Pharmacy. A gun lay on the cement floor right next to him, and Nicole was in shock."

I try to listen, but I can't concentrate. "You found him?" I eke out my next question. "How is he?"

"Alive. He's at Harborview in Seattle, a great hospital, great doctors. He's getting the best care." Lorissa stops, catches her breath. "But Meaghan, it's not good."

"Not good?"

"He's in a coma, according to the police. They suspect it's a bullet to the brain." She tries to muffle her cries, but I can hear. "The doctors say his chance of making it—well, there's some hope." I close my eyes. Say nothing. Too many emotions flood through me. This can't be true.

"Meaghan?"

"He might not make it? He might die?" I feel the water dripping from my eyes, and yet I am numb. It's not really happening.

"We don't know."

My throat clamps up like a severe allergic reaction. I can't breathe. I don't know what to think. "Do they know what happened? Who shot him?"

"No one knows anything. I called you right away."

My hand grips the phone like a vise. Vertigo sets in.

"I'm so sorry," she says. "I know he means so much to you."

My mouth is dry, parched. I'm about to hang up when I remember. "Lorissa, will you take care of Chumley?"

"Of course, we will. Of course."

A moment passed. "It's Brandon." I say, my voice is strong, cold.

"What?"

"It's Brandon." I speak harshly, bitter, though now my tears are streaming. "Brandon is behind this. I know he is."

28

Meaghan Farren

I rinse my face with cold water and stare in the mirror at my smudged mascara, the black circles under my eyes. I look like a wet rag doll. What a mess. I sit on the edge of the cold porcelain bathtub, elbows on knees. I've gone and fallen for someone who's been shot. Who might die. And it's my fault. Brandon would never have come after Scott if it weren't for me. I don't know how he did it, how he found Scott, but I'm so sure. Brandon is evil. Pure evil.

There's a crevice in my heart cracking open, an avalanche of feelings exploding. I totter into the living room where Corey and Anastasia are loafing on the sofa, feet on the coffee table, glasses of wine in hand. Such a normal couple. Isn't this what couples do? Come home, bitch about the boss, be excited about progress at work, bummed about the latest screwup? I had imagined this happening with Scott and me: being like a real couple. A normal one. Maybe even adopt some kids. White picket fence. The works.

When he sees me, Corey jumps up so fast his horn-rimmed glasses nearly fall off. "What happened?" I see the concern in his eyes. Anastasia looks up at me, wine in hand, wiggling her purple toenails. "Do you need something to drink? Wine? Water? Juice?"

"Just some water for now."

Anastasia runs to the kitchen, while Corey stands next to me awkwardly, clearly wanting to help but not knowing what to do. Anastasia returns and puts her arm around my shoulders while I drink the water.

"Thank you," I sputter.

"Meaghan," she says in a soft voice. "Can we help?" When she opens her lips, the tiny chip on her front tooth brightens her smile. I hear a Mozart waltz playing faintly. I haven't shared much about my life with Anastasia and Corey. Graham had told them I was hiding from an abusive husband, but that's all. Now I sit on the rattan chair and pour it all out: Brandon, moving West, Scott— and now, I gasp for a breath as I finish—Scott lying in the hospital with a bullet in his brain.

"Oh, Meaghan!" Anastasia comes over and hugs me. "I'm so sorry. That's so much to deal with." She gets a tissue from the kitchen and hands it to me. "Scott sounds like a great guy."

I wipe my nose with the tissue. "He was. Is. Oh, I just can't believe it!" My tears begin again.

Corey clears his throat. "Dinner's about ready. Do you think you could eat? It might do you some good."

The Brazilian steak smells delicious, bringing back my ten-year-old self's memories of Dad barbecuing on our decrepit Victorian's porch. I loved that house, even with its missing boards on the deck, its chipped paint in the kitchen, its hanging shutter that snapped against the window in the rain. I nod, yes.

Anastasia tosses a salad and Corey cuts the steak onto our plates, then serves the old-fashioned American meal—steak, baked potatoes, tossed green salad. "Maybe you should postpone starting work," Corey says. "You've been through so much."

"Well, I told your neighbor I'd start right away." I feel numb and so alone despite their kindness.

Corey takes my hand, like he is my own nephew. "With all that's going on? Nearly beaten to death, a bare escape, traveling all the way to a new continent just to feel safe, and now the man you love is shot? Do you know how that would rank on the table of stressors? Over the top!"

I manage a wobbly smile. "Well, if you put it that way."

Anastasia agrees. "You need someplace to chill. Like a real retreat. You said you've got a little savings, right? You don't have to start work right away?" I think about it, then finally nod. "Well, then, give yourself a break."

Everything they're saying is true. So true. "You don't think your neighbor would mind?" My voice cracks.

"Nah. Not at all."

"But what would I do?" My voice quavers. If I were home, I'd try those things other women do, like a spa, a yoga retreat, some healing road trip.

"Mmm," Anastasia takes a bite of steak. "I was a vegetarian for years before I met this guy." She sends Corey a wry smile, and he nudges her with his elbow. "I know!" Anastasia says. Corey and I both stare. "You can rent a car, right?" Anastasia leans toward me, excitement in her voice.

"There's this *amazing* little village high in the mountains. An itty-bitty place called Cochiquaz. It's the spiritual capital of the world!"

29

Meaghan Farren

After dinner last night, Corey and Anastasia had brought out a map and shown me how to find Cochiquaz. They sold me on the idea of a mini-adventure to "the spiritual capital of the world," whatever that means. This morning I pack my small suitcase. They've been so wonderful to me, but I really need to be alone now. To grieve. To figure out my next step.

So much has happened so fast. One night I'm with my love, having a candlelight dinner, and now a few days later, he's shot in the head, maybe dying, and I'm in the mountains of Chile heading off to who knows where. Cochiquaz —a quiet place for me to sort out my thoughts.

Corey drives me into La Serena, through neighborhoods of pink and yellow and blue adobe houses, boys playing soccer in the alleys, girls huddling on corners, whispering. We arrive at the auto rental place, which seems like an exact replica of ones in America. I rent a Subaru Outback just like the one I'd purchased on my road trip, but with a few more dents and chips in the paint.

Once I'm behind the wheel, I feel lighter. Not free from sadness or grief, but I can feel my lungs, I can breathe, and that's a step. I recite Spanish to myself, reading all the signs and billboards. Little by little my high school Spanish begins to return, and while I drive the narrow road into the mountains, I try to name all the sights along the way.

After several hours, the road shrinks to little more than one lane, its switchbacks winding higher and higher into the Andes. Above are sharp cliffs and below are acres and acres of grapes grown for *pisco*, the favorite sweet Chilean alcohol.

Twisting up into the mountains reminds me of my evening drives in Massachusetts over the lush green hills covered with maples and oaks. After Brandon pummeled me one time, I finally figured out how to play the game—or so I'd thought. I began to act compliant. So much so, that after many months Brandon began to loosen the reins. I followed his orders: cleaned the shower so it didn't just glisten, it shone like polished silver. I never talked back, no matter how many times he told me I was fat, ugly. I stayed thin, barely eating, and he'd patted my head when he weighed me every day. I was his "good girl."

That was when I started jogging. Though I was still his captive, he'd allowed me to run because I had convinced him I'd look better—that is, be a better showpiece—if I were more fit. I carefully applied my makeup, blush, and mascara at four each afternoon because the better I looked when he arrived home at six or six-thirty—or even eleven o'clock—the better he'd treat me. I obeyed his every word, and if I did see that glint of his belt buckle, my insides would explode with fear, but I'd hold up my chin. Not too high. Not in defiance. Still, I didn't cower.

And my reward for this compliance was spending the cool evenings up on Mount Sugarloaf, watching the purple skies as the sun set. I'd drive the winding road, drinking in the scent of the woods, up to the parking lot on top. I'd gaze below at the lights twinkling from the New England farms and villages, swaths of green rectangles the size of postage stamps; old-fashioned red barns and white houses, so picturesque, like an Andrew Wyeth painting. I'd turn off the car, and in the silence, I'd dream of my escape. I couldn't just run away, not without a plan. I needed money, a disguise, a destination far, far away. Someplace Brandon had never heard of. I remembered the alumni magazine. The article on Graham, living on a remote island, and his innovations at Amazon. Could I go there? To Graham and Lorissa's?

I'd planned, plotted every detail, saved money, ordered clothes to blend in to Washington State, chose the perfect day to leave—when Brandon had such an important luncheon, he paid little attention to me. He didn't notice the anxiety on my face, hear the hope in my voice when I said, "Good luck with your luncheon." I had decided on my gamble.

And how did that gamble work out? I ask myself as I drive by more of the neatly planted grapes, sweet smelling in the hot Chilean sun. Brandon not only found me, but it was probably he who had shot an innocent man, a man whose grievous sin was being kind to me. A friend. A man whom I had begun to love.

I tighten my hands on the wheel and bite my lips as the thin, paved road turns to dirt, the car climbing higher and higher. Hours after leaving La Serena, I arrive at the end of the road and a hand-carved sign with crooked letters announcing "Cochiquaz." Behind the aged wooden sign sits a white stone building—an inn and restaurant—the white so bright it's blinding under the flaming sun. The two-story, six-unit inn makes me feel like I've traveled in a time warp, back to an older, primitive era when cell-phone reception wasn't something you missed. "The only way anyone can reach you is through their landline," Corey had warned me.

"It's fine. No one's going to try," I'd said.

I park on a dusty patch of dirt that must be a parking lot, but there is only one car. The one other building, another white adobe, is bordered by stooped gray trees hanging low to the ground, with one path leading up the mountain, one path leading down.

This is the end of the world as far as I can tell. At the entrance to the inn, an old man offers a toothless welcome behind a rickety hand-carved table. "Hello," he says, his only English word, I suspect, as he begins to pantomime, pointing to the calendar, a small map of the surrounding area. Pablo, I learn, is his name. He checks me in with some rapid words of Spanish and hands me a key.

As the sun is setting, I wander behind the inn, thinking of Lorissa. She sounded as devastated as I am. Imagine finding a bloodied body, someone shot in safe little Yachts Village. She knew Scott had come through for me, stood up for me, and started me on the path that ended with me being here, in this safe place, here in Cochiquaz, Chile. What does that say? I think it says Lorissa cares deeply for both me and Scott. Maybe that she forgives me.

Forgiveness can be so powerful—both for me and for her. Maybe we'll never be best friends again, like the old adage about friendship, "The crack will always remain." Still, she felt for me and knew how destroyed I would be about Scott.

Oh, Scott. I am on the verge of love. My heart skips when I think of you. Although I've rarely prayed, now might be a good time. I make my way around the inn, dust dancing through the rays of the broiling sun, when suddenly I stop. Stunned.

Before me are two enormous round crimson and orange reflecting pools. They mirror the brilliant red evening sky. Beyond them, giant Buddha heads, eight feet tall at least. I step closer. Submerged in the water is a boulder-sized amethyst.

What is this place? Why are these here? If only my Spanish was better and I could ask Pablo.

I bend my neck back so my eyes scale the daunting Andes. I hear a strange bird singing from afar. Alone in this strange sanctuary, I dip my ankles into the cool pools, splash lightly, taste the dust, and feel humble against the ten-thousand-foot mountains towering above me. When I inhale, I sense the Divine, the sacred, and say a prayer for Scott, for his recovery, for his healing. I feel touched by a Spirit and at peace—a wretchedly sad peace, but peace nonetheless. The sun slowly dips below the horizon and the lilac sky morphs to black. Then stars and more stars, brighter stars than I ever imagined. Millions of stars dot the world around me. The Southern Cross! There it is. The Southern Cross.

I eat dinner at the restaurant at the inn—a small room with a bar and a half dozen wooden tables and chairs. I drink my pisco sour, place my napkin in my lap, and reflect on how it had all gone wrong. Brandon and I had moved to Northampton, hoping his prep school job would lead to a professorship after he finished his PhD. Then, in a shock that had reverberated through my soul, three fifteen-year-old girls accused him of assault and rape. No, I'd thought, not my husband. We'd been married more than ten years. I'd been on his side. Believed him when he'd said those girls were rich, spoiled liars, trying to get an "easy A", so they made up that ridiculous story that would ruin his reputation forever. He'd never get another job teaching because of those false accusations. He was innocent. I'd defended him to anyone who asked. I was proud of my professor husband. Thought it a shame he had to begin brand-new, start in a new field.

But he had stumbled home a year after beginning in real estate, drunk, angry, mean. At first it was words, hateful words, and a week later fists, then, after months, pounding, smacking, boots kicking. Of course, now I've read so much, learned so much more. I know now he had followed the pattern of every abuser, and I should have left after that first punch. Should have thrown away the flowers he bought me the next day. Should have packed instead of listening to his apologies. Should have driven back to my dad, who was still alive back in Port

Townsend. Should have explained—and suddenly I freeze, like I've been struck by a diesel truck.

I sit taller, stretch my neck, place my glass on the table. Oh, why hadn't I seen it before? I can hear those footsteps now, like I'm living in a movie, those footsteps of Brandon's stomping up to our godforsaken apartment. I had shooed Chumley off my lap, let her scoot under the bed so Brandon wouldn't see her, and stood next to the stove, like I hadn't been sitting, rocking all afternoon. Those footsteps? Those footsteps that turned my veins to ice? They were the same steps as my father's, my father before he killed my mother.

Why hadn't I seen it before? Why hadn't I seen that I was just following the same pattern when I fell for Brandon? Why had it taken visiting this tiny spiritual village in Chile to recognize the obvious? That, indeed, I had married my father. Why hadn't I put it together before now? That the most obvious insight of all I couldn't see. And why is it I understand now?

The next day, the intensity of the sun nearly blinds me. I plan to see a shaman after breakfast, the eldest, wisest man here, whom Anastasia had described before I left La Serena. "You must see him," she'd said.

I'm finishing my coffee at the little restaurant when Pablo calls to me. "Meaghan," he's trying to say, and he holds out the phone toward me like I have a call—but why would anyone reach me here? I place my napkin on the table, and fear strikes my heart. Scott can't be dead. He can't be.

"Meaghan." Ah, Lorissa. "I called Corey, who gave me this number." And then I hear her voice quiver. She's gasping. I smell fresh herbs in the restaurant while my stomach knots. What's going on, I want to scream, but I wait till she catches her breath. Then, finally, I ask.

"Is Scott dead?"

Lorissa sniffs, stutters. "No. It's not that." I wait. He'll never recover from the bullet in his brain? Mind gone? Paralyzed?

"Nicole says that Connor shot Scott."

I squeeze my eyes together, absorbing this. "What?" Suddenly I am outside of myself, outside of my own selfish self-pity.

"Lorissa," I say, but she cries louder.

"Lorissa, I don't know your son that well, but still, I get feelings about people and I just know he couldn't shoot anyone. Why would Nicole say such a thing?"

"Nicole called the police the day before Scott was shot, saying there had been a robbery at the Harvard Street Pharmacy." Lorissa inhales. "Someone stole some sort of opioid. Lots of them. Like a thousand? Roxicodone."

"Roxicodone?" I'd never heard of that.

"Roxies, I guess the kids call them. Some super addictive opioid. I never heard of them before, but they're like oxycodone. Anyway, bad, bad stuff. The police didn't tell us much, but I get the impression Nicole implicated Scott in the theft without actually accusing him and then she said Connor bought stolen Roxies from Scott.

"She called the police the day before Scott was shot?" I'm confused. This doesn't make sense. This is not the Scott I know. "Why? Why him? Them?"

"Nicole says she and Scott were working in the back of the pharmacy and Connor charged in, his eyes all crazed, pupils like pins, pointing a gun at Scott. 'Where are my Roxies? You ripped me off. You owe me five hundred Roxies,' and Scott brushed him off, they yelled, and then …Lorissa is crying so hard she cannot speak.

"Take your time," I say.

When Lorissa catches her breath, she says, "Nicole said Connor shot him! Shot Scott, tossed the gun, and ran out the back."

My chest pounds, and now Lorissa is howling. "My son! My son!"

I wish I were there to hold her tightly, envelop her in my arms. "I don't believe it," I blurt out.

"My son is a troublemaker. I know that better than anyone. But Meaghan, believe me. Connor couldn't have done it." She's begging, beseeching. I picture her face so red, raw. Agony in every word. "Connor is a delinquent. I know that. But," she raises her voice, firm, unequivocal, unquestioning, "he didn't shoot anybody!" She's yelling. "He gets in fights. He smokes pot. I know he does. But he was getting so much better with that new counselor and new meds."

"Oh, Lorissa. How can I help?" I wish I could think of something.

"I just don't know." Someone turns off the Spanish television that I hadn't noticed, it sounded like white background noise, but now I hear the rapid conversations of diners behind me.

"Meaghan, do you think Scott was dealing drugs?"

"Oh, Lorissa, no! Do you think I'd hang out with a drug dealer if I knew? No. Not at all. I don't believe it, either."

And then it hits me, like I've been stabbed. I can't trust my own heart. I'd never dreamed I would marry a psychopath like Brandon. I'd been so naïve. I just don't know anything anymore. "I…I just had to ask." Lorissa sounds apologetic.

"Well," I pause—I'm not sure I want to say this, but she deserves to know: "Scott *was* mysterious. I honestly felt—feel—like he's been holding something back. But drug dealing? No. I don't buy it." Scott seems like such a good guy. *Is* such a good guy. So patient. Thoughtful. Fun. Determined to keep me safe. Can I have been that wrong about him? Just like I'd been wrong about Brandon?

"You know I've pulled my hair out about Connor over the years," Lorissa says. "Screamed, cried, stood for hours in the shower, just so I didn't have to face the next crisis. But shoot somebody? No. Connor would not do that."

A waiter places a plate with toast and a wedge of cheese on the bar in front of me. "A bullet in the brain! Oh, Meaghan! You know if Scott dies, Connor could be charged with murder!

My boy didn't do this. I've got to figure out why Nicole came up with this horrid, ridiculous claim."

I'm right there with Lorissa—emotionally, if not physically—but when she says "if Scott dies," I feel like a boomerang has swung around and struck me in the gut. I cringe. *Oh, please no. Please don't let him die.* But Lorissa. I must support Lorissa. I must be the friend to her that I wasn't twenty years ago.

"Nicole claims Connor shot Scott right in front of her and ran out the back door. They're going to test the gun for DNA. Apparently, that takes a while. If the DNA on it matches Connor's, well. . ." No need to finish the sentence: Connor would be up shit creek. In jail.

I hope and pray Scott won't die—and not just for me. For Connor and Lorissa, too. Is it possible Connor did shoot Scott? Can you ever truly know anyone? Even your own son? "Of course, he didn't shoot Scott," I say. "I'm so, so sorry Lorissa. If there's any way I can help. . ."

"You know, I wish you were here," Lorissa says. I smile. I wish I were there too.

I pay my bill and meander back out into the sunshine, but feel a headache surging through my head, my shoulders, my back. I used to get headaches all the time in Northampton, but when I moved to Washington State, they'd nearly disappeared. Today, though, my head begins to throb in the bright, white sun. Craggy trees separate me from the rocky desert path that leads higher up the mountain. I feel dust in my hair, in my nails, like a layered veil rising from the ground.

Drawn by the Buddhas, I return to the reflecting ponds and sit by the edge of the pool, crossing my legs and stretching my back and neck so I'm sitting tall. I fold my hands in a Buddhist mudra, close my eyes, and meditate. I breathe slowly, inhaling the mountains, the water, the Buddhas, the dust. I imagine veils—mine and Scott's, Brandon's, Connor's—all hiding and covering and distorting the truth of who we really are.

I continue breathing, and slowly my headache dissolves. Eventually, I rise to my feet and stroll back to my room. I dress in a sleeveless blouse and a cotton skirt, put on sunscreen, fill a bottle with water. Anastasia gave me directions, which I follow, even in the raging heat.

I trek the dirt path until I come upon a branch hanging over the road holding a wooden sign with indecipherable writing. Past the sign, I discover twenty small homes made of stone. Between the buildings hang red and purple and green printed fabrics, like thin bedspreads from an import-export store, dangling from ropes that remind me of clotheslines, connecting each of the houses to one another. Wind chimes made of sticks and bones resonate melodically in the stifling desert heat. I lift the corner of a bedspread, striding through a dirt corridor that leads past home after home, until I reach a withered woman with long faded skirt and billowy blouse and a scarf around her head.

"Shaman?" I ask in English. She is bent, her face leathery, and she's missing most of her teeth. Grunting, she points her gnarled finger. Sweeping through a few more hanging cloths, I find a stone hut where an ancient man sits on a stool tied together with rope, his eyes milky with cataracts. He beckons me inside. I stop, but only for a moment, feeling surprisingly safe in this "other world."

He gestures for me to sit on a straw chair, then he departs, returning with a bowl of water. I smell—incense? Herbs? Rosemary? He dips his creased hand in the water, then sprinkles drops on my forehead as though baptizing me. He moves his hand inches above my body, going from my head to my toes, up and back down again, up and down. I can feel his energy, as though he's touching me, but he's not. I can feel my own energy being tracked by his hands. I close my eyes, the desert heat on my skin like a thin cotton sheet. My chakras are truly coming to life. Tears trickle down my face. I feel my emptiness, my hollow center, and then, ever so slowly, I am filled with love and care and serenity. I see pink.

I open my eyes to the elder, note the compassionate smile on his bronzed, wrinkled face, his knuckles lumpy with thick, rounded bone. What did he just say? "You are depleted." Yes, I am depleted. Completely depleted. I rest a few minutes more, like I would after a massage—that's how I feel, like I've had a deep Swedish massage. And then I rise, nod, and bow— for some reason, the bow comes automatically as I drop coins in the bowl at the door.

"Gracias."

Dazed in a dreamlike state, I wander back to my room, past dried, short trees with spikes for branches, and sleep the rest of the afternoon and through the night.

The next morning, I stop by the mysterious meditation pools, then hike along a path that leads past more barren trees. What has happened to me? The man I love was shot, the son of a friend is accused of shooting him, and my depleted spirit has been cleansed by an ancient spiritual shaman who has given a sense of peace and gratitude. I'm not sure what my next step will be, but I will help. I will find a way to help the woman I hurt so badly all those years ago. Somehow. I want to see Scott, who may or may not live. And yet I am here, in the southern hemisphere, because of Brandon. Is he holding me captive as much here as he did when I lived in Massachusetts? Am I letting him rule my life? Still?

I wander the rocky trail, through trees with branches that are mere gray sticks, pointy and ragged as a witch's broom. I'm surprised to find water: a creek, clear and blue, bubbling over stones, and next to it a mud shack where a short dark man wearing a torn plaid shirt and faded jeans reties ropes for his fences. "*Hola*," he waves with a grin that bursts from his round cheeks. His wife bends her head through the narrow doorway of their house, her hand on the shoulder of a small boy with a tousle of black hair, wearing a Vanderbilt tee shirt. Crazy, the tee shirts that end up here. A sign, "Caballo," is drawn with a marker on a piece of board nailed to the fence. Horseback rides.

Almost surrealistic: Buddhas, shamans, horses—squirreled away
in a remote piece of the Andes Mountains desert.

The man and I pantomime, I hand him money, and we
both mount horses with hard black saddles of torn leather.
Together, we trot up into the hills, past remnants of trees, fallen
wood, and then mammoth rocks the size of the very horses we
are riding.

Some people might criticize my going off with a strange
man on a strange horse in a strange place, but I still feel so
trusting and peaceful after my time with the shaman. Besides,
what have I got to lose? I have no family. My marriage only
isolated me. Any friends I had in Northampton disappeared one
by one after my husband attacked those girls and I foolishly
defended him. No, all I had in Northampton was Chumley, and
all I had on Wilkes Island was Chumley and Lorissa and Scott
and Graham.

Our trot becomes a canter, and I gallop with a sense of
freedom I haven't known since I was a child, when I rode with
my dad along the Washington beaches. I can almost smell the
ocean beaches. Dad and I would stop to examine the shells, then
poke at the sea anemones, squatting on our haunches, watching
them fold into themselves.

I haven't ridden for years, but now as I duck under a low
branch, I truly feel like the vessel for a prayer. I hadn't even
noticed how lonely I'd become. Maybe how lonely I'd always
been. I'd hidden from myself as much as I'd hidden from
everyone else. At this moment, though my thighs are sore and I

hate to think of the blisters from the hard saddle, I feel truly, fully alive for the first time since Brandon smashed my spirit with his initial blow years ago.

At dinner Pablo pantomimes that Lorissa is going to call again. Between the shaman and the horseback ride, I feel renewed, so much so that I'm actually eager to speak to her. She might be calling to say they removed the bullet from Scott's head and he is fine, or that Nicole, no longer in shock, has confessed she made up everything about Connor. Still, I dread bad news. No matter how hopeful I try to be, when Pablo hands me the phone, I hesitate to take it.

When Lorissa asks how I am, I launch into what I've come to understand about this bizarre place. Apparently, the spiritual center of the earth used to be a place in India, and then in the age of Aquarius. "Remember hearing about that? Like that old movie, *Hair*? 1970ish? Anyway, the earth's axis shifted, and we're at the exact pole-opposite end of the earth from there."

No sound from the other end of the phone for a moment. "So that makes it the most spiritual place in the universe?"

Of course, I had been so cynical before I experienced it firsthand. "Well, earth, anyway. Maybe not the universe." Is that a chuckle I hear? "Anyway, enough about me. What's going on?"

"Do you want the long version or the short?"

"Long is good," I say. "I'll just order another cup of coffee."

30

Lorissa Orondo

Lorissa hasn't slept for days—not since Nicole accused Connor of shooting Scott; since she learned the police were going to question Connor. She expected them to show up at her door any minute. The same questions keep circling her brain: How could Nicole do that? Why would she?

Lorissa pours herself some mango juice, sweet and tangy, watching the sun rise above the horizon, a brilliant orange outline of the Cascade Mountains. Graham left a note next to the coffee pot. He's gone to the dump with the freezer that broke a month ago.

The doorbell breaks her reverie. She glances at her robe—coffee stains on the white terry cloth. Her hair all snarled. No makeup. She peers out the window: it's Jim Thorp, the police detective who was at the pharmacy when Scott was shot. She rushes to her bedroom, throws on some tights and a long sweater, slips a brush through her hair.

The doorbell rings again. She opens the door, overwhelmed by the sight of the uniforms and their badges. "Hello." Her most polite voice behind gritted teeth.

"Mrs. Orondo, we're sorry to bother you." Lorissa remains still, soldier stiff, while her heart thumps. "We have a search warrant."

She wants to scream "Get the hell out of here," but instead tightens her grip on the doorknob. "A search warrant? For what?"

"We're going to search Connor's room for any pharmaceuticals."

"Drugs?"

"Yes, ma'am. Stolen drugs."

Lorissa rakes her fingers through her hair. "May I see it?" She's never seen a warrant, but hopes to stall until Graham returns. Holding the paper in both hands, she tries to read the legalese. The words "everything looks in order" come to mind, but of course she has no idea what it's supposed to look like. "Well, Connor's asleep. Let me go wake him."

"No, ma'am. We'll go right in."

"Let me just wake him! Let him get dressed!"

"No." Thorp says in his kindest manner, which also means, "Get out of my way."

Lorissa leads them down the hall to Connor's room, where she knocks, then opens the door.

"Mom!" Connor says with his eyes closed, clearly annoyed. When his eyes open and he sees Thorp, he sits up and brings the sheets to his chest, half covering his Husky Dawg tee shirt.

"Connor." Lorissa modulates her voice, sounding steady. "They have a search warrant. They're looking for drugs." Connor's eyes shift from his mom to Thorp. "Come on with me," Lorissa says, "while they do their work." She sounds more composed than she feels.

The officers begin opening and shutting drawers. Connor and Lorissa leave the bedroom while they lift the mattress, check underneath, removing the pillowcase, shake out the pillow. Lorissa's hand is shaking as she punches in Jasmine's number.

"Jasmine, please! Can you get over here? They have a search warrant. Thorp! He and his partner are ransacking Connor's room!" The words couldn't spill out fast enough. Please, Jasmine."

"Take a breath. I'll be right there." Thank goodness for a lawyer who lives around the block. She hangs up, relieved, just as Thorp steps out of Connor's room dangling a baggie filled with pills. She and Connor are huddled in their small front hallway, and when she sees the little plastic bag dangling from Thorp's fingers, she shoots a dagger look at Connor, furious. Here she's been ready to believe every word he's said—*no drugs, not involved with Crowley*—and yet what is this?

"Are these yours, Connor?" asks Thorp. His eyes are sharp and his thick cheeks remind Lorissa of a vicious bulldog. His tone reveals no emotion. He repeats the question.

Lorissa feels a fright she hasn't known since her dad died, a sense of loss and anguish and anger rolled into one. "Don't say a word, Connor." She glares at Thorp with his precious little baggie. "Not a word!"

"We'll need to speak to you at the station," Thorp says.

"Is that necessary?" Lorissa is at a loss, stalling. "Our lawyer will be here in a minute."

"Tell her to meet you at the station."

Lorissa rubs her forehead. Think! Think! she tells herself. She straightens her back and says with as much calm as she can muster, "We'll get dressed and we'll meet you with our lawyer at the station within the hour. Does that suit you?" The term "flight risk" comes to mind.

His partner begins to object, but Jim says, "Within the hour." Lorissa guesses the police could have taken Connor now, but this is Wilkes Island and the Yachts Village police. "My husband will be home shortly, and we'll all meet you at the station." She pauses. "With bells on." She can't resist a little snark.

"Mrs. Orondo, if Connor is not at the station within"— he checks his phone— "one and a half hours, we'll send a squad car for him." Lorissa leans her head against the closed door, her hand still on the knob. No, this cannot be happening.

An hour later Connor enters the Yachts Village police station, flanked by Lorissa and Jasmine, with Graham close behind. This police station, not at all like *Law and Order,* shocks most people. It's stunning. Maybe not the Hilton, but close. Set on green acreage with a skateboard park directly to the north and forest trails to the south, it is housed in a log-style building with the city council and staff offices, police station, and jail—all together like a cozy Northwest ski lodge. This is surely the town to be arrested in.

Jasmine speaks through a glass partition that reminds Lorissa of a fast-food take-out window, although this one is bulletproof. A policewoman buzzes them into a small reception area reminiscent of a doctor's office, with upholstered blue chairs, a coffee table, and against the wall a rack of leaflets and brochures, some relating to laws, others with tourist activities in Yachts Village. Kind of a bizarre twist: "Get out of jail and be a tourist, rent a boat down at the pier. Get out of Dodge."

A door to a small, windowless room is open and Lorissa sees Rhys and a stranger. Rhys' Dad? A police woman quickly shuts the door.

In the car ride here, Graham had begged Connor to tell him where he'd gotten the drugs, but he'd refused. Now, seeing Rhys, Lorissa feels relief. She decides Rhys was the one who had a drug deal with Scott. Connor just doesn't want to rat out his friend. Connor must have tagged along with Rhys when Rhys met Scott at the park. Scott probably showed him a box of drugs he'd pilfered from the pharmacy. Maybe Connor said he'd keep the pills for Rhys because—why would Connor do that? Of course! Because Rhys wanted to save some for a concert and was scared he'd take them all. That was it. Connor was just keeping them safe for Rhys. Lorissa relaxes, glad she's figured it all out. They'll be out of this police station in an hour.

"Come in." Thorp leads Connor, Lorissa, Graham, and Jasmine into another small square room, closing the door behind them. No one offers the Orondos coffee or water. Still not like *Law and Order*.

"Why is my client here?" asks Jasmine.

"As you may have heard, Nicole Whyrrl has stated that Connor Orondo shot Scott Crowley, presumably in a drug deal gone bad."

"But, there's no evidence." Jasmine was on point and straight forward, not in the least intimidated. Lorissa was glad to have her on her side.

"That's changed." Connor wiggled in his chair, while we waited for Jim to continue. "We found some unopened drugs from a pharmaceutical rep in Connor's underwear drawer." Connor's eyes are glued to his hands. Oh, brother, Lorissa thinks. That's where they found them? He could have at least picked a better place to hide them. When Lorissa was in high school, she'd hidden her birth control pills in the toes of ballet shoes.

"And we have some new evidence," says Thorp. Lorissa catches her breath and reaches for Graham's hand. "Connor, describe your day when Scott Crowley was shot. Detail by detail."

Connor hesitates. Speak up, Lorissa tries to convey telepathically. Just tell them about getting kicked out of high school. The room's institutional disinfectant makes Lorissa's nose itch. "I had a fight with my mom at school and rode my bike," he muttered. Why do they all use that same disgusting cleanser? Hospitals, schools, and now, apparently, police stations.

"You left your mom, then started riding your bike? Where?" Thorp asks.

"I dunno, all over." Connor balances his chair back on two legs. He smirks.

Lorissa juts out her jaw, pissed he's acting like a jerk. She feels a shot of embarrassment. Her only son is acting so cocky in front of these police who may be about to bust him. She digs her nails into her palm.

"A long bike ride?"

"Yeah, I'm trying to get in shape." Graham's face is expressionless. Is their son lying? Is he really trying to get in shape? This is the first she's heard about it.

"Yeah, ask my counselor, Jonathan Fleury. He thinks I should do the STP—the Seattle to Portland bike ride." Lorissa eyes widen. Really? The STP? The 200-plus mile ride through valleys, forests, farmlands? Graham had thought about riding it once years ago, but never took the time to work out and prepare. More than 10,000 riders.

Lorissa's eyes drift to the small window above Thorp's head, from where a draft ruffles Connor's hair. If he hasn't told her about the STP, an activity she approves, then what else isn't he telling her? And why didn't he?

Actually, she understands. He's failed at so many things—soccer, the clarinet, school—he doesn't want to start one more thing and fail. He probably doesn't want her to nag him about it. Would she nag? Yes, she probably would.

She feels sad suddenly, not for the drugs, not for Crowley, but for her little boy, her toddler son, who'd been her "date" everywhere before he'd started kindergarten. She missed that soft little hand in hers, those big gentle eyes, those hugs that said, "You're the world to me." And now here is this boy—this near stranger—swaggering, acting cool at the worst possible time. If there is any time to be humble, this is it.

"We will," Thorp said. "We'll ask." Connor nods as though saying "Gotcha!"

"Excuse me a moment." Thorp cracks open the adjoining door and before he slips out, Lorissa catches a glimpse of Rhys with arms folded across his chest, his cheeks flushed, head facing down toward his chubby belly. She hears him stutter before the door shuts. She almost feels sorry for him, probably would have if he hadn't dragged Connor into so much trouble over the years.

With the door closed, Jasmine snaps at Connor. She's known him since he was three. "Quit acting like a jerk. They've got something on you. Something that made them search your room. What is it? Where did the pills come from? What happened?" Lorissa is glad to see Jasmine take over. "Connor, tell us," Jasmine demands. Connor opens his mouth, his eyes going between Lorissa's, Graham's, and Jasmines, about to speak, when Thorp reenters.

"Connor, I'd like to remind you that you are at the police station now and we're conducting a murder investigation." Lorissa snaps to attention. "Murder?" she shouts.

"Murder? I thought this was about drugs."

"Mrs. Orondo, be silent while Connor answers the question."

She's almost embarrassed by her outburst, but not really. "When did the conversation about drugs switch to murder? What on earth are you talking about?"

"A witness stepped forward."

Lorissa squints. "Murder? Is he dead? Is Scott Crowley dead?"

"Crowley's prognosis is extremely poor. No, he is not dead. Yet. He's in a medically induced coma, and a bullet to the brain is never good. His chances of a full recovery are less than five percent."

Lorissa gasps. She pictures the last time she saw him, lying on the gurney, perfectly still. She isn't surprised—there was so much blood, a hole carved in his head. Still, it's a shock to hear. "Right now, we're talking assault with intent to kill. That could be twenty years. Murder, of course, could mean life. Any minute the charge could change to murder."

Outside, a seagull swoops and cries. The sky is muted, a dull gray, the Northwest's prime fall color. Thorp's partner enters the room and whispers to him, then hands him a photograph. "Do you recognize this boy?" Thorp asks Connor.

Connor looks closely at the photo, then asks his dad, "Isn't this the kid you helped out with that soccer scholarship? His grandma's sick and all? Mom, isn't she the one we brought casseroles to once in a while when she was in bed?"

Graham and Lorissa both examine the photo. "Yes. Damian Walker," Graham says.

"Yeah, that's the name. Damian," Connor agrees.

"And," Thorp says to Connor, "you were nowhere near the pharmacy when Mr. Crowley was shot."

Connor shifts his weight, wiggling on his chair like he had in preschool when he couldn't sit still one more minute.

"Connor," says Jasmine. She speaks slowly, enunciating each word carefully. "Answer Officer Thorp honestly or not at all. Okay?"

When Connor pushes back his plastic chair on the linoleum, it sounds like a fingernail on a blackboard. "What's this kid got to do with it?" he asks.

"This boy saw you enter the pharmacy around 11:00 a.m., and a few minutes later, he heard a gunshot. He never saw you leave, but he did see your mom go in shortly after that. Connor, Nicole identifies you as the shooter, as you know. Says you shot Crowley because of a drug deal gone bad. And we've found stolen drugs in your room."

Lorissa's head swirls as vertigo sets in. Connor blanches, blood draining from his face, matching the whiteness of the wall behind him. Lorissa's mouth tastes like plaster, and she imagines his does too. "No, it wasn't him!" Her mom instincts take over. "If anyone, it was Rhys. Did you ask him? Where was he that morning?"

"Lorissa." Graham rests his hand on hers.

"Detective Thorp, you're making some broad insinuations here. Are you planning on making an arrest?" Jasmine asks.

"No! Where was he?" Lorissa's world is spinning out of control. "Where was Rhys? Let's say Nicole saw some kid. It was probably Rhys, not Connor. Or any other kid from Yachts Village High. Or from anywhere, for that matter."

"Rhys has a solid alibi, Mrs. Orondo."

"Solid. Like what? Where was he?" Lorissa can see herself as though from a distance, a jabbering mom defending her son, flinging accusations that make no sense, that the police have no need to answer. And yet they do.

"Rhys was at your house that morning. Rhys was with Mackenzie."

Lorissa's head spins, wilder and wilder. She holds her hands to her ears, trying to stop the dizziness. "Mackenzie? With Mackenzie? No, that couldn't be."

Jasmine places her hand on Lorissa's arm, bringing her back to earth, to this room where Connor nods, his head bobbing up and down, agreeing with Thorp. "Mom. Stop. Rhys was with Mackenzie until he went to the park. She told me."

Lorissa opens her mouth. It couldn't be. And yet it is. There is so much she doesn't know about her own family.

"Jim. I'd like some time alone with my client," Jasmine says. "Otherwise, I'm going to advise him not to answer any more questions." The fluorescent lights buzz loudly. Thorp agrees.

As soon as the door shuts behind him, Jasmine snarls at Connor. "What's going on here? What is Thorp saying? Nicole and the boy's accusations, the drugs. You need to tell me the truth." Connor slumps, that arrogant expression gone. "Start from the beginning, Connor, and tell the truth."

Connor clears his throat and stretches his fingers in and out, in and out. "You won't believe me. You won't believe anything I say." He hangs his head for a full minute before he finally answers. "I rode around. I said that. I rode to the park."

We all nod. "But, first." Lorissa holds her breath. "First, I rode to the Harvard Street Pharmacy."

We all sit in silence, letting that sink in. "So, the boy told the truth? Damian?" Jasmine asks.

Lorissa thinks back on that awful day. She and Connor had argued after he'd been suspended one more time, she'd driven off in her car, he'd left by bike. She couldn't get to work, which she'd desperately wanted to do, so after crying a million tears, she'd decided to go see her old friend Nicole. She tried to visualize the Harvard Street Pharmacy parking lot in her mind: mostly empty, the sidewalk too, then she entered the pharmacy and, yes! Yes, Damian—had been there! Little Damian, so scrawny, in torn, dirty clothes. She'd grazed right past him, so upset about Connor and her job, but yes. He'd been standing there.

Now, in the interrogation room, a silver slant of light shines on the tuft of hair on Connor's chin. "Yes," he says. "I stopped by the pharmacy before I rode to the park. I left my bike in back, but the back door was locked, so I had to enter the front."

"Connor!" Lorissa groans. She won't say it. She won't say what she is thinking: For heaven's sake, Scott could die! Thorp is talking murder!

Lorissa folds her hands, like in prayer, just as her mom had taught her. She bites the inside of her cheek, telling herself let Jasmine do the talking. Jasmine continues, "So, you went to the Harvard Street Pharmacy to get drugs from Crowley and then what happened?"

"No, I didn't! I had nothing to do with drugs! Yes, I stopped by the pharmacy, but not to see Crowley. Why would I want to see him? I hardly know him, and besides I don't do drugs anymore except maybe a little pot now and then!"

"Okay, so you went into the pharmacy and what happened?"

"Well, I opened the door and that little bell rang and. . . No! I'm not saying anything. You won't believe anything I say; it will get all twisted, and … *no!*" He crosses his arms defiantly and rests his chin on his chest.

It's now two in the afternoon. They've been at it for four hours. Lorissa's blood sugar drops. She needs to eat. What can she do to make Connor tell them what happened? She feels completely defeated, drained. She's about to search for a vending machine when Thorp reenters, grave eyes and a pinched forehead. Lorissa falls back in her chair. This does not look good.

"Connor, the pills we found in your room are Roxicodone."

Connor's brows shoot up in surprise. Thorp isn't going to cut Connor any slack. "Where did you get the Roxies? Did you steal them from the pharmacy? Is that why you shot Scott Crowley? He ripped you off and you wanted to make him pay, didn't you, Connor?"

"Hey," Graham interjects. "Don't you talk to my son like that. What happened to 'innocent until proven guilty'?" Graham flings back his chair and stands, slamming his hands on the table. "That's my son you're talking to!"

"Sit down, Mr. Orondo! Sit down or you will be escorted out. Do I make myself clear?" Graham's face flushes, he's fuming, but he sits. Thorp continues. "You wanted Crowley gone, didn't you, Connor? Dead!"

"No! No, I didn't!" Connor's arrogance has melted and now he's near tears. "I didn't use any Roxies; I didn't try to kill anyone, I didn't!"

"Connor Orondo, I'm arresting you for assault with a deadly weapon with intention to kill Mr. Scott Crowley."

"Mom, Dad!" Connor cries out. "Mom, I didn't do it!"

"No!" This cannot be happening. Lorissa's son cannot be arrested—not for a charge that could turn into murder.

"I didn't even do any of those pills. That's why they were all in that baggie. I didn't do any of that!"

"Wait a minute, Thorp," says Jasmine. "You're arresting him on what evidence?"

"Evidence? Drugs in his possession, one witness who saw him shoot Crowley, another saw him enter moments before the shooting. . ."

"But I told you that myself." A bead of sweat rolls off Connor's forehead.

"You have the right to remain. . ."

"Mom! Jasmine! You've got to do something. Dad!" The officer takes Connor by the arm and starts to walk out of the room. "Mom!"

"Stop!" Graham shoots out of his seat again. "The word of one little half-starved boy isn't enough to arrest someone for

something as big as this, is it, Jasmine? How do you know
Damian didn't do it, if he was standing right there?"

"Mr. Orondo," Thorp says, "everyone's guilty but your
son, is that it? No, Damian's word would not be enough. But all
the other evidence against your son? We have a solid case.
Nicole Whyrll will swear in a court of law that it was your son
who entered the pharmacy, pulled out the gun, and shot
Crowley."

"No! That's ridiculous. Nicole is one of my oldest
friends." Lorissa stands as tall as any mother could. "He didn't
do it! Okay? My son is not a shooter, and he's certainly not a
killer. He didn't do any of this, and we'll prove it!"

31

Lorissa Orondo

As Graham and Lorissa drive home from the station, brown leaves portending the beginning of winter skip across the road. A maple tree among the firs swings its barren branches, reminding Lorissa of playing pickup sticks with Connor in preschool. When she had been pregnant with MacKenzie she'd felt tired, so, so tired, but her sweet toddler son had adored her. Her husband had been devoted as he'd moved up the corporate ladder, and she was filled with hope, the kind of hope that seems completely absent in her life today. *My son did not shoot Scott Crowley.* Graham slams the brakes at the red light, and Lorissa's head bounces on the headrest.

"Sorry," he says.

She watches Graham squint, imagines he's thinking that this accusation, this shooting, this screwed-up family is a problem, a puzzle he can figure out. They pass Barton Elementary School where Connor and Mackenzie had started kindergarten, pass holly bushes entwined in geometric shapes.

Ten minutes later, Graham pulls in their driveway. "I'm going to the office."

"*Now*?!" Lorissa thinks she'll throw up like a drunken teenager on her own front lawn. "Today? Now? When your son's been accused. . .?"

"I know what my son's been accused of. I'll be gone only a half day. I need to think. And you need to. . ." His voice drifts. He sounds so hard. Lorissa is glad he doesn't finish the sentence. I need to what? she thinks. Get hold of myself? Calm down? Get a grip? He stirs her anger, which is good, because anger is energy. She bangs the car door shut and slogs toward the house as though returning home after a brutal surgery. Dragging her steps, it's like a million-mile walk to the front door.

Moments later, tires screech. The car reels back up the driveway, and Graham jumps out of the car, catching Lorissa in his arms. She nuzzles her face in his shoulders, and they cry and cry together, all the tears they've held inside since she'd first seen that bloody body on the concrete floor of the pharmacy.

"I'm sorry, sweetheart," Graham says. "I just can't stand this."

"He didn't do it," she says.

"I know." Graham squeezes her tightly as she tucks her head under his chin and he kisses the top of her head. Across the Sound, a foghorn blows. There's no more talk of going to the office today.

Lorissa wipes her eyes and nose. Inside, she boils water for tea. She and Graham settle on the couch, facing their massive window, watching Jim Corcoran check his mailbox with Guru wagging by his side. Lorissa smiles—that sweet, mischievous beast!

To love a dog, to love a person, with all their mistakes, with all their digging holes and rolling eyes, that is in the DNA. At least in her DNA, and ol' Jim Corcoran's. And it's not like it's easy to look past the foibles—not Guru's, not Connor's. No, she muses, you have to deal with their mistakes one by one. But how did Connor's screwups blow up so big that her son has been arrested for attempted murder?

Lorissa places their cups in the dishwasher and pads to the hall mirror. Her dark eyes are dull against her blushed cheeks, but when she tosses her hair, it furls over her shoulder and she looks pretty. How can that be? How can she appear so lovely when she feels so awful? How can she be pretty when her whole world is falling apart?

"Mom!"

Mackenzie home already? Is it four in the afternoon? Mackenzie barrels up the steps, nearly crashing into her. "Mom. It's all over school. Connor's been arrested? They think he shot Mr. Crowley?"

In her jeans and Yachts High tee shirt, with her hair pulled back, her blue and white handblown-glass earrings, Mackenzie seems so mature. Mascara, just a tad, and barely visible pink lip gloss, perfect for highlighting her cheeks. Is this girl the same chubby daughter who once aggravated Lorissa no end? Suddenly Mackenzie seems perfect, the girl who can do no wrong.

But she had. She had seen Rhys behind Lorissa's back. No. Lorissa is too drained to care about Rhys. She pulls Mackenzie to her and wraps her arms around her. "Yes, sweetheart. But he didn't do it. I can assure you, we'll find out who did."

32

Meaghan Farren

I am still at the restaurant, my meal served, eaten, cleared. Only one couple is left in the dining room, an older grey-haired pair who hold hands under the table. Pablo isn't exactly hovering, but by the way he checks on me, I can tell he's ready to close the restaurant.

By the time Lorissa finishes her recap of Connor's situation, I am struggling for words of support. "You'll get through this, Lorissa. I'll be there for you. So glad Graham is back home." We make plans to talk tomorrow, and when we hang up, I imagine she's feeling as helpless and impotent as I am, not knowing how to turn this mess around.

I thank Pablo and return to my room. Where I lie wide awake staring at the moon through the muslin curtain. Finally, I throw on my cotton robe and step outside to see the sky is the color of onyx and the stars remind me of dotted swiss fabric, with the Southern Cross as brilliant as neon. The desert air feels like a comforting shroud, even at midnight. I taste the open desert as though it's tangible, something I can touch. I think about Lorissa and Scott, about Connor—about Brandon, who, I have no doubt, has made it his mission to track me down no matter where I am. Do I want to be a refugee the rest of my life? Or do I want to face my fear, possibly face my husband, and return to Wilkes Island to support Lorissa?

As I ponder, I realize this spiritual oasis has given me courage, strength. I'd told Lorissa when I'd first arrived on her doorstep that I'd do anything to make up for my cruelty back in college. Now, here's that chance, lying at my feet. I can continue to hide, or I can go stand by Lorissa's side.

I close my eyes, stretch out my arms, hands upward toward the sky, and I smell the trees and dirt and air. Yes, I think, the decision is made: I'm going to be there for Lorissa, for Scott, even for Connor. I'm not going to be a slave to my fear of Brandon anymore.

The next morning, I ramble once again up a dusty path that heads into the hills where the earth smells as thick and rich as a freshly planted garden. Yesterday Lorissa had said she'd call at 3:00 p.m. my time, so after my walk I head to the bar and order a coke, watching the minute hand circling around the old-fashioned black-and-white clock. When the phone rings, I watch anxiously as Pablo answers. When he hands me the phone, I say, "Hey, Lorissa," excited to tell her my decision. I wait in silence, hear only quiet weeping. She tries to speak, but few words come out. At last she says it. "Connor's DNA is on the gun."

"*Oh, no!*" I speak in a whisper, her pain like a sharp spear in my gut. "They found out already?" I hate to think what this means. "That seems impossible. I thought it would take much longer."

"Usually it does. Almost always, but the police expedited the results."

"What does Connor say?"

"He won't talk about it. Not to me, not to Jasmine. Says we won't believe him."

"Oh, Lorissa."

"We've begged, we've pleaded, but he is a rock and says every time he opens his mouth, it gets him into more trouble." These are the tears of a mother who would do anything for her son. Anything. A mother who loves her child to the core, a mom whose heart is being ripped in shreds as she stands by, helpless.

Her sobs become fainter—I picture her going through tissue after tissue. "Lorissa," I say, "I'm coming back to Wilkes Island. I'm going to help you. We're going to fix this together."

She sniffs. "You can't do that. What about Brandon?"

"Lorissa, since I've been in Cochiquaz, my priorities have shifted. I want to help." I want to redeem myself. "I'll report Brandon to the police, get a restraining order that most likely won't help, but I refuse to cave to fear any longer. I'll watch my back every minute, but Lorissa, I'm going to be there for you."

"Why would you do that for me, Meaghan? Really, why?" Her devastation has turned to anger and I'm the target. With our history, I can see why she'd question my kindness.

"I want to make up for. . ."

"No, that's not what I'm asking."

I hear crows cawing faintly from her end of the phone. I see what she means. "Lorissa, I think it's because of this village, this land. I can't explain. I feel courage I haven't felt before. Courage to do what's most important. Courage to help a friend."

"Meaghan, that would mean so much to me," she stammers. "Graham argued with his boss about getting time off, and his boss agreed, but he has to finish up this one small project they've been working on for a year," she says through tears. "He's back in California. With him gone, and my two best friends off-limits—Nicole is a flat-out liar, and I can't talk to Jasmine in the same way now that she's Connor's attorney— your being here would mean so much."

Did she really say that? Being there would mean so much to her? I feel a lightness, joy, and my eyes moisten. "I'll leave Cochiquaz today and will be back to Wilkes Island in just a few days." But before I can hang up, I need to ask. "Any more news on Scott?"

"Only through Jasmine. He's still in a coma." Pots and pans being washed bang in the restaurant kitchen. "But apparently doctors may be able to operate on Scott's brain. Remove the bullet."

"He might be okay? Like Gabby Giffords?"

"Oh, Meaghan, I have no idea."

"Of course, she doesn't. Silly of me to ask. "So, Lorissa, how are you doing? Really."

There's a pause. "Honestly?" I can't tell if the sound she utters is a laugh or a cry. "You know, like in cartoons, when a steamroller flattens Mickey Mouse? That's me."

33

Meaghan Farren

Layers of dust sheathe the windshield as I drive out of Cochiquaz, past dead limbs that were once trees, past remnants of paths hundreds of years old, past the vineyards for *pisco* waiting for harvest. I smell a delicious sweetness, all while hearing Scott's voice in my mind—so melodic, so kind, so sincere. "Darling." One word, in the right tone, can mean so much. Still, I find myself asking, almost unwillingly, was he dealing opiates? Those killers?

I just can't believe it. Yesterday, when I'd called Graham's nephew, Corey, and let him know I'd be driving the rental back to La Serena and then returning to America, he'd sounded surprised but understanding. "If you ever want to return, you're always welcome." You'd think I'd known him for months or years, not a day. I'd also called his neighbor and apologized for quitting my job before I had even started. "No worries. Come back when you can."

Seventy-two hours later, I disembark at the Seattle-Tacoma airport, hair tangled, makeup smudged, so tired. I rent a Toyota Camry and start through the fumes of bumper-to-bumper traffic down I-5 made worse by early torrential rains. Once I cross the tiny bridge onto Wilkes Island, relaxation descends over me. I arrive at Lorissa's doorstep at 9:00 p.m. and remember the other times I've stood in the dark facing her front door. "Oh, Meaghan." Her hug is as tight as any I've felt.

"Hey," I say, but when we pull away, I am struck by Lorissa's face, gray, drawn, gaunt. Her eyes are red and her hair, though pulled back in a ponytail in her usual style, looks dirty, stringy. She takes my wet coat and leads me to the spare bedroom, where Chumley lifts her head, then breaks into a rocket-engine purr. I decline a cup of tea and instead shower, then fall asleep within minutes.

At the dining room table the next morning, Lorissa and I gaze outside. Call it silver, call it slate, call it brushed stainless—they're all variations of the same: the water, the sky, the air, each blending into the other, barely lines of demarcation between them. No one would believe there's a fifteen thousand-foot volcanic mountain buried behind the clouds. "You're welcome to stay with us as long as you like," Lorissa says, but I'm hoping it will be only a week or so. Connor will be cleared, the shooter found, and Brandon apprehended. I will see Scott, awake from the coma, recovering from the bullet. Now there's a rosy spin.

"You okay?" I ask Lorissa, savoring my first cup of coffee. I never got used to that instant Nescafé in Cochiquaz.

"Connor is in the local jail in Yachts Village, which isn't that bad, to tell you the truth. When it was built a few years back, we had a tour with Mackenzie's Girl Scout troop. Let me tell you, it's a far cry from *Blue Bloods*. Clean; decent food, more like a hotel. But he'll be leaving there soon for Grayson Center, the juvie center in Tacoma." I see the strain on her face—pillows under her eyes, tight lines stemming from her mouth. "He'll be the innocent island kid with all these hard-core guys from the city. That's what scares me. Oh, Meaghan, I'm so worried about how he'll survive."

I don't blame her. Connor may have gotten in a lot of trouble, might be labeled a "delinquent" on Wilkes Island and in Yachts Village, but I doubt if he has any street smarts. "When will they transfer him?"

"I don't know. Today, tomorrow."

"And Graham?"

"His flight was delayed, but he should be home from San Francisco by then." Lorissa reaches across the table and touches my hand. "I'm so glad you're here, Meaghan."

"I feel like I belong here. For you, for Connor, for Scott." Lorissa's weak smile expresses a palpable sense of gratitude. "So, Connor still isn't saying why his DNA's on the gun?"

Lorissa shakes her head. "Or where he got the Roxies. Or why he went to the pharmacy. Only that, yes, he did go there before he went to the park. Apparently, Nicole's DNA is on the gun too, but it's her gun, I believe. She just had it out of the safe for. . . I'm not sure why."

I unwrap a package of English muffins, making myself at home. "Would you like one?"

"No."

"Are you eating at all, Lorissa?" Before she answers, I say, "I'll fix you one," getting the butter from the refrigerator and the knife from the drawer. Two minutes later, I smell the muffin, burned, although I'm standing right next to the toaster.

"Oh." Lorissa perks up, if only a bit. "Meaghan, sorry. The toaster is on the fritz." With the bamboo tongs, I pull out the black crusts and throw them away, drop a new muffin in, and turn the dial to lower the heat.

"I have a meeting with Jasmine today," Lorissa says. "And then I'm going to see Connor. Want to come?" Her eyes plead— she does not want to go through this alone. "Be Graham's proxy till he gets home?"

"I'd be glad to, Lorissa."

We drive downtown to Jasmine's office, a block off the main street. Since Yachts Village is at the tip of a peninsula, every kind of water-centered business is here—paddleboard rentals, kayaks, a fly-fishing shop. Lorissa shuffles from the car. "I should have known," she mutters.

"Known what?"

She looks up at me with those bleak eyes. "That things were bad. Really bad with Connor. When he stole my bracelet." I tilt my head, questioning. "You know that bracelet we got together?"

"Absolutely. You mean after our first midterms, that time we traipsed into town our freshman year of college?"

"And we gaped in the jewelry store window? Forty minutes later we strolled out, each with a shiny matching charm bracelet?

"We both blew all our money for the semester. Oh, Lorissa, how did that clerk ever talk us into buying them?"

"I know. Right? We were both so broke." That was one of those times I'll always cherish with Lorissa. We had so many fun times, in the beginning. I hope she remembers more of the good times, not just our wretched ending.

"You know, I kept the charm bracelet from all those years ago." I lift my wrist and jingle the Eiffel tower, the musical note, the sewing machine.

"I've got my matching bracelet, too." Now Lorissa drags her feet more slowly. "Or had it."

The gulls overhead squawk; a splat hits the asphalt inches from my feet. "What happened?"

She describes catching Connor digging through her jewelry box a few months ago. "I didn't think too much about it. Then, when I noticed you wearing your identical one, I looked for mine." She reaches behind her neck and pulls on her ponytail as though it's falling out—a nervous gesture; it looks just fine. "I found the little red box empty—a square of cotton, and that was all. I thought Connor stole it, but tried to block it out. Deny it to myself."

She looks as miserable as I've ever seen her. "Then he practically confessed he stole it. After our fight at the high school that horrible day, he said he'd get it back for me." The fateful day—the day Scott was shot. "It's like chewing glass," she says, massaging her forehead. "Meaghan, sorry to dump all this on you."

"No problem, Lorissa." My heart goes out to Lorissa, but I also feel torn. I want to see Scott so badly, but he is in a coma, he won't know I'm there. Lorissa needs me, depends on me. I'll wait before I go all the way to Seattle to see him.

An hour later we enter Jasmine's stylish small office. The leather, the bouquet of chrysanthemums, the oak furniture all say "small practice, competent attorney." Her receptionist hangs up the phone. "I'll let her know you're here." A minute later, she beckons us into the office where Jasmine sits behind a sprawling mahogany desk, just a shade darker than her own skin. We exchange small talk—nice to see you again; yes, good flight, Chile was amazing—and then we get down to business.

"Lorissa." Jasmine's voice takes on a different tone—urgent, demanding. "You've got to get Connor to tell his side of things. With his DNA on the gun, with Nicole and Damian's statements, Roxies in his drawer, let me tell you, it doesn't look good. He's being held and there will be a hearing to set bail. Tomorrow."

"Tomorrow?" Lorissa pulls a tissue from her purse, twisting and turning it. "We didn't know things would go this quickly."

"Four p.m.," Jasmine adds.

No one speaks for a moment, and I notice quiet jazz playing in the background. Lorissa continues to shred her tissue.

"And if Scott dies, Connor could be charged with murder?" Lorissa's voice is meek.

Jasmine leans forward, presses her waist against her desk, taps her pen just once. Her voice is low and deadly serious.

"Lorissa, Connor is seven months away from his eighteenth birthday. They could charge him as an adult."

It's as if someone took a suction hose and sapped every ounce of Lorissa's strength. I squeeze her hand. Jasmine continues. "Lorissa, I'm Connor's attorney. I need to tell you the facts as I know them. If Connor is completely innocent, as he says he is, he must tell us what happened." She waits for this to sink in. "Now."

Lorissa's mouth opens. Incoherent sounds escape as if she wants to speak, but no words come forth.

"You need to get your son to talk. To save his sorry butt. I don't mean to be crude, but there is nothing, nothing we can do if we don't know his side of the story."

Lorissa slumps in her chair. "I know. I know." I take a fresh tissue from the top of Jasmine's desk and hand it to her.

"Is there any news?" I ask, meaning about Scott as well as Connor.

Jasmine directs her attention to me. "You were close to Scott Crowley, right?" I'm suddenly intimidated by her coal-black eyes drilling into me.

"Yes."

"Was he dealing drugs?"

She's so frank, no warning before this shot; I freeze momentarily. I weigh my words before I respond. "No, I don't think so. I'm not saying he would have told me, but he just didn't seem like the type. I mean, he seemed so nice. Seems."

I won't add that he was more than nice, that I fell head over heels for him, that I've dreamed about him so many nights. I won't say that he had a mysterious air, that he started to tell me something before Brandon appeared at my doorstep. What had he said? "Old Mrs. Lucas. . ."? And then that sickening snarl from Brandon, pounding on my door, telling me to open up.

"The police are investigating him, as you can imagine they would. Nicole claims he stole Roxicodone from the pharmacy and sold it to Connor. That's the case the police have. The drug deal went awry between Connor and Scott, and so Connor shot Scott. With the opioid epidemic that's raging, cops aren't messing around."

"Lorissa told me, but I just don't believe it." The room feels so stuffy, and my only desire is to leave this office and never come back. I don't want to find out anything bad about Scott. I truly loved—love? —him. Truly love him.

"Well, the news today is that police found one hundred Roxicodone in a little sliced pocket in the upholstery of the backseat of Scott's truck."

No. Can this be true? It can't be. Can it? My eyes dart to the painting behind Jasmine, a red and black and blue Jackson Pollock imitation with splatters and spills. "No. He couldn't have," but then I stop myself. Could he?

"What *do* you know about him? The police may question you since they can't question him. And the fact that you left town right before the shooting doesn't look good."

I feel a sharp stab. "What?"

Jasmine sounds reassuring now. "Yes, Lorissa explained to me all about your escape from an abusive husband. Don't worry."

I grip my chair arms. I never thought about that—that I could be under suspicion because I flew to South America just before Scott was shot.

"What can you tell me about Scott Crowley?" Jasmine repeats, twirling a pen between her fingers.

"I don't know much, I guess, when it comes right down to it. A foster kid from Tacoma, but that's about it."

Jasmine shuffles some papers on her desk. "Honestly, it doesn't look good for Scott, although surgeons plan to operate, take the bullet out of his head." Jasmine rubs her nose where her reading glasses pinch. "So, Lorissa, promise me you'll find out more from your son. What happened in the pharmacy?"

So much for reassurance. Jasmine's so sharp, curt—she's nothing like that warm-hearted, fun woman I'd met at the barbecue last spring. This is business, and she's not messing around. We stand, dismissed. "Thanks, Jas," Lorissa says as we step to the door.

Outside, Lorissa looks as if she's been thrashed.

"Hey, Lorissa." I know I'm walking on eggshells here. "Is there any way I could try?"

"Try?"

"You know... try talking to Connor? I mean, who knows? For whatever reason, Connor and I seem to have some kind of rapport, a connection. I mean, maybe he'll open up to me. It couldn't hurt."

Lorissa bites her bottom lip, presses her fingers into her eyes as though completely defeated. "Anything. I'll try anything."

The policewoman runs a wand over us and guides us to the back of police station/jail to see Connor, the lone jail tenant, who looks wilted on the edge of his cot in his tee shirt, jeans—no belt—and white terrycloth slippers. White sheets, white walls, beige floor tiles, sparkly clean. I smell a speck of ammonia.

Connor's haggard face is oily, and he looks like a scared kid, not someone who belongs in jail. He doesn't stand, doesn't lift his head, doesn't utter a sound. "Hey, Connor," Lorissa speaks quietly. He raises his head, meets his mom's eyes, ignores me. With her back against the open cell door, Lorissa describes our meeting with Jasmine. "Sweetie, you've got to tell us what happened."

Is it my imagination, or do his cheeks fill out like he's holding on to his words with all the strength he has? He sits up, crosses his arms, and glares. "No one believes anything I say. They believe that lying friend of yours who's a two-timing druggie. Nicole is what?" he says, "President of the Rotary? President of the Chamber of Commerce? Some such thing, and I'm a low-life loser."

"Don't call yourself a loser."

"Why, Mom? Everyone else does, although you'd never know—you're always singing on that stupid video game in

Seattle. You always want to blame anyone—anyone but
yourself."

"What does that mean?"

Whoa. This is off to a bad start. "Hey, guys," I interject.
"Let's stop a minute." I didn't come to be referee between mom
and son, but somebody's got to.

"Rhys, for example," Connor says. "Everything's always
Rhys's fault. Tell that to Mackenzie."

"Connor." My voice is as firm and neutral as I can make
it.

He looks at me as though seeing me for the first time.
"Hey," I say.

He nods by way of greeting.

Lorissa is furious, her face a brilliant red, hands on hips.
"Stop it, Connor," she screams. "This is your life we're talking
about. Stop messing around and tell us what happened."

A guard appears who'd been out of sight, but apparently
within hearing distance. He watches us, then speaks to Lorissa.

"Would you like to come with me?"

She eyes me, then Connor, confused, as if she's so
upset, she's lost her senses.

"Do you want to get a soda or something?" I ask her.
Her face looks perplexed, as though she doesn't know what to
do. It's almost as though she's in shock, seeing her son in this jail
cell.

Finally, she follows the guard down the hall, and I'm left
alone with Connor. He scrutinizes his slippers as though he has

a keen interest in their threads. Oh boy. We hear his mom crying, then it fades as she walks away. Neither of us speaks for several minutes.

Okay then. Enough. "You were awfully hard on your mom."

Connor raises his eyes. "Yeah, well. She was hard on me." But his tone has changed and he sounds remorseful, and maybe, just maybe, he regrets his side of the outbursts.

"You understand what's going on here, right? If anything happens to Scott"— which means "if he dies," but no, I can't go there. I squash my emotions, can't think about it. "You'll be charged with murder. You get that, right?"

Connor grimaces. Clearly, he hasn't thought this through. "That's why your mom's acting nutso. Why she's terrified for you." He shifts uncomfortably as reality begins to strike. "And Connor? You could be charged as an adult since you turn eighteen in just a few months." I'm not going to say those two poisonous words, "death penalty," though I hope he realizes them himself and starts to understand how serious this all is.

"May I sit down?" He shifts over on his cot, and I sit next to him, lean my elbows on my knees, mirroring his posture. He tugs at his chin thoughtfully.

"Connor." What on earth do I know about talking to a teenager? Nothing. But with his life on the line, I'll try. Maybe if I'm honest, he'll be honest. "I kind of know what it's like to feel like the whole world is against you, like there's no point in even trying. It's easier to keep secrets, wear a mask, pretend everything's fine, when it's absolutely not fine." For the first time, he pays attention. Once I begin, my words spill, sparing none of the gory details. I describe my dad killing my mom, Brandon's abuse, my escape to Wilkes Island, and my second escape, to Chile. My shame.

He lifts his eyes, questioning as though to ask Really? You went through all that? What he says is, "So that's why you had that chopped-off, dyed-black hair when you first came here? You did that to escape that dude?"

"Yep. Although, honestly, I don't know how it could have helped. I wasn't thinking very well at the time."

"Oh, man. I thought it was 'cuz you were some kind of cool, old punk rocker." We both snicker—a tentative laugh, but we're connected. Just a little.

"So, Connor. What happened? Why were you at the Harvard Street Pharmacy that morning?" I didn't have to say which morning. Connor begins to pace his ten-by-ten cinderblock cell. Its open window is barred, yes, but it allows fresh air in. The cell is only a notch down from my college dorm. Talk about fancy.

He addresses his feet. "What's the point of talking?"

"To save your sorry buns," I yell. "That's the point." I didn't mean to shout. I get a grip and speak more gently. "Give me a try." The acrid smell of the sanitizer, which didn't bother me before, now seems overwhelming. I'm afraid I'll be sick.

Connor lifts his head. "Okay." He meets my eyes and begins. "I went to the pharmacy to get my mom's bracelet back. She probably told you I stole it from her?"

"Sort of."

"Well, it's kind of a long story. See, first I just stole it from Mom's drawer 'cuz, I don't know, I was pissed or something. Just to get back at her for always being down on me. But then Rhys and me—we came up with an idea. Since the bracelet didn't seem all that important to Mom—I never saw her wear it, not ever, and it was buried under a bunch of other jewelry boxes—Rhys and I thought, 'Hey, let's pawn it.'" Connor swallows hard. "We go to this pawnshop in Tacoma and, well. . ." A gulp. "Well, whatever, it doesn't happen, I end up not pawning it, so Rhys and I go to that park, Sunrise Beach Park, that one I saw you at." I nod, following.

"All of a sudden, I can't find the bracelet," he says. "We look all through the grass, everywhere. Then a few days later, I see Nicole's there at the same park and she's wearing the bracelet."

Connor cracks his knuckles. "Rhys and I—we go there all the time. It must have fallen out of my pocket and she found it."

"So, Nicole had it, and you wanted to get it back?"

"To give it back to Mom 'cuz she and I had this big fight at the high school that morning. I got suspended again, and she was worried about losing her job—which she did lose—and I said some things that…well, I felt kinda bad."

"You went to the Harvard Street Pharmacy to get the bracelet from Nicole. Then what? Tell me the details." Connor fidgets with his fingernails as though deciding whether or not to talk. Whether to trust me. I fold my hands, wait. "Okay. I was so pissed at Mom after that fight we had at the high school that I decided I'd get her stupid bracelet back, and at least she wouldn't have that on me. I started riding my bike." He meets my eyes. "Anyway, I got there, to the pharmacy, and realized I didn't have my lock, so I rode around back, left my bike there, and went in the front."

"Then what?"

"Well, it felt a little weird."

"How so?" I ask.

"I don't know. Weird, that's all. Like super quiet." I nod.

"I called 'Nicole,' then heard something—loud. A bang. Like a really loud sound. Like a gunshot. Then, a thud. Then, another bang, like maybe a door."

He stopped. Checked to see if I was still listening.

"And?"

"Well, I didn't know what to do. Should I run to the back where the sound came from? Or should I just call 9-1-1?"

He paused again. This was the part he hadn't told anyone. "I decided I needed to check out what happened. Maybe someone was hurt. Maybe I could help them."

I waited, then prompted him. "What happened next?"

"I went to the back office, and as soon as I pushed the swinging door, I caught a whiff of—well, I think it was a sour smell. Then, blood. Lots of it. A puddle of blood by Scott's body on the floor. Blood everywhere. I met Scott once or twice so I knew it was him, and I thought for sure he was dead."

"Then you called 9-1-1?"

"No, 'cuz just then I saw Nicole sitting behind the desk holding a gun up to her head, touching her temple, like she was going to blow her head off."

"I never heard that part before."

"I never told anybody." His voice was hushed. "Yeah, she was holding this gun right up to her head, like she was ready to shoot herself, and her eyes were all weird, glazed over, like she couldn't even see me. I had to decide: *Do I deal with Scott, who's probably already dead? Or with Nicole, who's about to kill herself?* I went over to her and said, 'Nicole, what the hell are you doing?'

"Nicole said, 'It's over. It's all over.' And man, did she look serious, like she was going to pull the trigger. I go, 'Nicole, think of your daughter. Think of Torrie. She'd never get over it if you killed yourself. And Joel. You've got such a great family.'

"I kept repeating that kind of stuff, and finally she lowered the gun, and I grabbed it out of her hand, and just then I heard that little bell tinkling at the front door and my mom's voice calling 'Nicole, Nicole' and I panicked. I'd just had that fight with her a couple of hours earlier, and I didn't know what she would think, so I threw the gun down and ran out the back door and jumped on my bike and pedaled faster than I ever have in my life—I gotta tell you, the sweat was pouring off me by the time I got to the park and met up with Rhys."

Quite a story. He's got a point: no one is going to believe him except his parents, his sister and me. I sit for a few minutes, noticing a small bird swooping by the window. A swallow of some kind, I presume. He didn't even try to save Scott? But I get it—he'd never live with himself if Nicole killed herself and he could have prevented it.

"What about the whole story of the drug heist? Scott wasn't dealing drugs?"

"I wouldn't know anything about that." Connor leans against the cinder-block wall, as though it feels good to get his side of the story off his chest. "But I doubt it. I mean, I'm not saying Scott is a great guy, but. . ."

"You think Scott might have been dealing drugs to Rhys behind your back?"

"Nah. That's something Mom would have come up with. She's crazy when it comes to Rhys. Probably would blame him for 9/11 if he hadn't been in diapers at the time."

"Your time is about up." I jolt. I hadn't heard the guard approach. "Two more minutes for today." Then he retreats to the other side of the hallway.

I stand, wondering if I should hug Connor. Probably not allowed. "Okay if I tell your mom?"

"Yeah." He's back to staring at his slippers like when I first came in.

"Thanks."

"Sure, Meaghan." He sounds depressed, of course. Who wouldn't be, locked in a jail cell?

But I also notice his tone is somewhat lighter because maybe, just maybe, someone believes in him.

I rest my hand on the cell door. "Connor, you understand I'm trying to help you, right? That I'm on your side?" He nods, unconvinced. "Here's the thing. I just don't get what you and Nicole were doing at the park."

"It's not like we were together." He nearly spits at the idea. "I mean, yeah. Rhys and I like to go there to … you know." He glances up at the cell door, looking for the guard. He's not going to say, "smoke pot" out loud. "But sometimes when Rhys and I are just chilling, they show up." He chuckles. "Rhys and I usually go into the bushes."

"I don't get it."

Connor shifts on his cot, uncomfortable. "Okay, Meaghan. You want to know the truth. Nicole was there with Scott Crowley. Not a couple of times—a lot. Just not so much lately."

What is this? Suddenly we're in my personal territory. Nicole is flirtatious, but. . . I want to know—and I don't want to know. I clamp my trembling hands together so he can't see. So— Scott and Nicole? "Together? Like talking after work? That kind of thing?"

"Not exactly." Connor doesn't want to say it. "See, Nicole and Scott were getting pretty hot and heavy. Really into each other, to tell the truth. You know, holding hands, kissing, and, well, you know, and then two days before he was shot, they got in a huge fight. Scott took off in a huff, and Nicole had to drive his truck back to wherever."

I don't cry. My eyes don't water. I don't even feel sad. Numb, only for a second, and then my adrenalin shoots and I'm furious, angry, ferocious, like that feeling I used to get when Brandon's real estate deal fell through and he stopped at a tavern and came home itching for a fight. Bring it on, I'd think—before he threw me against the wall, that is. That's how I feel now, cold, hard. Scott Crowley—you and Nicole?

"You and Rhys spied on Scott and Nicole through the bushes—is that what you're saying?"

"I guess. Sort of pretending we're paparazzi or something."

A protective wall grows around my heart, around my emotions. Detachment. Scott was having an affair with Nicole. What business is that of mine? I grit my teeth. I can't stand this anymore. I can't breathe.

"Your time is up." The guard starts to unlock the cell door.

I turn abruptly, ready to hightail it out of there, when Connor says, "I think I heard your name."

"What?"

"I think they were fighting over you."

"What do you mean?" Here I am, ready to write Scott off. Another loser I hooked up with—another loser, and this one broke my heart. Ready to forget all those good feelings I had in Chile. And now what?

"That last time. Before he got shot. Maybe, like," Connor scratches his nose, "maybe it was some lover's thing. Like that's why she shot him."

"Lady. Time's up. Now." The guard has no more patience. He steps through the cell door, takes my arm, and guides me through the small reception area with its couch and table, through the foyer with its tall oak ceilings, past Lorissa who is anxiously waiting for me. When the guard lets go of my arm, I lunge at the revolving door to the outside, pushing it open with both hands, gasping until I can breathe again. I lean over, heaving.

Suddenly this is too hard for me. I hate men. All men. I hate falling in love. I hear the door spinning behind me and Lorissa jets out.

"What happened?"

I tip my head down, hunching over, fingers spread across my knees. I feel like I'm suffocating. Lorissa gently leads me to a bench and we sit, backs to the police station, facing the view of the Yachts Village bay. Fishing boats, sailboats, yachts, all claiming their space on the waterfront.

Lorissa is dying to know Connor's version of events, but she waits for me, seeing how shaken I am. "Scott was having an affair with Nicole." I catch my breath. "That whole time I was falling in love with him, he was having an affair with Nicole." I'm furious, not just at him, but at myself. *Why do I fall for such total jerks?*

Lorissa massages my back, trying to soothe me. I shake my head, snapping out of my own world of troubles and relay Connor's full story—bracelet, preventing Nicole's suicide, throwing the gun.

"Connor saved Nicole from killing herself? Why didn't he tell me? Or at least Jasmine?"

"He's so convinced the cops will twist anything he says, and after all, as he says, 'he's a loser, and Nicole's a rock-solid community member.'"

"Well, why. . ." Lorissa's forehead is creased in new angles, so perplexed, trying to figure out her son.

"Why did he talk to me?" I ask. "I suppose it was one loser to another." We both laugh. Not a natural, easygoing laugh, but enough to dispel the tension for a moment.

"No, really. I told him about all that came down in my life, plus—don't be pissed—I saw him and Rhys smoking pot at the park once and never told you." Lorissa squirms, as though deciding how she feels. "Anyway, I didn't think it was such a big deal, but since I hadn't told you, maybe he thought he could trust me."

Lorissa mutters so I can hardly hear. "Rhys."

"Don't go off on Rhys now. Connor went to his defense."

"Sure, he did." Lorissa nods impatiently. "Will Connor tell Thorp now? At least Jasmine? Maybe Thorp won't send him from Yachts Village jail to Grayson Center." Anything to keep him, the naïve island kid, in Yachts Village.

"I'm not sure."

"I need to call Graham."

While Lorissa steps away to phone her husband, I gaze out at a kayaker paddling past a yacht that could smoosh her with one wrong turn. The woman in the kayak, wearing sunglasses and a baseball cap, seems so peaceful, so calm. I was so close, I think. Or at least I thought I was, to that peaceful, serene life I'd always dreamed of. Now I wonder. Who is Scott, actually? What was his game with me? It's so hard to scream and yell at somebody who's lying in a coma. I'm furious. How dare another man mess with my heart. And Brandon's still out there! I know he fits in with shooting Scott somehow. I know he does.

Lorissa returns, phone in hand. "Graham's going to get on the next plane."

"Great!"

"Meaghan, thank you so much." Her smile is strained. "I'll see if I can get back in to Jasmine to tell her all this." She calls, exchanges the requisite polite conversation with the receptionist, then waits a few minutes.

"Jasmine will jam us into her tight schedule at five." Three hours to kill.

We mosey down to Java Café, order lattes, then cross the street to the grassy waterfront park. "Downtown" Yachts Village is such a misnomer. Only three blocks of shops and galleries and restaurants, capped by the crème, the history museum, for tourists who have had enough of dispensing their money on items they'd never purchase were it not for the lovely setting—paintings, dresses, jewelry.

Lorissa is more anxious than I've ever seen, her shoulders curled over like she's an ancient woman in need of a cane. "I keep thinking the worst," she says to me in a muffled voice, trying to hold back her emotion. I put my arm around her.

As we straighten up again, a fit young woman runs by with the sweetest golden retriever. With a leash in one hand, she holds a plastic bag for doggy poop in the other. "Jack," she calls, but the dog is the friendly sort; he noses his wet schnoz into my palms, licks them all over while his puppy face is practically grinning, so happy to make new friends.

"Hey, pooch." I rub his head and pat his back, his fluffy tail wagging wildly until he's had enough and scurries ahead.

"Sorry," the woman with the leash says.

"No worries." But by then they're past hearing distance.

"It's funny how dogs make it seem so easy." Lorissa hugs her arms around her stomach.

"What do you mean?"

"Oh, you know. Friends." She looks up at me, questioningly. "Nicole and I were close. So close. She told me so many secrets, so many things she'd done in high school and college and I've never repeated them. That's me. I just don't go for gossip. I think that's why most people trust me." I don't respond, don't say the obvious: Except me. I didn't trust you. One of the biggest mistakes of my life.

"I mean, the whole reason I went to the pharmacy that day," Lorissa says, "was because I needed someone to dump on. Someone to vent to. I was so mad at Connor, so upset at losing my job, and I could always turn to Nicole."

I nod, moving to the edge of the sidewalk as a man and woman jog by. "I'm just so bummed out," she continues. "On top of all my worries about Connor, I'm just sad about losing Nicole. How could Nicole do that? How could she just concoct that story about Connor?"

"I don't know, Lorissa." Again, I bite my lip, don't say what I'm thinking: You need to keep your focus on Connor. I lift my face to the sky on this unseasonably warm fall day, where white clouds have spread thin and the sun feels soothing against my cheek. We walk in silence.

"So, Meaghan." She catches me off guard. "What's the deal with Scott?"

I suck in my breath and notice she perks up thinking about something, anything, other than Connor and Nicole. "I fell in love," I say. "I didn't even realize how much in love until I arrived in Chile. And now I don't know what to think." I chew on my lip. "Did I tell you about when we adventured around Hurricane Ridge? Up in the mountains, near Port Angeles?"

"At the end of summer?"

"Right." I tell her about driving along the lush green Olympic Peninsula, past the lavender farms, and finding a trail through the woods, where yards of moss hung from limbs, little wood planks over streams, giant firs hundreds of years old. "We had a picnic—that was our thing: being outdoors, picnics, keeping an eye out for wild animals. I don't know what did it, but one moment, cutting a piece of sourdough bread, I sighed deeper than I ever had. I knew, I just knew, this man had touched me in a deep and faraway place." I giggle like a fifteen-year-old, remembering.

"Of course, I shelved those feelings, kept trying to escape them. After all, with all I'd gone through with Brandon, I certainly didn't need a new love in my heart. But. . ." and now I reflect on how much has changed. "But now, who knows who he is, what he is, who I even fell in love with?"

My laugh is a bit artificial. It's not actually funny, and yet it is. "Really, does the man I fell for even truly exist?"

34

Meaghan Farren

The receptionist escorts us into Jasmine's office, where Lorissa and I settle into the same red leather chairs in front of her sprawling desk. "Hey," says Jasmine, arms propped on her desk, professional and harried. "Connor opened up to you?" She looks at me, almost with suspicion. "Do you know why?"

I cough, regard her Persian rug, neatly crafted in red and blue and purple. I gather my thoughts. "For one, I'm an outsider, neither parent or lawyer." Lorissa and Jasmine don't smile. "I was less threatening, I guess." Jasmine acknowledges that with a slight tip of her head.

"One time I saw him smoking dope at the park and didn't say anything." I don't look at Lorissa. "Plus, we shared, I don't know. He and Rhys"—Lorissa seethes when I say 'Rhys'—"and Scott and I.. . we, well, we shared a 'moment.' That's the best way to put it. We saw an eagle, its wings spread, gliding over the water, and it was one of those magical days, and I don't know, we all just seemed to connect." Jasmine's eyes narrow. "And another time we talked in his parents' kitchen, and—I don't know, some people just hit it off, you know what I mean? Who can say why? It happens."

Jasmine swivels her chair, just a touch from left to right. The light from the high window above the Pollock replica casts a sheen on her mocha-colored face, and I can almost see her mind spinning. "What did Connor say, exactly?" I go through it all, from the bracelet to the park, to the fight with his mom, to the pharmacy, Nicole with the gun to her head, and then, more reluctantly, Nicole and Scott together.

Jasmine falls back into her chair, staring at her desk as though it's going to offer her answers. "What we've got is a detective story. Nicole had opportunity and motive. A detective's dream." I'm excited for about a half second until I realize the obvious, and Jasmine continues. "Scott and Nicole fight after their little tryst. She shoots him at the pharmacy. What we're missing is proof. We've got no proof except Connor's word, which isn't. . ."

Lorissa groans. She's at her breaking point, and I know it's killing her to have Graham in San Francisco, not here to help her through this morass of legal mumbo jumbo. "Pieces to this puzzle are missing," Jasmine says. "Now that Connor's begun to open up, there may be more he's either hiding or innocently forgot to say. Lorissa, you speak with Rhys. See if there's anything we might have overlooked."

"Rhys?" Lorissa sputters. "You want me to talk to *that* Rhys?" Jasmine's mouth twitches just enough to keep from bursting into a laugh. Lorissa is over the top with her anti-Rhys stance, and it would be almost funny—if we weren't dealing with the life of her son.

"You want to free Connor? Yes, Lorissa. You said Rhys is Connor's closest friend. Yes, you need to talk to him."

Jasmine now directs her gaze to me. "Meaghan. I know I asked you before, but please think hard. Can you tell me anything else about Scott that we haven't found in his records?"

"I didn't know him that well, apparently." Well enough to fall stupidly head over heels. Not well enough to know whether or not he sold drugs or if he did a drug heist. Not well enough to know that he was doing it with you know who. I can't stand to even say her name.

"We're finding out more and more about him." Jasmine says. I rub my lips, not sure I want to hear. "He has a record." I close my eyes, wishing this would all just disappear. I've been hoping the accusations against Scott were all mistakes. Stealing drugs? How could I have been such a fool.

Jasmine speaks slowly as she breaks the news. "He was a gigolo."

My jaw falls to my knees. Just knock me out with a feather. Of all the words I expected, these aren't the ones. "A *gigolo*?" I can't contain myself. I had prepared myself for him stealing drugs, even dealing drugs, but this? "Like that Richard Gere movie? A gigolo?" I start to laugh, laugh so hard tears flow down my face, laugh until my tears of laughter become tears of pain, and then they keep pouring. When my voice returns, I ask, "What did he do?"

"He swindled old ladies," Jasmine speaks gently, delicately, as though she knows my heart is breaking a little more with every word. "I guess there were a few old ladies he accompanied to dinner, to musical shows, and so forth, but this last one"—she lifts a manila folder from her desk, opens it, and reads through several papers— "the nephew of a Mrs. Lucas filed suit. Her nephew figured out Scott was stealing from her, and when Scott was escorting Mrs. Lucas to the show *Oklahoma*, he was apprehended in front of the Pantages Theater. Arrested, handcuffed, driven off in a police car. Mrs. Lucas was"— Jasmine checks her notes again—"eight one. Eighty-one years old."

I am incredulous. Horrified. First, despair and then fury, disorientation, as if I am in a house of mirrors and I keep seeing myself from one angle, then another and another. I think back to my last night with Scott, the candlelight dinner, the shrimp fettuccine tasting so yummy, the mood so romantic, and then Scott had begged to speak. What was it he'd said before Brandon banged on the door? "Mrs. Lucas. . ."

"What happened?" I ask.

"He embezzled two thousand dollars from her, was arrested, convicted, and sentenced to a year in jail."

"A year," I repeat, still trying to wrap my mind around this—that we are talking about Scott, my Scott.

"He completed his sentence, then met with his parole officer every month—until he was shot." Jasmine checks the file.

"It looks like he was released from jail, worked construction to pay restitution, then went to school to be a pharmacy tech."

I smell the coffee from the other side of the door, in the reception area. "I'm surprised he could even get a pharmacy license," I say. "I mean, with all the news about the opioid crisis and so forth, I'd think licensing laws for a pharmacy tech would be a bit more stringent."

Jasmine leans forward, her forearms back on the desk. "Oh, there are laws. He couldn't have gotten a license in this state."

"What?" I'm confused.

Jasmine continues. "No way could he get a pharmacy tech license. Want to hear my guess?" Lorissa and I say yes at the same time. "My guess is that Nicole held that over him. She knew he couldn't get a job anywhere else. No one else would hire him. It's illegal. She had him by the balls."

I absorb this. "So, you think, what? That he didn't willingly go to the park with Nicole? That he didn't want to have an affair with her?" I sit up straighter. "Because that's bullshit, you know." But it does add another dimension to Nicole and Scott's relationship. She was holding a lot of power over him. "How could he even go to school to study that?"

"Oh, it happens all the time," Jasmine explains. "The whole for-profit college machine. Recruiters wait outside the food stamp or welfare office or jail and push these schools. The kids, or men or women, pay a fortune, work their tail off, and end up with these degrees that can't be used for anything. These places love to sucker in felons. It's their bread and butter."

I rest my elbows on the chair arms, impressed by the softness of the leather, and begin to chew a fingernail. I'm so grateful for my time in Chile when I felt such emotional healing, like I had truly cleared my heart and soul. Who knows how I'd ever have dealt with this if I hadn't had that chance for renewal? What more can be said? I sit on the edge of my chair, ready to stand and leave.

"His parole officer doesn't think he was doing the drugs," Jasmine adds. "He thinks he's a 'con man who got conned,' as he put it." I chuckle faintly. And what does that make me? Just an easy mark? I'm ready to get out of here, but Lorissa is thinking more clearly than I am.

"We don't really know about the drugs, right? If Connor's telling the truth, which is what I care to believe, then Nicole is lying. If she's lying about Connor shooting Scott, she might be lying about everything."

Everything, I think. Connor, Scott and her, drugs, all of it.

"Are you wondering if there were any drugs stolen at all?" Jasmine asks. "You mean, maybe there never was a theft at Harvard Street Pharmacy? And yet Nicole called the police the day before Scott was shot to say drugs were stolen from the pharmacy." She tugs one of her dangling earrings. "No, we don't know. We just have Nicole's word, which. . ."

"Means nothing." Lorissa spits. "Nothing."

35

Lorissa Orondo

"Evidence," Lorissa says. We're back at her dining room table, two mugs of black tea steeping. Through her great room window, Mount Rainier is dusty white. Lorissa dips her tea bag in and out of the steaming water. I don't know if she wants input or if she's just thinking aloud when she says, "I still wonder if Rhys did it."

I knead the back of my sore, tense neck. "Connor was royally pissed that you blamed Rhys. He doesn't think there was any kind of drug deal going on."

"Mom!" Once again, I'm shocked it's this late in the afternoon, that school is already out. Mackenzie is breathless. "Was Connor sent to Grayson Center? That's the rumor in school. Is it true?" Lorissa greets her daughter with a mama-bear hug.

"Not yet. He's still in the Yachts Village jail. But we're going to get him out of there. Soon." Mackenzie unstraps her backpack and throws it on the floor. "Tea, Mackenzie?"

"Sure."

Lorissa brings a fresh cup of tea, some honey, and a spoon, to the table. Her daughter scavenges through the pantry and finds cheese crackers.

"Mackenzie," Lorissa says, "I wonder if maybe Rhys had something to do with the shooting, if he's the one who wanted the Roxies. I mean, with all the trouble he's gotten your brother into over the years. . ."

"Mom." Mackenzie spills her tea all over her jeans, she's so irritated. "No!" she screams as she goes to the kitchen for a towel to clean the mess. "No way Rhys did anything. Why would you even think that?"

Whoa! I've never heard Mackenzie so vehement. I can see Lorissa is trying to figure out how to phrase her response. "You sound pretty certain."

"Mom," Mackenzie says in exasperation. "Mom. Stop thinking that it's all Rhys' fault. Because it's not. He doesn't have a mother, at least he doesn't know where she is, and his dad's, like, never there—I think he's been in jail. And you've got to know Connor would have gotten in plenty of trouble without Rhys."

Mackenzie is mad, but at least she's talking to her mom, which is a lot better than Connor, who's sitting in a jail cell, mute to her.

"Mackenzie, what's going on?" Lorissa's voice is level, as if to say "Enough of this BS." A stripe of sunlight falls on Mackenzie's face, her glowing cheeks, her perky small nose.

"Okay." Mackenzie takes a deep breath. "You want to know? Rhys and I are friends. I know he doesn't do Roxies, and you know what else? I'll tell you the truth."

I sipped my tea. This was going to be good.

36

Meaghan Farren

"Rhys was here the morning that Scott was shot. *Here.* With me," Mackenzie says.

It's so quiet I almost hear a hummingbird's wings fluttering outside the window. I dare not look at Lorissa. This is one of those times I'm glad I'm not a mother. We all stiffen in our chairs, no one speaking, no one moving. Lorissa's bitter enemy is her son's best friend and her daughter's crush. What a mess. I silently push back from the table and move to the oak rocking chair at the other end of the great room, giving Lorissa and Mackenzie some space for their mother-daughter talk. The silence is broken by the dog barking across the street. That Guru. Lorissa finally finds her voice. "Detective Thorp told me he was here. You snuck behind my back and invited Rhys over here?"

Mackenzie's face is pink. "Mom. Nothing happened, okay? Chill. He's actually kind of shy around girls, to tell you the truth."

"Don't you dare tell me to chill." Lorissa's face contorts into a gargoyle, so angry.

"Mom!" Mackenzie is near tears. "I'm sorry." Mackenzie seems to truly want her mom's approval. Lorissa told me Mackenzie had been so easy compared to her brother. "We listened to music," Mackenzie says. "That's all."

"But. . .but." I can imagine what Lorissa would like to say. But he's a screwup. But he's not allowed in the house. But he's not even your friend; he's Connor's. Lorissa cringes, and I can see she's trying to be patient. It must be so hard to communicate with your teenage daughter—harder than the most difficult jigsaw puzzle. Her voice softens. "You like Rhys?"

Mackenzie watches the hummingbird drinking nectar from the feeder on the deck. "Yeah, I like him. It's not like I'm going to marry him or anything. But he's nice to me. He acts like I'm the most wonderful girl in the universe. I never had anybody who just, like, seemed to worship me. So, yeah, I like him. Kind of a lot."

Lorissa has made her feelings about Rhys clear to me more than once, and I can see that she knows how a wrong word now could alienate her daughter. Guru barks again, interrupting their conversation. "Oh, I wish that dog would shut up," Lorissa says. "Maybe we should buy him a muzzle, sneak over there and put it on him all day, then take it off right before the Corcorans come home after work."

Mackenzie giggles. "I can just imagine you sneaking over with a muzzle."

"Maybe we should have Rhys do it."

"Mom!" Mackenzie rolls her eyes.

"Sorry, Mackenzie. I just couldn't pass that up." A reprieve, a laugh of truce.

Mackenzie sighs, as though trying to make her mother understand. "Mom, no other guy shows any interest in me.

Nobody even acts nice to me." She brings her feet to the seat of her chair and her knees up to her nose, hugging her arms around her legs. "And I know it's because I'm so fat. If some boy's nice to me, of course I'm going to, you know, like them."

Oh, boy. Mackenzie's throwing her mom in a minefield. So many wrong things Lorissa could say: "You're not fat" or "why don't you eat a little less?" or "Come on, there are probably a million guys who'd love to take you out." Instead, Lorissa responds gently. "Well, sweetie, some guys can just be jerks, it's true. They don't know what they're missing."

Mackenzie's mouth tics—not a smile, but perhaps a positive acknowledgment that although she doesn't believe a word her mom just said, at least Lorissa isn't repeating the crap people usually say.

"So, Mackenzie." Lorissa is using her firmer "mom" voice, as though now it's time to get down to business. "How many times has Rhys been over when I wasn't home?"

Mackenzie's fingers move as though she's counting: "Thirteen, fourteen, fifteen," she whispers. Eavesdropper that I am, I can't help but turn and watch Lorissa's eyebrows crawl up to her hairline, her face reddening.

"Just kidding, Mom! Just that one time. Honest. I wanted to show him my new music." She raises her voice. "And by the way, if he hadn't come over, ya know, he might not have told me stuff about Connor's 'new side.' I guess that medicine Connor started taking in June is kicking in 'cuz Rhys says he's always talking about stuff that new counselor is saying, like how

Connor should really believe in himself and all that. Like he doesn't have to be good at everything just because Dad was." Lorissa leans forward, listening intently. Was Connor always comparing himself to Graham, and they never noticed?

"Yeah," Mackenzie continues. "It's pretty cool how Connor's so into his bike riding and Rhys is so into his photography. Connor's getting in shape for that big Seattle to Portland ride."

Lorissa's phone rings, startling Mackenzie and me. Before she answers, she checks the number. "Dad." As she listens to Graham, her jaw tightens. "There's got to be something you can do." I hear the anxiety. "What about Oakland?" Silence. "San Jose?" With each question, Lorissa's voice rises higher and higher. "What about the train? How long does that take?" A longer pause. "Okay. Love you, too." Click.

She throws the phone on the table. "Dad is fogged in at the San Francisco airport, and Oakland and San Jose aren't any better. He can't get a flight." She doesn't move, as though reconciling herself to the fact there's nothing she can do. Graham's devoted to his family, I know that. And now, he belongs here with Lorissa, not in San Fran. But while he's gone, I'll do my best to be supportive.

"Mackenzie." Lorissa reaches for her daughter's hand. "Connor's probably going to Grayson Center tomorrow."

"Oh, Mom." Mackenzie sinks in her chair, as depressed as Lorissa is about the prospect of Grayson Center. A few minutes later, she sits up and clears her throat. "So, Mom?" She looks like she's figuring out the best way to ask. "Is it okay if Rhys comes over sometime? Pleeease?"

"Ohh, sweetie." I know Lorissa wants to say "No, never," but I can also see that she feels so beaten down dealing with Connor, missing Graham, the fight just isn't in her. "Okay. But only when your dad or I are home, okay?"

Mackenzie smiles as though she's not too excited, but it's clear she is. "Okay. Love you, Mom." She rewards her mom with a huge hug.

For dinner Lorissa, Mackenzie, and I stick with pizza from the Wilkes Island store, then cap off the evening watching old episodes of *Gilmore Girls* with a bowl of buttery popcorn in their downstairs family room. Mackenzie is shocked I haven't seen the series and quickly catches me up on it. She and her mom cuddle up to each other, and the three of us share a fleece throw, flip off the lights, and begin the marathon. Two episodes in—right after a deer runs into Rory's car—Mackenzie's phone vibrates and she disappears into her room. So much for a girl's night together. Another two episodes later, she emerges from her bedroom.

"Mom," she says, "that was Rhys. He's worried about Connor too. And you know what else he said? He has pics on his phone of Nicole and Scott together at the park. Couldn't that help?"

Lorissa turns off the TV and switches on the lights. "Yes! At least that would show Nicole's not such a perfect citizen."

We all think for a minute. I speak tentatively. "If they're being romantic in the photos…" It's hard for me to say, but Lorissa picks up the thread.

"If they're being romantic, and then Crowley said he wanted to end it, like Connor said…"

"Then that's evidence—motivation—for Nicole to shoot Scott! She was jealous, just like on TV!" Mackenzie is so excited she's nearly bouncing on the couch.

"A woman scorned and all that!" says Lorissa.

Wow. Are they saying Nicole shot Scott because he was going to dump her for me? Was he trying to brush her off? Could the photos of Nicole and Scott together be the evidence we need to get Connor out of jail?

"But. . ." Mackenzie sighs, "Rhys lost his phone."

PART III
OCTOBER 20, 2014

37

Meaghan Farren

"He lost the phone with the pictures of Nicole and Scott Crowley?" Lorissa is exasperated.

"He thinks he lost it at the park," Mackenzie says.

It's like winning roulette, then losing everything with a single spin of the wheel.

"We're going to find that phone," Lorissa says. She is determined. "We will find it."

The next day, 10:00 a.m. Saturday, we three detectives—Lorissa, Mackenzie, and I—dress in our heaviest sweatshirts, raincoats, and boots and drive over the Wilkes Island bridge on what may be a wild goose chase. The windshield wipers swish the pounding rain, the sea below the bridge churns with whitecaps, and the chill feels more like twenty than forty degrees.

"Mom, it's been raining forever," Mackenzie sighs. "The phone's probably sunk in the mud. Even if we find it, there's no way in the world it will work. Rhys said it's an old phone, doesn't have Find My Phone or any stuff like that."

Lorissa's forehead crinkles in waves that match the water below the bridge. It's not that Mackenzie isn't right—it's that Lorissa is desperate. "Mackenzie," her mom explains, "Scott hasn't gotten one ounce better. If he dies, Connor will be charged with murder. We're going to try."

I feel Lorissa's anguish, worry, and exhaustion. Scott might die. He might leave this all unresolved. Mackenzie sucks in her lips, worried too. I can't imagine how hard it must be, having your brother in jail for attempted murder, especially when you've lived such a privileged fairy-tale life. "I love you, Mackenzie," Lorissa says, the only comfort she can give her daughter.

In the backseat, Mackenzie stares out the window as we pass forests, then her elementary school, and cross over Route 16, driving through Yachts Harbor, our town that's warring between maintaining its life as a fishing village and transforming into a fast-paced tourist mecca. We don't speak, even as our tires grind into the deserted lot, crunching the gravel next to the empty equipment shed at Sunrise Beach Park.

We each don gloves—gardening gloves, dishwashing gloves, stretchy acrylic gloves—and slog down the hill, the mud sucking our shoes like tentacles. It's rained on and off for a week, but now a patch of blue weaves through the clouds, and the rain lightens to a wispy drizzle coating the air. "Let's start by going all the way down to the beach, then work our way back up," Lorissa says.

"When I try Rhys's phone, it goes straight to voice mail."

"I'm sure the battery's dead," Mackenzie says.

Thirty minutes later, Lorissa lifts yet another moss-covered stone on the rocky beach, and a tiny hermit crab scurries out, then buries itself again. "Mom, this is hopeless."

"It's not hopeless." Her son's future is on the line. Over the sound of smashing waves, we hear a car park up the hill in the parking lot, then a door slam, and minutes later a boy in a green raincoat, a flannel shirt, and faded baggy jeans lumbers toward us.

"Rhys." Mackenzie claps her hands together as though keeping herself from jumping up and down.

"Well, I figure if you're gonna look for my phone, I might as well help." Rhys's shoulders are broad, his stomach paunchy, and all I can see of his face under his hood is his mouth, a tender smile. Genuine. A bit like Hagrid—big and burly, but ultimately kind. A good person to have on your side. "Any luck?" he asks.

"Not yet." Lorissa searches for—and finds—her most enthusiastic, welcoming voice. Whatever her real feelings are, now she needs Rhys on her side. She needs his help. I bet she'd love to ask him about this "new side of Connor" that Mackenzie mentioned, but her pride is too great. Her son should tell her about his bike riding goals himself.

We inch up the trail from the beach, moving ever so slowly, the four of us spreading out like a CSI team in search of evidence. Well, that's what we are. A crazy kind of investigative team.

"That's where Connor and I used to stand." Rhys points to an opening in the blackberry bushes, which, I see as I inspect more closely, stretches back several feet. "I mean, it's not like we planned to be spying on them or nothin,' but we just didn't want to be seen, ya know?"

Didn't want to be seen getting high? I don't say it, but he gives me a knowing look. No need to upset Lorissa any more than she already is. Oh, well. I was his age once.

In high school, I'd never gotten into trouble, even though a lot of other kids smoked pot. No, it was Lorissa who'd run away—to the U District in Seattle, hanging out on the street busking for change, sleeping in an alley. Her dad had moved out when she was eleven, and a year later he died. She'd had a tough time dealing with it.

Then one day she really blew it. She was supposed to be at the high school, watching out for her sister, but she traipsed off with her boyfriend for ice cream. When she remembered she'd forgotten her books, she returned to the school and heard squeals of terror coming from the locker room. Lorissa always remembered running towards those cries, the smell of chlorine from the school swimming pool, the boys circling Ashley in the locker room, taunting her. Ashley trembling, shaking, wailing as they edged in closer, heckling, ignoring Ashley's pink face, her desperate sobs. When Lorissa thinks about that day, she still feels that a raw, open wound. Yes, Lorissa arrived just in time before those monsters did who knows what to Ashley, but what if she hadn't? What if she hadn't gotten there a split second before…she quivers remembering. Ashley couldn't sleep alone in her room for months. Her terror left a life-long scar. She never overcame her fear of men she didn't know. This was Lorissa's biggest shame— not being there to protect her sister with Down Syndrome. Not being there for Ashley.

The incident had scared Lorissa straight, so to speak, and led her mother to decide to stay in Washington where Ashley could have treatment for her trauma, move into a group home when she was older. One time her mom had hugged Lorissa and said, "I was afraid I'd lost you both." Afterwards, Lorissa stayed close to Ashley and even took karate lessons—got a brown belt— "just in case."

That night at college, when Lorissa had confided her shame about not keeping her sister safe, I'd felt so close, so bonded, like we were soul sisters. But she'd gotten too close, and by then I was terrified that in some unsuspecting moment I'd spill my guts and tell her about my dad. A few days later I cut her off.

Brutally and ruthlessly severed the connection—for twenty years. And that was my shame.

Now, all these years later, I wonder if Lorissa sees a part of herself in Rhys. A part of herself she'd rather her kids never knew. The difference between her and Rhys is that she had a loving, attentive mom who helped her back on her feet. Rhys, apparently, has no one.

"And here," Rhys points to a grassy area by a stump in the middle of the field, "here's where that hot pharmacist lady Nicole and that dude Scott fought the day before he got shot. They screamed and yelled and finally she whopped him right here in the chest."

"Connor mentioned they got into a fight," I say, hoping for more details.

"Oh, yeah. Man, they fought." Rhys waves his arms dramatically. "She starts to get hot, rubbing up against him, then he pushes her away."

"You must have been pretty close," Lorissa says.

"Well, yeah." Rhys looks embarrassed.

"What happened next?" I want to hear the story; I don't want to hear it. Curiosity wins over jealousy.

"He's got her wrists; not like he's hurting her or nothin'. I think he just wanted her attention. I couldn't hear his exact words, but . . . Connor and me—we both heard your name, Meaghan. We talked about that later. We couldn't hear as well as we could see, but we sure heard your name."

"What happened?" Mackenzie is impatient.

"Scott looked furious. He shoved her away from him...and that's when we noticed she was wearing your bracelet, Mrs. Orondo." He glances up at Lorissa. Waits for a reaction. Gets none. "Scott stomped off, hoofing right past his own truck," he indicates up the hill— "without turning back once. He was royally pissed. That was some fight."

"What did she do?" I ask, all the time pretending to myself we're not talking about the man I thought I loved and the woman he was having an affair with.

"Kind of hard to tell." Rhys's eyes shift, as though trying to picture it. "She climbed in the backseat of his truck, and we couldn't see what she was doing, but we could see her rounded back for—I don't know—awhile, and then she climbed back into the front where she fiddled around—looking for Scott's keys, maybe? Anyway, she fired up the truck, and zoomed off. I mean really hauled ass. Glad no one was coming the other way. That would have been a nasty crash."

I crouch down and continue raking my fingers through mushy fallen leaves, through grass clippings, through more blackberry bushes, searching for the phone. Even though the rain has stopped, my hair drips down my back, and I'm as cold as on a winter day in Massachusetts. We all move up another foot. So tedious.

That's it. The detective life is not for me. I'm glad to help Lorissa and Connor, but that glamorous job of Nancy Drew's is off the bucket list. I scratch my neck, putting pieces together. "Rhys, you said Nicole did something in the backseat of the truck. Could she have hidden the Roxies there? Police said that they found a whole bunch in a slit in the upholstery."

"*Mmm*," he ponders. "Maybe. I dunno."

Raindrops drip from the fir boughs. Lorissa halts, puts her hands on her hips, stiff, like an army sergeant. "Rhys." She stands in front of him, fierce. "You never bought drugs from Scott Crowley?"

"No, Mrs. Orondo. Never!"

"And you never saw Scott Crowley selling drugs?"

"No." A crooked smile forms with half his lips. "I mean, Crowley doesn't seem like the type, does he? He's kind of cocky, if you know what I mean. But drug dealer? I don't believe that whole story."

I must have moved or jerked because Rhys quickly backtracks. "I mean, he seems like a nice guy. But a two-timer. That's all. I mean, he sounded kind of nice at first when he tried to break it off with Nicole—at least that's what Connor and me thought was going on—but shit, did he get pissed when she said whatever it was. I think he was really hung up on you, Meaghan. That's what me and Connor were saying after that big fight."

His words sound good, but what do I believe? I don't know. I just don't know.

Lorissa doesn't cut him any slack. "But you did drugs? You do drugs?"

Poor Rhys. I feel sorry for the kid. No one wants to tangle with a mama bear like Lorissa. "I never did no Roxies, if that's what you're asking. I never did none of them. As for smoking a little pot, yeah, maybe. But I don't see how that makes any difference."

Good point. Air somewhat cleared. We all continue our search, stooping over, examining each side of the path, then hike up through the middle where the grassy area opens to the size of a football field before it reaches the parking lot.

After two hours of useless search, we finally arrive back at the cars, cold, miserable, empty-handed. Mackenzie was right. How stupid. How could we possibly find a cell phone here?

"Bummer," Rhys says. He opens the door to his car, plastic and duct tape covering the hole where the back window should be. After a few minutes of awkward silence, he starts his ignition, the engine sputtering like it's going to start, then kaput.

We stand next to his car, waiting. "Hey, Rhys. You checked your car for the phone, right?" Mackenzie asks. He unlatches his glove compartment, pulling out a packet from Les Schwab tires, aspirin, a pipe, some rolling papers—which he quickly puts in his lap. "Well. I found a flashlight." He holds it up. Once again, he turns his key, his engine engages this time, for just a minute, and then it whimpers dead.

"We have Triple A if you need it." Lorissa sounds reluctant.

"Thanks, but this is how the car starts sometimes. I'll get it." We hear Rhys swear—not at Lorissa, I'm sure.

Lorissa is despondent and defeated. As she slowly turns the key to start the car, Mackenzie hurls her door open without warning and flies out. "Mom!" She dashes to the equipment shed, where a spark of silver shines at its base, half-buried in the mud.

Rhys tries to start his car a third time, and finally he sputters out of the parking lot.

"Mom. Meaghan. The phone!" Mackenzie leaps back in the car. "It won't start, though. The battery's dead."

"Oh, Mackenzie!" Lorissa leans over the seat to hug her daughter. "Great work!"

"Mom, it's soaked. It won't start. It won't do anything. We need to get Rhys and have him take it to the store!"

The car idles for a minute, then Lorissa hits the accelerator and winds up the hill out of the park, spotting Rhys up ahead. She pounds on the horn. "Let's go to Verizon." I block my ears to the screech of the honking that goes on and on and on until finally Rhys pulls over.

Mackenzie rolls down her window. "Rhys, we found your phone. Jump in. Mom can take you to the Verizon store." Rhys drives ahead a few thousand feet so he can leave his car at the city park.

Mackenzie slides over, making room for Rhys, who fills more than half the back seat. I watch Lorissa as she eyes the boy she's hated for years and her daughter in the rearview mirror. What a predicament. The key to her son's release seems to lie with the boy she blames for everything that's ever gone wrong in Connor's life. Then, to make it worse, Mackenzie's face radiates, her face one big smile that sure looks like true, albeit teenage, love. "It will be okay, Lorissa," I whisper, patting her back.

"Cool," Rhys says. "Man, I was so bummed about those eagle shots."

"What?" I peer over my seat.

"Oh, I mean I want to help get Connor out of jail, for sure. I mean, there's no way he shot Scott or nobody else. I bet he couldn't even hold a gun without his hand shaking." Was he calling Connor a wuss? In the kindest of ways?

"What do you mean about eagle shots?"

"Ya know, Meaghan? Like those ones I took when we ran into you and Scott down there? I've got a bunch more, plus some great ones for my photography class."

"That's so cool." Mackenzie's voice lilts as if she's a fan talking with Justin Bieber.

Oh, brother.

"Yeah. I got some amazing shots of smoke rising up from the mills in Tacoma, in front of Mount Rainier. Looks kind of—I don't know—all trippy and stuff." He clears his throat.

It's like I can see inside Lorissa's head: Okay—one point for this. . .this hooligan. "You like photography?" she asks.

Forty minutes later, the motley four of us tumble out of Lorissa's car: neatly groomed Lorissa in her designer jeans with the designer holes in the knee; bright, fit teenage Mackenzie; rough and tumble Rhys; and me, barely put together in jeans and a Columbia rain jacket, a woman with a broken heart, confused yet determined. My hair's grown out, I've dyed it back to its natural dirty blonde, and my wrinkles have eased after my spiritual time in Chile. I'm actually in pretty good shape because I've started a daily running routine like I had when I was younger. I try to reconjure the peace of the desert mountains, though that seems centuries ago.

When we file into the store one by one, I see a man with dark hair and from the back, he looks like Brandon. I feel the old familiar terror. When he turns, I see I'm mistaken, but I'm still shaking.

I haven't thought much about Brandon at all, but as soon as I remember him, a shudder springs up my spine. I imagine his face, like a rubber mask with curves and creases, his vicious green eyes peering at me. It's one thing for me to relax, another to be less than vigilant. I bet he wishes he had opened the kitchen drawer in our ramshackle apartment and pulled out the longest carving knife, gleaming under the bare lightbulb, and slit my throat like some carrion he found flailing on our maple-lined street. I've adjusted my mind-set to a "screw him" attitude and refuse to recoil, and yet I need to pay attention every moment. Every second.

I hadn't thought of Brandon because I've been so wrapped up in helping Lorissa, and now I like being part of our oddball foursome, working like detectives, trying to set Connor free. It's been so long since I've been part of anything that I'm actually having fun. I'd spent so many years in my desolate second-floor apartment alone with Chumley, my only companion, dreading the return of Brandon. We humans get used to situations, even rotten situations, so easily. Adapt. I'd forgotten how it feels to be with other people, out for a ride, out for an adventure, out in the world. Free. The very opposite of Connor, locked in a jail cell.

The Tacoma Verizon clerk, short with curly blue hair and a nose ring, snorts derisively, turning the phone over in her hands. "I doubt I can, like, do anything with this old phone. I mean, this is oold."

"Can't you just put it in rice or in silicone or something?" Lorissa sounds so desperate.

"Not anymore, Mom." Mackenzie sounds embarrassed that her mom is so out of touch.

"See this red line here?" the nose ring asks. "If it were, like, pink, we'd probably be able get the phone to work." Then, "no pink line." Kind of like a pregnancy test, I think. "See this? Red."

If it would be any help, Lorissa would be on her knees begging. "We don't even need it to work," she pleads. "All we need are the pictures."

The girl behind the counter tosses her fingers through her hair and explains with the irritation of an eight-year-old talking to her four-year-old sister: "Every once in a while we, like, get a phone with red to work, but that hardly ever happens. I've never seen it myself."

"Hey, man," says Rhys. "Give it a try. I need my phone."

"Whatever," she says. She takes the phone, hands it off to the girl who'll work with it, and calls the next person in line.

We awkwardly hover around glass displays of newer phones until I say, "Let's go to Starbucks while we're waiting."

We pile back in the car and fifteen minutes later stroll into the Starbucks at Tacoma's University of Washington campus. We're on Pacific Avenue where twenty years ago, Scott once told me, heroin needles used to lay in the cracks of the weed-filled sidewalks, windows were boarded up, addicts flung beer bottles so they'd break in the middle of the street. Since then, an epic metamorphosis: clean, wide sidewalks; an art museum filled with Chihuly glass; brand-new shops selling flowers and running shoes and cupcakes; a light-rail train looping from the bus station to the hundred-acre zoo and park; a history museum much loved by children and adults alike. Trees now grow next to the side walk, flower baskets hang from the street lamps.

A city can change—people can change. I have changed; I will change. I will no longer be captured—emotionally or physically—by a man, I say to myself. I think of both Brandon and Scott, wondering how on earth I could be such a horrendous judge of character.

When Lorissa opens the door to the Starbucks, my eyes blink to adjust to the dark lighting as we amble past a couch, tables, and chairs to join the line to order at the counter.

"This is where Scott told me he first met Joel," I say.

"Oh?" Lorissa pulls out her wallet. "Joel as in Nicole's husband?"

"Yeah." Scott had told me that it was crowded one day. He was scrolling on his laptop for pharmacy tech jobs, when Joel and Torrie ended up at the table next to him. They got to talking, and Joel said his wife owned a pharmacy. The espresso machine blares, blocking out all conversation. When it stops, Lorissa asks, "And Scott went from here to the Harvard Street Pharmacy? And Nicole hired him on the spot?"

"That's my understanding. And you know what else?" The smell of coffee is so strong I think I could get my caffeine fix just standing here. "Scott said she wasn't even looking for a tech. Apparently, the pharmacy isn't doing too well. All the big chains have pharmacies now. Small family drug stores are getting killed."

"And she hired him anyway? I noticed how empty the shelves were the day that. . ." We all know which day.

"Scott was surprised the pharmacy stayed in business at all," I say. "He never saw the account books, but he did see the customers—or lack of them. He said that one day not a single person came in all afternoon."

"That bad?"

I nod. Scott had told me he'd figured that as long as he received his paycheck every two weeks, he'd stick around. "And it all started with a conversation with Joel, right here." The line moves forward a few inches, but everyone orders such complicated drinks. "It might have been exam time when they met," I muse.

"This place can fill up with kids studying, taking up all the tables. Scott said Joel bought Torrie a bagel and sat her on his lap while they waited for the zoo to open so they could see the puffins."

"He's such a doting stay-at-home dad," Lorissa says with a wistful tone, like, what happened to that wonderful family? "I've taken Torrie—you know she's my goddaughter? —to the zoo over and over, and she's mesmerized by those cute puffins diving and splashing and flapping the water off their wings." The line has progressed. I order my double tall latte with skim milk—I hate calling it a "skinny" like you're supposed to. Lorissa and Mackenzie order their mochas; Rhys scans the scene around him, over his shoulder, side to side.

"Sir," the barista says, "may I get you a drink?" Rhys's paw-sized hands hang loosely by his side, his red plaid shirt opened to the third button, dark hairs curling on his chest. It dawns on me that not only has he never been here before, maybe he's never been in any Starbucks. I'm not the only one emerging from an insular world.

Mackenzie comes to the rescue. "Want what I'm having?"

"Sure." He stares in the glass counter at the croissants, scones, and banana bread.

"Hey, guys, how about some croissants?" Lorissa orders four, lays a twenty on the table, then recalculates, adds another ten to cover all our food and drinks.

We find a burl-wood table by the door. Teens and twentysomething girls and boys with backpacks trot by, busily punching their thumbs into their phones. I toss out the dirty napkins and crumbs left on the table, continuing our conversation.

"Are Graham and Joel still good friends?"

"Well, Graham hasn't seen him since. . ." We know. Since Joel's wife accused their son of attempted murder. "Graham honestly doesn't know what to think. Sex must be steaming hot to put up with her antics." Mackenzie glances at Rhys and they both laugh, listening to Lorissa talk about their neighbor's sex life.

I add a half packet of sweetener to my coffee and sip slowly, so it doesn't burn my tongue. None of us are speaking. Instead, we're each so emotional: Lorissa, in the pits of desperation, trying to save her son; Mackenzie absolutely glowing, being with Rhys; Rhys seeming content and curious, as though he needs to watch his p's and q's, but he's not exactly sure what that means. What's the right way to talk, the right way to behave around Lorissa, who's blamed him for Connor's trouble all these years? "Thanks, Mrs. Orondo," he says. Can't go wrong with that.

"Sure, Rhys." In the speck of sun lighting Lorissa's face, I notice how much weight she's lost. She stirs in her seat, almost as uncomfortable as Rhys, and folds her hands neatly on the table. Her back is straight, tall, prim. "I just don't understand about those drugs Connor stole from the pharmacy. Why did he do that? He doesn't seem all strung out on those Roxicodones."

Rhys puts down his coffee. "Oh, no, Mrs. Orondo! He didn't steal no drugs from any pharmacy." Rhys is certain, no doubt in his voice. "No way."

Lorissa pinches her eyebrows together, clearly perplexed. "Well, the cops found that baggie of Roxies in his drawer. He must have gotten them somewhere." She's been hiding her contempt, her disdain, but not any longer. She sounds indignant, ready to lash out, but Rhys interrupts.

"You thought he stole them drugs from the pharmacy?" Rhys is appalled. "I can't believe you'd even think that! Connor? Never."

Lorissa's shoulders drop, truly humbled. It's as if Rhys believes in Connor more than she does and, clearly, Rhys knows more about her son.

"No way. He got them from Nicole's house. You know? That time you guys had that neighborhood barbecue?"

She scowls. "You mean way back last spring? What are you saying?" Lorissa shoots Mackenzie a glance, like Why didn't you tell me?

"I didn't know. Honest, Mom."

"What did Connor do? He rummaged through her medicine cabinet and found some pills and just pilfered them?"

"Hell, no." Rhys snorts, then tells a story that shocks us all. Connor had spilled his beer all over his shorts at the barbecue, beer that he knew he wasn't supposed to be drinking, so he went looking for a towel in her bathroom. And surprise, surprise, he finds this baggie buried under the towels, and he opens it up, and—I'm sure the three of us have eyes widening to saucers as we listen to Rhys. The Roxies were in a baggie in the drawer, under the towels, so Connor just took them. "But," and now Rhys sounds disgusted, "he didn't even eat any of them. Never. That's how come the cops found them all. Connor told me he didn't even remember he put them in his drawer, it had been so long since that barbecue."

Alanis Morrissette sings from the speakers; kids chatter at the table next to us. A girl with thick eyeliner says, "My econ teacher's so cute!" which is followed by a mass of giggles.

At our table, it's as if we've each turned to granite, reflecting on Rhys's words. I repeat what I think I heard him say. "Nicole had Roxicodone, a really addictive opioid, in her towel drawer?" We're mulling this over, all coming up with the same conclusion. "So, who would hide Roxicodone in their drawer under the towels?"

"Somebody who's strung out," Rhys says. "That's who'd keep Roxies in a towel drawer. With a kid in the house even!"

38

Meaghan Farren

His words echo in my head. In everyone's, I'm guessing. Mackenzie picks up her cup and holds it, not drinking. Lorissa's eyes move toward the door as another gaggle of girls meander in. I start to count all the laptops open on the tables around us. Nine, all belonging to twentysomethings with white wires connected to their ears.

Well, a puzzle piece has clicked into place. So that's why Nicole screams and yells and flips out so easily. She's not just psycho. She's an addict.

"No," says Lorissa. "I don't believe it. Torrie could have found them! Nicole loves her daughter. She'd never put her daughter in danger."

"Yep," Rhys says. "Pretty screwed up."

"No. She wouldn't have done that. She's not an addict. She's been my friend, was my closest friend, for a decade. I would have known."

"Not so." Rhys, big and brawny like a lumberman who's spent weeks in the woods, rests his thick arms on the table and speaks without filters, calling it like it is. "I've known loads of people who are strung out. A lot of them just keep on going, lying and scheming, and all the time no one knows. She's a pharmacist. That's like being queen of the candy store."

We're all quiet once more, barely hearing the chatter around us. I'm worried about Lorissa. She just doesn't want to believe it, and yet if Nicole is addicted to Roxicodone, everything makes sense. "But she's my friend."

Was your friend, I want to say, but I don't. Lorissa's whole body crumples, like she's shrinking, curling up, crushed. I pull out my phone and type "Roxicodone addict" into Google. "Does this sound like Nicole? Here are symptoms listed on the Internet for people addicted to Roxies: 'mood swings, irritable, anger, euphoria, change in vocal pitch, light-headed, itching, nose drips, brain fog, withdrawing from once-pleasurable activities'?"

Lorissa crosses her arms and lowers her head, shaking. "But she was my friend." I feel a dagger in my heart. I was the friend who'd once hurt her, and now here's another. I wrap my arm around her to comfort her, but she pushes me away. Mackenzie, Rhys, and I sit in silence. I sip my latte and bite my croissant as quietly as possible, trying not to disturb Lorissa as she absorbs this all.

She lifts her head and rubs her eyes. "Well."

Yes, well. Lorissa drinks her coffee. She seems to be in that funny place between laughter and tears, not quite sure how she feels. "I can't help but ask myself, why didn't I see this before?" She scratches the back of her neck, wondering. "All these years. Now it makes so much sense."

"So that bitch made up the whole story about Connor stealing the drugs just 'cuz Scott was going to dump her!" says Mackenzie. Lorissa sends her the evil eye. I guess saying "bitch" isn't appropriate for her clean-cut daughter, but at this point, when her son is in jail for what could end up being attempted murder, we are far, far beyond appropriate.

Lorissa's phone vibrates on the table, and she quickly answers. "Okay, thank you." Her voice is leaden. Monotone. Oh no, I think. Lorissa looks grim for a moment, but then her eyes suddenly flash and she shoots her arms into the air. "Yes! Yes! They've managed to save the photos!" We hoot and holler like the Seahawks just won. We gather our cups and napkins and throw them in the garbage—or should it have been the recycling can? — and hustle out to the car, speed to the Verizon store.

How could Lorissa be so playful with us when I know she's feeling empty inside? Maybe the curious chemistry of the four of us oddballs, all together solving this puzzle, gives her more energy. Maybe figuring out that Nicole is the true addict answers a lot of hanging questions.

Rhys runs into Verizon, grabs his phone, and we're off to the next stop—Bartell Drugs. Rhys connects his phone to the cord on the photo machine to see the photos. While they're uploading, Lorissa's phone rings. She turns her back to answer as Rhys begins scrolling through all his pictures. Mackenzie and I huddle over his shoulder—eagles flying over the Sound; another carrying salmon; one picture focused on the sky through the filter of the pine needles, so clear, so well defined I can almost smell the tree; Mount Rainier surrounded by pink and blue and violet sky. That boy has talent! Beautiful nature—yeah, that's great, but can we get to the people pics?

Lorissa rejoins us. Now we see Scott and Nicole, smiles on their face. My stomach aches, like I'll be ill. A perfect couple, holding hands. I don't think I can do this. See them together. I move away, but my curiosity gets the best of me. Nicole and Scott by the water, skipping rocks into the sea; embracing; kissing. I step back again. I can't stand to look any longer.

Rhys, Mackenzie, and Lorissa flip through photo after photo. "You have a knack for this, Rhys. You might have a paparazzi life in your future." He takes Lorissa's words as a compliment. I'm listening to them from the other side of the aisle, where I'm leafing through a magazine, catching up on the latest celebrity gossip.

"Hey!" Mackenzie says. "Look at that picture! Nicole in the backseat of Scott's truck. She could be planting those Roxies in his seat, couldn't she?"

Okay, okay. I've got to see this. I replace the magazine and return to the photos, seeing a person's rounded back in the rear seat of Scott's truck. Doesn't seem to me like it proves anything.

"Well, if you look at the whole series together. . ." Rhys has six photos that include Nicole getting into the truck's backseat, hunching over, then moving up front to the driver's seat and driving out of the park.

"I don't get it," I say to Rhys. "Why did you take all these?"

Rhys pinches his nose as though that will help him think. "I dunno. At first Connor wanted something, you know, in case she figured Connor took those Roxies from her towel drawer."

"You mean like blackmail," Lorissa says.

I return to my magazine. Anything to distract me from my feelings. Rhys shrugs.

"What about this one—it's just some random guy at the beach. Who's he?" Mackenzie asks.

I don't bother to look. I've already seen too much. "I dunno. I saw him once before." Rhys clears his throat and coughs, seeming to stumble over his words. "He was there and I took the shot. Later, he met Nicole. I mean, I'm not a voyeur or anything; I just kind of get into taking pics."

Lorissa checks the time. "That was Graham who called. The fog is clearing and he'll be able to get a flight out. And I completely forgot I promised Ashley I'd take her out to dinner. Rhys, I'll pay for the printing. Will you order eight-by-tens of all the pics of the people?" Lorissa is talking as though she's had eight espressos. "I'll take them to Jasmine in the morning. She'll know if they'll help get Connor out of jail."

"Lorissa," I say. "Mackenzie and I can take Ashley to dinner while you go pick up Graham." That way she and Graham can have some time alone together. "After we drop Rhys off at his car, we can go back to your place and I'll take my car."

It doesn't take a moment for Lorissa to agree. "Rhys," she says, reaching out her hands to his. "Thank you. Thank you so much. Your photos prove Nicole had reason, had a motive, to shoot Scott. The oldest reason in the book. A strong dose of jealous rage."

"And don't forget about the drugs," Mackenzie pipes in. "If it weren't for Rhys, we'd never have figured out that Nicole is the addict." True, I think. Lorissa owes that boy a lot.

"No prob," Rhys says, embarrassed by the kind words.

Ashley opens the door to the group home before Mackenzie has a chance to knock. "It's me, Aunt Ashley, instead of Mom. Is it okay for Meaghan to come to dinner with us?"

"It's okay." As Mackenzie signs her aunt out in the guest book, Ashley says, "Darcy made me mad today. She kept singing that song 'It's a Small World' over and over and wouldn't stop. Your grandma used to sing that song to Lorissa and me on our long car rides." She wipes her nose, then sneezes.

Mackenzie gives her a warm hug. "Sounds like a cold. You sure you want to go out?"

"Of course, I am."

At Ashley's favorite restaurant, she tells the waitress where she wants to sit, pointing to a table by the window facing the parking lot. We all pretend to read our menus, although I assume Ashley goes by the photos. No matter. Mackenzie and Ashley, apparently regulars, always get the same meal. Mackenzie: soup of the day and a tossed green salad with water. Ashley: waffles with whipped cream and a diet Coke.

"They hardly ever have waffles or pop at the group home," Mackenzie explains to me, then turns to Ashley. "Sorry I haven't seen you much lately, Ash. Did you hear Connor got into trouble?"

"What happened?" Ashley bends her straw to sip her soda.

"Well, he's accused of doing something bad that he didn't do." Ashley sneezes, reaches into her pocket, and pulls out a balled-up tissue. "Wait a sec," Mackenzie says. "Let me find you a fresh one." She fishes around in her purse, then dumps its contents onto the table. "I know I have one in here."

"Gee, Mackenzie, you have a lot of crap," Ashley says.

Mackenzie laughs. Ashley is not one to beat around the bush. "I know!"

One by one, Mackenzie sorts through her cell phone, her wallet, the glasses she wears to see the blackboard at school, the photos they printed at Bartell, her small hairbrush, lipstick, two pens, and, at last, a small package of tissue. "Here!" She hands a tissue to Ashley. "You think I should clean out my purse?"

The waitress startles us by asking for our order. I ask for a BLT and an ice tea, and while Mackenzie and Ashley order, I unclip the envelope of photos and begin to examine them one by one. There they are, Nicole and Scott, an intimate, loving couple, gazing into each other's eyes like teenagers, laughing. Are they dancing in the park? Ugh! I throw the photos back on the table and flip them over so I can't see them.

Yet a twinge of curiosity jabs me, and before I can stop myself, I go through the photos one by one. There they are,

Nicole and Scott—so lovey-dovey—cheeks close together, smiles, white teeth flashing. Another one with their arms wrapped around each other, Scott's dimple a tiny crater in his chin, eyes shining green as the trees. And *her*, waves of thick red hair rolling over her shoulders, blue high heels. Heels in that Sunrise Beach muddy park! Ridiculous!

Ahh! There's the one with them fighting. First, Scott's mouth is wide, as though yelling, his arms waving. Then, he's pivoted toward Nicole, and even in this phone photo I see her eyes flared, her mouth taking up half her face, snarling. Next, there's the one of Scott hiking up the hill, alone. Rhys is a great paparazzi! He and Connor followed Nicole up the hill, and... yep. There's the series: climbing in the back door of Scott's truck, a hunched back, Nicole then climbing into the front seat, and driving off. The last photo in the series even catches the truck's exhaust fumes.

And then one more photo. A knot suddenly curls in my gut, twisting and burning. "No!" I shout. The waitress stops in her tracks, nearly spilling our three dinner plates. "No!" I scream. A skinny man with glassy eyes at the table next to us stares at me. I'm suddenly self-conscious. "Sorry," I mutter. I stare at the photo of the slick man with shiny shoes standing by himself at the park.

"Brandon!" I poke my finger into the photo. "This is Brandon. My husband!" I lift my face to see Mackenzie and Ashley, eyes round, waiting for an explanation for my outburst. "The monster! This is him talking to Nicole."

Ashley lifts her necklace off her chest and nervously circles her fingers around the beads, as though afraid of me. She looks at the photo too. "I saw that guy before."

What? No, she must be mistaken. She takes a big bite of her waffle, which smells so sweet, so delicious. "Are you sure, Ashley?" Mackenzie asks. "Where?"

Ashley turns her lips out, almost pouting. "Well, I guess I'm not sure. I just thought maybe."

Now I'm confused. When I flew back here from Chile, I was determined to help Lorissa, determined not to give in to my fear of Brandon, determined to be free. As soon as she told me Scott was shot, I was sure Brandon was behind it. My gut screamed it. *Brandon.* Now my courage is washing away as I see his face in this photo. My courage is slipping. I had this secret hope that he'd give up, that he'd leave the state, that he was out of my life. Hope is not enough.

"I guess I made a mistake," continues Ashley. "I thought I saw him at that place with Connor and Rhys. But— oops!" Ashley covers her mouth with her hand. "Oops. That was a secret."

Mackenzie leans her face inches from Ashley. She speaks slowly. "Auntie Ash. I know you're good at keeping secrets, but you've got to tell us this. Connor is in big trouble and you could help him."

Ashley's eyes focus on me, as though wondering if I am trustworthy. Thankfully, I pass the test. "Well, okay." She then tells us that one day, when Connor came to take her out to lunch, Rhys was with him. He asked if she wanted to go on an adventure, and they all drove to Tacoma. Connor went into "that funny store with bars on the window, and that mean guy" she points at the photo "yelled at Connor and that guy had a gun, and I don't think it was a toy gun, I really don't, and Rhys and me were watching from the car and then Connor ran out of there super-fast and he seemed kind of scared and then we went to Denny's and I had a butterscotch sundae, my favorite kind. Vanilla ice cream with butterscotch sauce. But no cherry. I don't like cherries."

"And Ash, it was this guy?"

"Yes, it was." We all sit in silence for several minutes. Mackenzie asks, "Meaghan, do you think your husband might have something to do with shooting Scott?"

"I do. I just don't know how or why." I bite into my BLT. The bacon tastes like pure decadence. Ashley dumps syrup on her waffles, pouring and pouring until the waffles are drowning in their own lake of maple. "Aunt Ash—that's probably enough. Here, let me help you." Mackenzie picks up her fork and knife and cuts the waffles into bites.

"I wonder," I say, my eyes gazing at the couple at a table across the restaurant, he with a graying beard that hasn't been trimmed in years, she in a flowered red blouse, her arms jiggling as she picks up the menu. "Brandon was at Sunrise Beach Park with Nicole? I mean, that's a pretty out-of-the-way park, right, Mackenzie?" I'd only been there that one time with Scott.

"Oh, yeah. I've lived in Yachts Village since I was one years old, and I've hardly ever been there. Kopachuck Park is so much closer to us."

"How's this for a theory?" I think out loud. "Maybe Brandon and Nicole joined forces—him jealous of Scott, her jealous of me? Maybe Scott was trying to break it off with Nicole and..." Ashley sips her diet Coke until she's down to ice cubes, slurping for a few extra seconds. "And? Nah. What a crazy thought."

"Rhys said he heard your name when they were fighting," Mackenzie says. "Remember? And they were arguing really loud." Connor had said the same thing. Scott was two-timing me, but wanted to leave Nicole for me. They both said that. He picked me over her? I hate thinking about this, wondering about Scott. I hate him. I'm so angry I want to smack him, but I can't because he's lying in a coma in the hospital in Seattle. I can't even be mad at him, but now I'm even more furious, because he might die on me. I have no idea where to go with all these emotions.

"So, Ashley, you and Rhys and Connor saw this guy at the 'funny store with bars'?"

"Yep." She takes a big bite of waffle.

"Hey," says Mackenzie. "Did you see *Dancing with the Stars* last week? Can you believe who was kicked off?"

"I know," says Ashley. "And that shiny purple dress! That was so pretty."

"Right! The way it swirled around and around. I felt dizzy just watching!"

While they talk about *Dancing with the Stars*, my mind spins. I'm missing something. There's a puzzle piece that doesn't fit.

After we drop Ashley back at the group home, Mackenzie calls Lorissa while I'm driving. She tells her everything Ashley told us, about a place with bars that Rhys and Connor secretly went, where a man had a gun; that I identified Brandon as being that guy from Rhys's photos; that Ashley thinks maybe Brandon was the same guy that she saw at the "funny shop with bars." Mackenzie listens for a few minutes. "Okay, Mom. Yeah, I'll finish it tonight. Love you!"

She hands me the phone. "Mom wants to talk with you. I'll put the phone on speaker."

"No, Mac, I need to speak to Meaghan alone." Mackenzie doesn't like the idea of her mom and me having secrets from her. I pull over at a weigh station and hear panic in Lorissa's voice.

"Meaghan, I just got a call from Jasmine. They started to move Connor from the jail to Grayson Center and..." She's breathing loud and fast. "And he ran! Connor escaped!"

39

Meaghan Farren

I'm about to say "What?" but I eye Mackenzie. Clearly, Lorissa doesn't want Mackenzie to know about the escape or she would have told her. Mackenzie has enough worries for a fifteen-year-old. "Here's the thing," Lorissa says. "I'm at the airport. Graham's flight got stuck on the tarmac in San Francisco, so he'll be even later."

"How can I help?" I try to speak as if I'm bored, not giving away the crisis to Mackenzie, who's staring at me.

"I've racked my brain, and I think I know where Connor went. You know that tiny little island that you see when you cross the Wilkes Island bridge? It's called Jacob's Island, and there's an old footbridge between it and Wilkes Island. Only four houses on the whole island—it couldn't be more than a quarter mile long, but once there was a camp, so there are some deserted old cabins. We used to visit friends there when Connor was little, and he always called it his favorite secret place." I scribble on a scrap of paper like I'm writing down a grocery list or something.

Lorissa groans. "Oh, Meaghan, do you know how much trouble he'll be in if he doesn't turn himself in? He's an escaped fugitive! Jasmine's afraid the judge will crucify him."

I nod and say "mmm-hmmm" as I add to the faux shopping list, trying to avoid Mackenzie's gaze.

"Please, Meaghan, could you help me? I bet he might be hiding out in one of those empty cabins. Please, just do this one more thing and find Connor? I'll drive home from the airport, and Graham can take the shuttle when his plane lands, but still, it will take me over an hour. Would you mind, Meaghan?"

Poor Lorissa. She's losing it. "No problem," I say as nonchalantly as possible, my eyes on Mackenzie as I curve my lips in a smile I don't feel. "I'll just drop Mackenzie off at your house, then run your errand. No worries."

"Thank you! Mackenzie has a project due tomorrow, by the way."

"What is it?" Mackenzie wants to know when I end the call.

"Oh, your mom just wants me to run a quick errand for her. Do you have much homework? Your mom mentioned something about a project due."

"Oh, yeah." She grits her teeth. "I kind of forgot. A twenty-page paper on women in business."

"That could be fascinating. Who are you studying? Coco Chanel—someone like that?"

"Well, she provides good historical context but. . ." With that, Mackenzie is distracted, talking about Sheryl Sandberg and Indra Nooyi and Irene Rosenfeld, and by the time we arrive at her house, she has no curiosity about Lorissa's errand.

"Since your dad's plane has been delayed, I'm not exactly sure when your parents will be home," I tell her.

After I drop her off, I look for road signs that I've never paid attention to. I'd noticed tiny Jacob's Island in my peripheral vision when I crossed the Wilkes Island bridge in the past; just a thousand feet offshore to the east, it has a lighthouse whose top had caved in and now stood as just a funny-looking cylinder. I finally find a sign that points to a dirt parking lot where Jacob's Island residents leave their cars.

But there are no cars here tonight. It's pitch black, clouds covering the moon, and I can barely see. I search the glove compartment for a flashlight and follow its beam. Eventually, I find an overgrown trail heading down to the dock where an old skiff is tied and, farther along, a twenty-foot-long bridge that swings in the slight breeze.

I aim my flashlight so it skims the whole footbridge, which appears to be constructed of frail boards strung together with rope railings on both sides, leading all the way to the tiny island. The bridge might be called many things, but steady and sturdy aren't two of them. If it weren't for Lorissa's son, if it weren't for how much I wanted to make amends, I would never step foot on this poor excuse for a bridge.

With one of the rope railings in one hand, my flashlight in the other, I take my first step. There's a creak that sounds like the wood will break under my feet. The wind whistles through the forests on both ends of the bridge. My ears are on high alert, and I can't tell the difference between hallucinations and reality. Is that a pack of coyotes at the other side of the bridge? A shark below me in the water? *Ha*. No sharks anywhere near here. My mind is playing tricks on me. But I'm not imagining the yowling of some feral animal.

Goose pimples rise on my skin as I manage another step, then a third. That groaning of the wood beneath my feet jars me, and I grab the other rope railing, nearly dropping my flashlight. I hear another animal call, but I can't tell if it's in front of me or behind me. Then a scratching sound, like the rope is unraveling. Another step—I am halfway there. The bay smells salty, filled with fish. One jumps and I hear the splash. I wish the clouds weren't covering most of the moon. Without the flashlight, I'd be blind.

"Connor," I call out in a loud whisper, wondering if I am on private property. I imagine that in daylight I'd see several *No Trespassing* signs. "Connor!" The only response is the wind tossing leaves. I am both sweaty and freezing at the same time. "Connor," I try again, my voice hoarse.

I am close to shore when I hear a rip. In half a second, the right side of the railing plunges into the water, the flashlight flies from my hand, and just in time I grip the left side of the rope railing with both hands. I dangle above the water. There are no killer fish, I know, but I'm frightened just the same. I claw my way, clinging with both hands on the remaining rope until finally my feet find solid ground. *I made it!* I catch my breath— relieved.

Pulling my phone from my pocket, I cast the tiny beam of the flashlight app from left to right, surveying the darkness around me—and there are Connor's eyes, inches away. He's just waiting for me to spot him.

"Connor."

"Jeez, Meaghan, you made enough noise." His sweatshirt hood covers his head, his hands planted inside the single pocket in front, his legs spread slightly apart, Clint Eastwood style.

"I did?" I laugh shakily. "Did you hear the rope on the bridge tear?"

"Oh, yeah. The water is only ten inches deep, though. You wouldn't have drowned."

It all feels so casual, as if we are camping together and next, we'll start a bonfire on the beach. "Your mom asked me to come and get you. She's been at the airport waiting for your dad, but his flight has been delayed over and over, so now she's just heading home and letting him catch a shuttle." I pause. "She's worried about you, Connor."

Waiting for him to say something, I look around. "Is there someplace we can sit down? My legs are kind of wobbly from that bridge." I'm about to say how scary it is, but it's nothing compared to what he's going through. He leads me to some old steps that go down to the beach.

"This was once a camp?" I ask, trying to get him to talk.

"Yeah, Mom and Dad used to bring Mackenzie and me over here when their old friends, the Banks, lived up there." Lights glow from an old-fashioned bungalow with a large storybook porch—rocking chairs, hanging plants, chimes lilting lightly in the evening air. My hands feel cold and damp, but there's magic to being in nature, hearing the ripple of salt water, smelling the forest around us. I am reminded of riding horses in Chile, when I had virtually no sign of humanity around me—just the wide-open mountain desert, that same feeling of being removed from humanity, a sense of the Divine in a place that is safe. I can see why Connor would run here, and why Lorissa would guess his hiding place. It's so serene, so peaceful—so far and yet so close.

"When I was around six years old," Connor finally opens up, "I was fascinated by Indian history: how natives migrated during summers to collect berries on Jacob's Island, and then they'd come back to bury their dead, not underground, but up there." He indicates the limbs of the trees above us. "They'd hang the canoes with the bodies and all their possessions in the trees, so the Great Spirit would come for them. I always thought that was cool." I nod in agreement but keep silent so he'll go on talking.

"Some old cabins around the other side were once part of a boy's summer camp. That's where I planned to stay, but everything's boarded up pretty tight." I sit in the dark, listening to the soft murmur of the Sound lapping against the shore, hearing Connor's melodic voice. I feel a thousand miles from civilization. Finally, he asks, "How did you find me?"

"Your mom said you always called Jacob's Island your secret place. You used to pretend that you were a storybook adventurer."

Connor nods as he stares through the thick fir trees to the water. "She sent you here?"

"She's so worried, Connor." A gust tickles my nose.

"They were going to take me to Grayson Center." His voice rises urgently. "I didn't shoot Scott! I didn't!"

"I believe you, Connor." I inhale the pine needles carpeting the ground. "And so does your mom. We all believe you. But running away makes you an escaped fugitive. It's only going to get worse, the longer you stay away."

"I'm not going back." Connor stares down at his sneakered feet. "How come Nicole is blaming this on me?"

"Maybe because she did it? Or is protecting someone? We're trying to figure it out. Your mom and sister and Rhys and me—we found Rhys's lost phone, and it has pictures of Nicole and Scott." I take a deep breath. How can I put this? "But Connor, you've got to come back. How did you get here, anyway? Did you walk or hitch a ride with someone?"

"Yeah, I caught a ride partway, then walked the rest."

"Listen, Connor. I have faith in Jasmine. She seems like a great lawyer, and she's going all out for you. But Connor, you can't stay out here, because the judge won't show you any mercy." I pause, hoping he'll respond.

"Come on," I say at last. "We'll get you out of Grayson Center as fast as we possibly can. I promise. The longer you're away, the worse it will be for you."

"No, Meaghan! No!"

I look across the water into the blackness and sigh.

After an hour of arguing like this, with me trying to be persuasive even though I'm seething with impatience, Connor reluctantly says he'll return.

Just then we hear soft paddling not far from us in the dark. A small beam of light from somewhere seems to be coming toward us.

"Connor! Meaghan!" I recognize Lorissa's voice, and my eyes have adjusted enough to the darkness so that I can see she's in a double kayak.

"We're over here," I whisper. My voice carries eerily across the quiet water. Lorissa paddles to us, lands and gets out, then gives Connor a hug like she's never going to let go.

"Mom! You're strangling me!"

Lorissa steps back. "Oh, Connor!" I can tell by her voice that she's been crying.

"I told Connor we know he's innocent," I say, "and we're working on proving it. And now he's willing to go back."

"Oh, thank God." She is about to say more but stops herself.

I look up at him. He hangs his head but nods in agreement. "Okay."

"I can take you both over one at a time," she says, and turns to Connor, "then drive you back to the Yachts Village police station. They'll probably take you to Grayson Center in the morning. I'll call Jasmine, but my guess is, you'll have a hearing."

I say nothing, but honestly, I think Connor's in deep trouble after running away from jail. I hope he can get out on bail, but he may have blown his chances. "Connor, how on earth did you run away?" Lorissa asks.

"Oh. . ." The moonlight casts a ray on his face, and I see his white teeth. He's a little gleeful, proud maybe, of his grand escape. "Thorp and I got to talking—he likes a lot of the same stuff I do, biking and hiking and fishing and all—so when he took me to the car to drive to Grayson Center, I asked if I could sit in the front.

"'Hell, no,' he said, like I knew he would. When I got in the backseat, I said, 'Well, you don't have to put those cuffs on me, do you? They hurt like hell.' So, he didn't, and then he forgot some paperwork and when he went back into the station, I took off. I ran through backyards, down side streets, and when I reached the coffee shop, I saw a guy from school and he dropped me off at the the bridge and I walked from there."

Connor's voice fades as they paddle into the darkness. "Yeah. I feel bad about screwing Thorp. I'll apologize to him."

Hurting Thorp's feelings is the least of Connor's problems. What he needs to worry about is the judge, who I'm sure won't take too kindly to this sort of move. Connor will find out soon enough for himself.

Back on Wilkes Island, we tie the kayak onto Lorissa's car, then she and Connor head for the Yachts Village police station and I drive back to her house. It's beginning to seem like my own home, but I wonder if I've overstayed my welcome.

Mackenzie's still studying at the dining table. How much should I say about tonight's escapade with Connor? How much should I leave to Lorissa? I decide it's up to Lorissa and Graham to explain Connor's running away, and it's not too difficult to remain silent, because Mackenzie barely lifts her head from her school books to say goodnight.

"Goodnight, Mackenzie," I reply. "I imagine both your mom and dad will be home soon."

"Okay, Aunt Meaghan."

I love the sound of that. *Aunt Meaghan.* There's something about those words that gives me a feeling of completion, of wholeness. I'm not ever going to have kids, but that's okay. Being Aunt Meaghan to Mackenzie and Connor— that sounds good. I reach over and hug her, maybe a little too tightly, but she doesn't complain, and I hustle down the stairs to bed.

The next morning, I wake up around six. No one else is up. After eating half a plain bagel, then lacing my running shoes, I set some eighties music on my phone, wrap it on my sleeve, stick in my earbuds, and sprint down the driveway.

I pick up speed and tear around the corner, where the road makes its ninety-degree turn around the woods. I dash past a two-story white house with red shutters and three carved pumpkins withering on the steps; another house with cedar siding has window boxes sprouting Halloween witches on brooms instead of geraniums. A lone deer stands in an empty lot covered with dried blackberries turned brown on the vine. My

mind churns through all I've learned about Brandon, Scott,
Nicole, the drug Roxicodone. Surely there's enough evidence to,
if not to free Connor, at least investigate more deeply.

As I run by Nicole's, I'm surprised to see Joel Whyrll
pounding a blue-and-white For Sale sign in their front lawn.
Nicole, whose name I can't stand to say out loud, is moving?
What do you know? I wonder where they're going, and why. In
their side yard, little Torrie's in a yellow jacket, pumping her legs
on the swings. Nicole and Joel used to be Lorissa and Graham's
best friends? Why on earth? I'm tempted to stop and say, "Joel,
you seem like a good guy. So why did you marry such a
conniving woman?" Instead, I pick up my pace.

What about Brandon? As long as he's around, I'm not
safe. I run harder through the neighborhood, hear his creepy
voice in my head; hear him banging on Scott's door, threatening
me; feel that vicious kick to my stomach, not knowing then what
I learned later, what that kick meant: No children. Ever.

I run harder and faster, my tears bubbling in my eyes,
and I push myself even more. I'm not going to give in to him.
I'm scared, I'm frightened, but if he ever shows his face, I'll fight
him with all I've got. My teeth are clenched and I'm so angry, I
do an extra loop around the neighborhood block.

A half block from the Orondos', I begin my cool-down
walk, remembering the peace I'd felt in Chile. Not just in
Cochiquaz, that odd little spiritual haven, but in all of La Serena.
I want to go back to Chile to sort out my feelings about Scott
and well, my whole life. I don't know whether I want to see him.

One minute he's the love of my life, the next he's a cheater and a louse. Maybe even a drug dealer. I'm so mad, I can't imagine what I'll say while he's lying there helplessly in a coma. Wake up so I can give you a piece of my mind? Somehow, I suspect the nurses wouldn't go for that.

I return to the Orondos' with sweat trickling from my face, my arms, down my back. "Good run?" asks Graham as I refill my water bottle. He pours milk into his coffee, cereal into his bowl, and sits at the kitchen table with his newspaper.

"Hey, Graham. Welcome back." I drink my water slowly. "Did you end up taking the shuttle last night? Lorissa sure was missing you."

"And I was missing her." He puts down the paper. "Meaghan, it's been so hard being away while all this is happening with Connor. In jail, for God's sake."

I rip off a paper towel to wipe my face, feel the ache in my legs. I pushed myself too hard.

"So, Graham, why weren't you here?" It's been over twenty years since we dated, but I still feel comfortable speaking my mind with him. "Your wife needed you. Your children needed you."

40

Meaghan Farren

"Here's the thing," Graham says. "I keep my job to pay the mortgage, so Lorissa can be here when the kids need her, and honestly, with all the trouble that Connor's gotten into over the years, it's been important for her to be available. But," he shakes his head, "it's hard to find a good-paying job that doesn't mean a lot of travel. I mean, we've got college tuition coming up."

Graham is such a handsome man, the dark eyes, the ruffled hair, serious yet playful. "Thank God for Skype, that's all I can say. And for friends like you." It's nice to be acknowledged, but that doesn't really answer my question. "I've just put in for PTO—paid time off—for a few weeks, although I'll still work a little from home. I'm not going to let my son rot in jail, and I'm not going to let my family be pulled apart by some druggie neighbor friend."

"Good to hear." And it is. There are still good men left in the world. Too bad I never find them—or, if I do, I let them go. Oh well, Graham just didn't "do it" for me back in college any more than he does now, but he feels like a big brother, and that's something I never had. He's a good man, this Graham Orondo.

"By the way, Jim Thorp just called from the police station," he says. "Wants Lorissa and me there at 8:30 sharp."

I check my phone. It's 7:30 a.m. "Is she still asleep?"

"Yeah. I told her I'd wake her at the last possible moment. Mackenzie kissed her good-bye as she headed off to school this morning." He takes a sip of coffee. "Jasmine apparently told Thorp all about the photos of Nicole and Scott, and Lorissa is hoping they'll release Connor right away, what with all that new evidence showing Nicole having an affair with Scott, something she never told the cops." Graham sounds wistful as he lowers his voice. "Honestly, Meaghan, I know it won't be that easy. Not after Connor's escape last night. I don't know what that boy was thinking."

I pour myself some coffee. "He was scared. That's all. Just a scared kid who saw an opportunity. Or so he thought." I see the fear and sadness Graham's been trying to hide, so worried about his son and his wife and Mackenzie. I can't imagine what he's going through.

I wonder what exactly Jasmine told Thorp about Scott. If Scott dies, not only will I lose my confusing love-of-my-life, as I had thought he was, but Connor could end up on death row. We have to prove Connor didn't shoot Scott.

A half hour later, Lorissa and Graham are dressed in their professional clothes: Lorissa in gray wool slacks, a silk scarf, small gray heels; Graham, his hair combed though still unruly, in a navy jacket, a striped tie with an OWU tie pin, oxfords—so unlike the jeans and tee shirt he wears to work at Amazon. Their mission is to free their son, and they'll do whatever it takes to convince Officer Thorp that Connor is innocent. Whatever Thorp thinks will be influential with the judge.

With coffee mug in hand, I watch their car head down the driveway, wishing them the best. I toss the other half of my bagel into the toaster, then when it pops, spread it with cream cheese. Settled on the Adirondack chair on the deck, I cross my legs under me, fold my hands, and begin my meditation. I've hardly meditated since I returned from Chile, but here in the silence of the island, with the house to myself, I find I am deeply entwined in my spiritual self.

Twenty minutes later, Chumley dashes through the bushes, jumps up and circles my lap, then purrs, just like old times in Northampton—which reminds me that although I'm mostly relaxed, the specter of my abusive husband still haunts me.

Rhys's photos of Brandon at the beach where Nicole met Scott don't prove anything, but my gut says my husband is involved. Why did Nicole meet him at the park? Today I'll call and start the process for a restraining order—something I should have done the first day I got back from Chile. I'm glad I carry bear spray, just in case. Now I'm getting frazzled just picturing his face. So much for the calm of Puget Sound, the eagle overhead, the lone boat puttering by in the water.

Guru barks across the street, digging. Again. Always digging. What did he find this time? A toy army man? He's got a pile of toys and tools and junk he's dug up from neighbors' lawns every time the battery in his electric fence dies, which is often, judging by the size of the pile. I can't imagine a more beautiful day, yet now that I'm alone, I lurch at the sound of the single car that drives by the house.

I go inside, strip off my clothes, and step into the steaming shower. I'm exhausted from worrying about Brandon, from trying to understand Scott, who he is and what he means to me, the mystery of who shot him. Let's see—he was a gigolo and went to jail, then he had an affair with a married woman at the same time he was dating me, but then broke up with her because of me? How do I deal with that?

Fifteen minutes later, I turn off the shower and stand naked, drip drying as the steam begins to dissipate. I picture the shriveled shaman in Chile, his gnarly fingers, saying I was depleted. Depleted before, depleted again. I keep returning to the fact that I don't know what or who I can trust when I can't trust my own heart.

I pat myself dry with Lorissa's thick towel. I hear the front door open, then Graham and Lorissa's voices speaking low, hushed. I can't distinguish their words, but judging by their tone, it doesn't sound good. I quickly throw on a robe, wrap the towel around my head, and patter upstairs to the kitchen.

Before I can even ask, Lorissa says to me, "Thorp is not going to let Connor out. The photos weren't enough." Her eyes are streaked with red—so much so, it's hard to see any white. Graham cloaks his arms around his wife. "I was so sure that the photos of Nicole and Scott and of her hiding pills in his truck would be enough to get him released."

Graham lifts a lock from Lorissa's forehead and smooths it to the side, a comforting gesture when they are both aching. "They're going to broaden the investigation, though—consider that Connor might not be a slam dunk," Graham says. Lorissa whimpers into Graham's shoulder, and I take my cue, heading downstairs to get dressed.

When I return in jeans and cotton blouse, Graham has disappeared into his office and Lorissa is emptying the dishwasher. "One thing about being a housewife," she says. "The work is twenty-four seven, so you never have to worry about what to do."

"You've got a little humor back."

Color has returned to her cheeks. "Not much." With her fingers stringing the handles of the mugs, she places five in the cupboard above the coffeemaker. "I thought Thorp would be convinced."

I pull out the silverware basket and place the forks and spoons in the drawer. "What happened?"

"Oh, such bull." She puts two glasses up to the light, finds streaks in them, returns them to the dishwasher. She describes being crammed in the same tiny room they'd sat in before, around a table that barely fit—Connor, Graham, Jasmine, Thorp, and her, with a woman officer standing by the door. "I don't know if she thought we were going to bolt or what. She left periodically, then came back and whispered something in Thorp's ear. There was just one little window, no pictures on the wall, and the only smell was burned popcorn on the other side of the door. Popcorn at 9:00 a.m.!"

"What happened?" I ask again.

"After looking at all the photos, Thorp says something articulate like, 'mmm,' or maybe it was 'ahh.' You know he's royally pissed about Connor's escape. It looks bad on him."

"I bet." And I wonder again what the judge will think.

Thorp had agreed that the photos were of Scott and Nicole, definitely they were intimate and then fighting. Possibly, just possibly, she could have been hiding Roxies in the truck. "But," and now Lorissa twists her jaw to the side in ultimate frustration. "But, as for believing she's the addict? Or her motive for shooting Scott being jealous of you? He said he'd 'give it consideration.'"

"But what about Rhys? All he saw and heard? And what about the photo of Nicole with Brandon?"

Lorissa scratches her cheek. "I hate to admit it, but we should have brought Rhys in with us. It might have moved things along more quickly." She pours herself another cup of coffee. "Want one?"

"No, thanks."

"He didn't say anything about the photo of Brandon and Nicole. Honestly, Meaghan, who knows how Brandon ties in, or if he does. But Thorp's going to at least consider the possibility that someone other than Connor did it. Before, he was treating it like a closed case."

"That's great!"

"Not great. Great would be him getting released. Yesterday. Great would be us not being in this mess in the first place. Great would be him not escaping. . ."

"Lorissa, stop. You'll drive yourself crazy."

She places a stack of plates in the cupboard. "You're right. That's what I'm doing. I just wish. . ." We all wish the same thing, that Connor is released, but this is her son, her baby who has riled her as only a beloved child can do. I might not be a mom, but I know that much. "Thorp said it's up to the judge to deal with the consequences of running away—of escaping custody, to use his words. Connor is being shipped to Grayson Juvenile Center as we speak." Her eyes moisten. "Graham and I are going to head over there once he gets off his conference call."

I return to the guest bedroom and sort my dirty clothes for a long-overdue wash. Just as I'm about to push the wash cycle, I hear arguing upstairs. I've rarely heard Lorissa and Graham argue, but this is a big one. I try not to listen, but the screaming "your son," "your work," "multi-million" filters through. Everyone's nerves are stretched to the max. I push "heavy wash" and the machine starts rumbling. The scent of detergent fills the laundry room, and it dawns on me that I've added too much of this double strength variety of soap.

A few minutes later, Lorissa bangs on my door. "Meaghan, do you want to go with me to Grayson Center to see Connor?"

"Isn't Graham. . .?" I stop myself. That must have been what they were fighting over.

"Graham's got this major crisis, and he's supposed to be on paid time off, but his boss says. . .anyway, some multi-million- dollar deal that his job depends on with Tokyo. Or Shanghai. He has to work today, even if he's at home." She lets out an explosive sigh.

"It just pisses me off. It pisses him off too, don't get me wrong. But here we are."

Lorissa needs all the support I can give her. "Of course, I'll go with you."

41

Meaghan Farren

An hour later we're in the visitor's line at Grayson Center—I'm just behind Lorissa, who's added more makeup than I've ever seen: blush, eyeliner, uncharacteristic bright red lipstick. Behind us is a large woman with thick orange hair and way too much cheap gardenia perfume. She cries noiselessly, a mother who has no idea how to help the child she desperately loves. Lorissa, clutching the large manila envelope of photos, closes her eyes as if she wishes she could make it all go away. I close my nose to see if I can make that horrid smell of cleanser disappear.

We endure the requisite frisking, the gloved hands up and down our arms and legs, which gives me the heebie-jeebies. The last person who touched me so intrusively was Brandon, and it always led to slaps or kicks or punches. Once cleared, we rush to the visitor's room door and see Connor, dressed in an orange jumpsuit, shuffling to us from a back door. Lorissa runs to him with arms outstretched, but she's stopped short by a guard: "No, ma'am."

I remain at the entrance to the room, once again an awkward bystander, but Lorissa signals for me to join her and Connor on metal chairs at a small table topped with cracked Formica, like from a fifty's kitchen. Connor's cheeks are concave, his eyes circled with gray; his skin is slightly green. He's been here just a few hours and he already looks ill. I try not to stare. Lorissa opens her mouth, as if she is going to ask "How are you?" but it's clear Grayson Center is a living hell, and Connor is doing anything but fine. "What are the goddamn detectives doing?" he barks. "How come they haven't arrested her?"

Lorissa ignores his attitude. "We're making progress, Connor."

"Hey, Connor, we're still trying to figure out who shot Scott." Up until now, he hasn't acknowledged me, but I might as well cut to the chase. "Here's the thing. We're wondering if Nicole did it and if she got the gun from my ex-, my … um, husband." I'm still married to that vile thug.

Connor's face is blank; he doesn't know what I'm talking about. Better start from the beginning. "Ashley told us something about you going to a place with iron bars? And you told me you went to a pawnshop to sell your mom's bracelet 'but something happened.' I'm wondering, is what happened that you ran into a guy with a gun? Ashley said she saw a guy with a gun through your car window."

I see Connor is catching on, so I speak slower. "We have a photo of my husband, Brandon, with Nicole at the park, and Ashley thought maybe that guy at the "store with bars" was Brandon."

Connor remains impassive, not revealing any emotion. He hesitates, as if knowing he's setting off a bomb with his mom.

"Well, yeah. Rhys and I, we checked out a pawnshop."
Lorissa's mouth tightens, and I see she is trying to restrain
herself, clutching hands together so tightly they're turning white.
She'd told me that she's practicing counting her breaths when
she gets upset. Breathing slowly. It looks like that's what she's
doing now: *let it go.*

"Damn it, Connor!" she screams. "You took Ashley to a
pawnshop where a man held a gun to you?"

Whoops.

"You put Ashley in danger? How could you?" Now
she's shaking her finger so hard I expect it to snap off and fly
across the room. "How could you do that to Ashley? Damn it,
Connor. I thought you were getting so much better this
summer."

Connor crosses his arms and looks down at his lap for
several seconds before he speaks. "Mom, I'm sorry," he says,
and he sounds earnest to me. "It's not like Ash was ever going to
be hurt. She stayed in the car with. . ." He wasn't about to say
"Rhys," knowing how his mom feels about him. He pauses, then
starts over. "Give me some credit. I *am* getting better. I ride my
bike everywhere. I even like my new counselor. Sure, he's kind
of a douche bag—Birkenstocks, all that mumbo jumbo—but
still, he's alright." His eyes implore her. "Mom, those new meds
are working. If Jacob Lawson wasn't such an asshole, calling me
a low-life loser and all that, I wouldn't have gotten in that fight
and gotten kicked out of school the day Scott got shot."

Lorissa doesn't respond. Her eyes are hooded—sad, angry, helpless. Love is a jumbled net, whether it's your son, your husband, or your bewildering lover.

"Connor," I say, "what happened at the pawnshop? We have only Ashley's version, and it was a bit muddled."

Connor wipes his hand across his mouth. Compared to being charged with attempted murder, going to a pawnshop is no big deal. "So, yeah. I was going to sell your charm bracelet, Mom. The one I took from your jewelry box, that matches Meaghan's." He looks sheepish. "I mean, I'd never been in a pawnshop before, and Rhys said. . ." He stops. He doesn't want to say anything bad about Rhys.

Murmurs from conversations at nearby tables fill in Connor's pause, and he turns to watch a boy with his mom. We hear the sound of sobs; in a far corner, a father argues with his son.

Lorissa closes her eyes, taking this all in. It seems to dawn on her that she can't dwell on her son stealing her bracelet, not right now. "What happened?"

"Okay. I was going to take Ashley to lunch, then. . ." He pauses and appears to rephrase how he's going to put it. "Rhys and I decided to take the bracelet and pawn it in Tacoma, so I went in while Rhys and Ashley waited in the car." Connor tells of entering this pawnshop in Tacoma that he'd driven by a million times, with neon lights in the window flashing "J wel y, Guns, To ls."

"I was thinking, 'Thank goodness Ashley doesn't play *Wheel of Fortune* because she'd never keep a secret, and Mom would kill me if I take her to a pawnshop'," Connor says. Lorissa is reluctant to laugh at her son's joke, but her slight smile forms almost involuntarily. "I pulled your charm bracelet out of my pocket. The clerk, a big guy with a Mariners baseball hat, helped some guy at the end of the counter who was checking out a handgun, inspecting the barrel, that sort of thing. It was taking forever. I said, 'Hey, how much can I get for this?'

"That's when they both noticed me, and two seconds later this dude, the customer, goes ballistic, screaming, 'Hey! That's my wife's bracelet! Where the hell did you get that?' At first, I glanced over my shoulder, thinking he was talking to someone else, but I was the only one there. Then the guy shouted even louder, 'Hey!' He came after me, waving the gun. I'm sure it wasn't loaded, but I gotta admit, it scared me a little."

'You got the wrong guy, mister,' I said, and hauled back to the car, then we barreled out of there to Denny's 'cuz that's where Ashley wanted to have lunch."

And you didn't think it was relevant to tell anyone? Great, Connor,

I think. "So, what were Rhys and Ashley doing the whole time?"

"Well, Rhys was just on his phone—Facebook or Reddit or something. I dunno. But Ashley watched like a hawk. When I was inside, I saw her watching through the window—me and everyone else in the shop—like she was watching TV."

Lorissa presses her lips together. She's still furious that Connor put her sister in danger.

"So, that's why Ashley saw the guy in the pawnshop, but Rhys didn't?" I ask, trying to work out why Rhys didn't mention recognizing the guy in the photo at the park with Nicole.

"I guess."

Lorissa shows the photo Rhys had snapped of Brandon at the park. "Connor, is this the guy from the pawnshop?"

"Mmm." He sucks in his lips. "Yeah. Yeah. For sure it is. Where did you get that pic?"

"Rhys took it at the park sometime when you weren't around."

"Mmm," he says again. "Usually it's only scuba divers there, us, and you know—Nicole and Scott. No one else. I mean it's crazy deserted."

Lorissa grits her teeth so hard I'm afraid she'll grind them down to nubs. I wonder if Lorissa's bottom lip will bleed, she's biting it so hard. I'm picking up some parenting tips here: bite your lip often. Too bad I'll never be able to use them.

Connor says in the kindest voice, "Meaghan, is that your husband? The guy you ran away from?"

Since I'd told my whole story to Connor in the jail cell, he can guess how worried I am. How scared I am about Brandon being in a pawnshop buying a gun. "Yes." I say. "He was there to buy a gun?"

"Oh, for sure," Connor answers.

I take a deep breath and sigh. What can I do? Be vigilant. That's it.

Lorissa lifts her shoulder bag from the back of her chair but remains seated. Our time is almost up, but before we leave, Connor asks, "So how is Scott?"

"We don't know," Lorissa says. "Thorp said they're planning on doing surgery and extracting the bullet from his brain, but I don't know when. He's still in an induced coma."

"I'm going to Seattle to find out," I say. And I know I'll be looking over my shoulder every minute.

42

Meaghan Farren

When we get to her car, Lorissa calls Jasmine to convey what Connor said. I can't help but overhear my friend's side of the conversation.

"Yes, Brandon was buying a gun at the pawnshop." Pause. "So that might have been the gun that shot Scott?" Another pause. "I know it's a long shot. I get that." A longer silence. "You think the pawnshop might have a serial number for the gun?" And of course, the important question: "Is there anything new about Connor's release?"

I can read Lorissa's face: nothing new. We're both drained. "Lorissa, I have to go to Seattle to see Scott. I've been putting it off. I'm so confused, but Nicole or not, I need to see him. Would you drop me off at the bus station?"

"Bus station? I'll drive you. Graham's working from home all day, and I'll go nuts doing nothing." Instead of starting the car, though, she rests her hands on the dashboard. "Meaghan, I have a confession." She turns to me with the crimson eyes and puffy cheeks of someone who hasn't had a decent night's sleep in a month. "I don't care who shot Scott. All I care is that my son didn't and that he gets out of jail. How's that for brutal honesty? That's how I feel. I just need to have my son home." She is grief personified.

"Lorissa, I get it. Really, I do. I can't put myself in your shoes. I don't have a son. Brandon took care of that for me. But

I do care who shot Scott. Very much. No matter if Scott was cheating on me with Nicole, no matter that he went to jail for being a gigolo, no matter any of that; he was kind to me when I needed someone to be kind. And if Brandon did it, you can be sure I want to get him behind bars as fast as I possibly can. There you have it. That's my brutal truth."

She smiles, and I do too, but they're mournful smiles, because that's the best we can do right now. Sitting in the front seat of Lorissa's car, our seat belts buckled, we both laugh, just a little.

"Okay, then," Lorissa says. "Off to Seattle."

The traffic up I-5 fluctuates from 70 mph to 20 and back to 70, from speeding to crawling, one accident after another. Then, construction. No surprise. How I hate the drive and appreciate Lorissa being behind the wheel.

Horns honk, brakes squeal, fumes cloud our lane. Lorissa switches lanes, then a truck comes up behind her and lays on the horn. She turns her head, sees an opening in the carpool lane, and moves over. "You wouldn't believe raising kids these days, Meaghan," she says. "You go to a PTA meeting and you see these Stepford wives all dolled up in the latest clothes, the perfect hair, the perfect children. But then you get on, say, an auction committee and meet these people: former architects, scientists, lawyers—powerful women who put their career in the backseat. Brilliant women. PhDs in charge of the elementary school field day. They all say something along the lines of 'It's only a twelve-year sabbatical from. . .going to Paris, Antarctica, winning the Pulitzer,' whatever." Lorissa catches her breath.

I don't know where to go with this. "Well, do you like it?"

"What, children? Of course. I love my children. I love them more than life itself. I love seeing them grow, evolve, become full human beings. Laugh, cry, giggle. But that's not the point."

"The point is," I paraphrase, "you can't win, being a professional mom. Is that what you're saying?"

"Oh, Meaghan. Honestly, I don't know what I'm saying." We reach the exit ramp to Seattle's hospital district with NPR droning on and on, neither of us listening. We stop at a red light where a homeless person limps between tarp-covered tents set up on the roadside. My mind switches to Scott, wondering how I'll react when I see him, unconscious, connected to IVs, a heart monitor, whatever else. I'm assuming he'll still be alive. I have to assume that. I won't let myself think anything else.

We reach the hospital and park, then walk through the doors that open automatically to a marble floor, Chihuly glass, a reception desk in what looks a five-star hotel lobby. This is where my insurance dollars are going?

"Hi," I ask the volunteer. "Could you direct us to Scott Crowley?"

Jasmine had given Lorissa his room number. "He's in room 638," she says.

"That's intensive care. No visitors allowed."

"We know no visitors are usually allowed," I say, like I'm speaking patiently to a child. "But we are his closest friends and he has no family."

She scrutinizes us. Really, I think, we look like terrorists? Give me a break. I imagine her asking, "Then why haven't we seen you here before?" but she doesn't. She points to an elevator. "It's that one, but I doubt if they'll let you see him."

I heave a deep breath, and even though this lobby décor— blues and greens in the paintings on the walls—is meant to relax visitors, I'm unnerved by those horrid hospital odors. We head toward the elevator. Lorissa stops, puts her hand on mine. "I'm going to just wait down here, okay?" Her eyes seemed so tired, almost drooping.

"Of course!" We hugged, then she walked back to comfortable leather chair.

"Good luck!"

Of course, Lorissa didn't want to see the comatose man her son was accused of shooting. I wasn't sure if I wanted to or not, either.

My eyes follow the lights above the elevator doors. One is coming down. Then it stops. I wait and wait. *Forget it*, I decide. I find the staircase down the hall, open the steel door, and run up the metal steps, my feet clanging and echoing like I'm wearing chains.

I arrive at the ICU. "I'm here to see Scott Crowley," I say to the woman at the desk.

"Are you family?"

I tell the same story I told the lobby volunteer.

"I'm sorry. He's not to be disturbed."

"But we're close. We're really close friends!" I dig for another argument: "I'm almost his sister. You've got to let me see him. Just for a minute!"

"No, ma'am. I'm sorry."

"I've got to see him! I came all the way from South America. I've got see him!"

"He's having surgery tomorrow. He needs his rest."

By now I'm furious. "Screw you," I say under my breath and spot a water fountain, where I linger until she turns her back. I run down the hall, looking for his room: 636, 637, there it is—638.

The machines, the sickly smells, Scott lying helpless, eyes closed, breathing through a tube in his mouth. I drop into the bedside chair, emotions welling through me. This is the man who, a month ago, I yearned for, the man I laughed with, who made me feel precious, who saved me from Brandon. This is the man I loved, who turns out to have cheated old women, stolen their money, and had an affair with a married woman.

But it seems he also broke off with her because of me. "Scott," I say. "Scott, it's me. Meaghan. You better wake up. You've been in a coma too long, and you have a bullet in your brain. Now, you and I have a lot of things to talk about." I've heard that people in comas can hear, and yet it feels stupid talking to him while he's unconscious.

The six-foot Nurse Ratchet appears in the doorway with hands on hips. "I told you. No visitors! I'll call security."

"I'm going," I say, rising slowly and taking Scott's hand. "Wake up, you. We need to have a conversation."

As I leave the room, I ask, "Has there been any change? What's the prognosis?"

"I certainly can't tell you. Confidentiality rules and all that. But I'll tell you this. We didn't expect him to make it through the first night, and every night he holds on, that's another good night."

What on earth does that mean? I must look really confused, because then she says, "We'll know more after tomorrow's surgery. They plan to remove the bullet tomorrow. Now you need to leave."

I step inside the elevator and the doors crush together, barely missing my nose.

Lorissa rises as soon as she sees me. She looks like she had a ten-minute nap here in the lobby. I'm glad she didn't see Scott. That's the last vision she needs, with all the stress she has going on. We leave in silence, through the front door, and once we're outside, the air feels amazingly refreshing. All the Dale Chihuly glass in the world can't make up for it being a hospital. "The nurse said he's going to have surgery tomorrow."

"Tomorrow?" We're both silent as we begin our drive south. Seeing Scott so helpless made me forget about those photos of him and Nicole, but back in the car, I'm furious again. I need to know what happened.

We reenter the I-5 chaos, bumper to bumper but not so many horns now. People just accept that the Seattle-Tacoma commute is hell. "Hey, Lorissa, this is kind of a crazy idea, but let's see if the guy at the pawnshop can identify Brandon. I mean, now that we've got his picture and we know he's involved somehow." Lorissa gives me that look: *Really?*

"Well," I stammer, "that photo with Nicole and Brandon means something. If we can find out what kind of gun he bought, that sure could help."

43

Nicole Whyrrl

Nicole hates this drive into the Olympic Mountains, especially on stormy days like this. She dreads limbs falling on her car, like the first time Joel had driven her up here to his family's old cabin. The road is notorious for wrecks. Tourists heading out to the mountains gawk at the ginormous trees whose boughs sway over the cars. Locals who need to pick up their kids from day care or get home to fix dinner, rev their cars, frustrated. Inevitably someone takes a corner too fast or passes in a perilous zone, and a car smashes into the woods as others pile up behind.

Today the road is particularly slippery, pine needles covering the asphalt like a thin sheet of black ice. Nicole swerves, taking S curve after S curve, past dozens of darkened houses squeezed between the highway and Hood Canal. Docks and floats, so much fun during the summer, now heave in the autumn waves.

Nicole's defroster is barely working, so she rolls down her window and smells the firs and the salt air. Her emotions roil. Damn it! How did he ever talk her into this? Nicole tries not to think about it. But of course, trying not to think about it only sharpens the images in her mind.

Her car creeps along the canal's shoreline, rain and wind blowing ever more fiercely. Though it's only two in the afternoon, it's so dark it looks like seven, with no lights in the houses she passes. The electricity must be out up and down the canal from the last big storm. She grips the steering wheel to keep the car from sliding on the slick road.

What on earth has she done? She'd made it through high school, even survived her idiot of a father. Still, she has never gotten rid of those memories, that shame. She remembers herself as a teenager, peeking behind the velvet curtain in *South Pacific*, the high school play, praying she wouldn't see her dad, relieved she didn't. She had surveyed the murmuring audience, excited for the production to begin. Then the auditorium door banged open and a gorilla of a man—huge chest, skinny legs, red veins in his cheeks— staggered in, shouting "Excuse me, excuse me" as he slithered his way across a middle aisle to a vacant seat. Of course; she recognized that voice.

Why did he have to be her dad? Why did he have to come to the play?

And then the moment she'd dreaded: her turn on stage, to say her bit part's one line addressing the female lead. "There's my girl," a voice from the audience had roared. "That's my Nicole." The lead had recited her lines, but no one could hear her over that bellowing voice: "Ain't she a pretty thing!" Nicole worked to keep from crying and tried to ignore him, to pretend it wasn't happening.

"That's my girl" had come the holler from the darkened audience. And after curtain call, everyone had spoken so politely to her, as though they knew how she felt. Some had whispered, glancing over their shoulders.

Freshman year, then sophomore year, she had felt nothing but shame. Nicole had begged her mom to switch schools. *My stupid mom*, thought Nicole. She'd worked her double shifts at the Dairy Queen and given Nicole what she could after paying for rent, utilities, food, and gas. Nicole had shopped for clothes at the St. Vincent de Paul in Aberdeen, trying to pick out donated clothes that fit, with shoulders that squared on hers.

Nicole had never gotten caught cheating on her tests in school, though she'd always studied hard so she hadn't needed to cheat too often. In college, she'd stolen clothes from other dorms on campus—few girls actually locked their doors—so she dressed well and acted smart. When Joel had fallen in love with her, she'd thought she'd hit the mark. She would live a life that looked normal; no one would ever call her white trash again. Of course, it was only later she learned that Joel had grown up dirt-poor, too, spending a good part of his life up in this shell of a cabin near Hood Canal. What a loser. Just what she'd been trying to avoid.

Joel had doted: devoted, innocent, naïve, never suspicious when she stepped out to bars, making up work conferences, visits to distant relatives who had never existed. And when he'd agreed to work half-time at Intel and stay home with Torrie, she'd had all the freedom she'd longed for.

And now she'd almost thrown it all away because of that bastard Scott Crowley. How had that happened? How had he gotten under her skin? She knew, really. He had secrets, too, and Scott and she were two of a kind, both pretending to be someone they weren't, drawn to each other like a magnet and screw.

She craved the danger Scott represented, the secrets about him she hadn't learned, and then he went and fell for that wimp Meaghan Perkins. What did he see in that woman?

Nicole's windshield wipers flap back and forth so fast she has to lean her face inches from the windshield. Even though she and Scott had a magnetism—she's sure he'd felt it as much as she had—she knows where it all went wrong. It was when that kid came into the drugstore begging, "Please. My gramma's so sick." The whining boy, Scott's defense of him, her hurtling the box cutter at Scott. That's when all that passion between her and Scott began to sour.

As she drives past the Hood Canal Winery, she momentarily considers stopping for a glass of chardonnay. No, with the winds still shrieking, the trees waving like flags, she wants to reach the cabin as soon as possible. She turns off the highway, then heads directly west toward Lake Cushman on a narrower road, fallen branches littering the roadside. After pulling her car over to drag a heavy limb covered with cones out of the middle of the road, she maneuvers up the dirt driveway to Joel's old family cabin, bouncing in and out of potholes, praying not to get stuck. It's a long drive to deliver a short message, but necessary to reach this off the grid cabin.

The sweet-smelling smoke of the wood fire hits her first, then she sees it swirling out of the stovepipe. The cabin looks like it came out of Laura Ingalls Wilder: a square log house with a covered porch tilting to the left, a dead plant in a half wine barrel converted to a large flower pot. The posts holding up the porch are thin trees with bark removed and knots remaining from sawed-off limbs. The cabin looks like one good blow would knock it down. Today's torrential rain and high winds might do the trick.

After parking, Nicole removes her shoes and switches to boots. Brandon stands by the cabin door with a shotgun in his hand as she sloshes through the mud up to the porch steps. "Put that damn thing away." She marches past him, opens the screen door, and checks out her husband's old family cabin. There's no electricity or heater or running water, so they used to bring in a tank of water from the city whenever they visited. Originally Joel's mom had had an outhouse, but Joel had upgraded to an environmental composting outdoor toilet a few months before she'd died. Nicole rubs her hands together in front of the woodstove. "Where's the coffee?"

Brandon sets a tarnished coffeepot on top of the woodstove to reheat. "What's the news?"

"Scott is alive, barely holding on by a thread."

"He's supposed to be dead. The asshole messed around with my wife. And Meaghan?"

"God only knows. Vanished. No one seems to know."

"Not even that friend of yours? What's her name? Lana?"

"Lorissa," Nicole says. "We're not talking."

He snickers, his scummy teeth a contrast to the slick image he had cast at the dark Pilchuck Tavern where they first created their stupid plan. "Hey, Nicole"—he nearly spits her name— "where's my part of the deal? I got you the gun, and you were supposed to get me Meaghan. Where is she?"

"I don't know. Okay? She could be anywhere. I still think Lorissa and Graham hid her somewhere. After all, they're her only friends. But whatever. Your time is up. You got me the gun. The deed is done. Now you've got to get out of here. What if Joel says, like he just might, 'Let's take a trip to the mountains'? He's going to know you've been here. The plan was you'd hide out just long enough to know the damage was done. Well, Scott's got a bullet in the brain, and now you've got to get out of here."

"Are you telling me what to do?"

"Don't threaten me." Nicole wonders why she'd never noticed his eyes are the green hue of a monster. "I wrote down everything that happened from the moment we met at the Pilchuck Tavern and put it in a safe deposit box. If anything happens to me, they'll find it."

Brandon's lips twitch. "Scott isn't dead and my wife isn't either, and that was our deal. I did my part. I got you the gun."

"Look, if Scott ever wakes up, which I doubt he will, his brain will be spaghetti. He might as well be dead."

Nicole pours herself some coffee. "I'm done. I'm going to close the pharmacy. We're moving to Aberdeen, out by the coast, where I'll work at Rite Aid."

"Aberdeen. Why would I know that name?"

"I don't know. Kurt Cobain? It's a small town, but we'll blend right in, me and Joel and our kid. It's where I grew up."

"Harvard Street Pharmacy will be no more?"

"No more. It was dying a slow, painful death. I'm taking it out of its misery."

"How's Joel feel about moving?"

"He's fine with it. His idea." She steps onto the porch. "Don't you know he's devoted to me? Now listen, *Al*, or whatever your name is, I don't care what you do, but don't do it from here. Your lease has expired. Stay away from me and find a new place to live."

"And what if I don't?"

"You will." She slams the screen door so hard one of the hinges breaks. She gave Brandon his orders—time to leave—and now she needed to get home before she is missed.

As she drives away, the rain stops, the dark clouds lighten, and soon the sky is splashed with purple and gray. When Nicole reaches the Key Peninsula highway, a raccoon waddles to the edge of the road, and she yanks her wheel, trying to hit it.

Vermin, she thinks. *The world is filled with such vermin.*

44

Meaghan Farren

Lorissa and I whiz along in the I-5 carpool lane. Clearly, she doesn't think much of my idea of going to the pawnshop, but I press on. "We can see if it's the same gun you found next to the body."

"Can they do that?"

"I don't know for sure, but isn't there a serial number or something?" Both of us are ridiculously naïve when it comes to guns.

We reach Tacoma and drive past the piano bar, the Starbucks, the costume shop. "I've driven by this little pawnshop a hundred times, but never dreamed of entering," Lorissa says as she backs into a spot in the empty parking lot. "Want to come in?"

This is what I'm here for, right? To support Lorissa? "Sure." I hope she doesn't see me gulp. This place looks creepy.

Ominous. "We're a team, right?" I say in a perky voice I don't feel.

"That's right!" Lorissa is also building her courage, checking her lipstick. She brushes her lashes with mascara, sighs, and unbuckles her seatbelt. I give her a thumbs up. "Just think Cagney and Lacey."

Alright then. Lori pulls her shoulders back and lifts her chin in a way that would make her genteel mom proud. "We can do this."

I'm assaulted by the dank smell as soon as I open the door. Must be from old watches, movie cameras, VHS players found in decrepit attics or storage sheds. Or maybe from the clerk bent over reading on his high metal chair, gray hair springing from his ears.

Lorissa remains three feet from the glass counter, poring over guns and bracelets and silver earrings. She steps forward.

"Hi," she says, but the man barely lifts his head from his *National Enquirer*. He sips his Slurpee. Lorissa taps her fingers on the glass.

"Excuse me." She clears her throat. His thick head lobs upward.

I'm scanning all around, wondering what on earth they sell in a pawnshop. Who buys this stuff? Enough stalling. Lorissa pulls out the photo of Brandon at the beach. "Have you seen this guy?" He returns to the magazine. "Nope."

"You didn't even look!"

"And ain't gonna." His Harley Davidson tee shirt ripples over his round belly, his left arm brandishes a tattoo, a bluish-green—snake? —swirling from his elbow to his wrist. I see letters but can't read it. "I don't get into personal matters."

"This is really important. My son." Lorissa stops herself, realizing how anxious, how desperate, she sounds. She straightens the collar on her blouse and begins more slowly. "Please."

He stares at her, assessing, then shrugs and takes the photo. "Maybe."

I can't stand it anymore. "Did he buy a gun?"

He lifts the straw from his drink and chews on it, not saying a word. We're a little slow on the uptake. Lorissa unsnaps her leather purse, takes out her wallet, and sets a twenty on the counter. The clerk's eyes are dull; his mouth doesn't move. She opens her wallet. Another twenty. His pock marks look as if his teenage acne never cleared. She's starting to take shallow breaths, on the edge of hyperventilating, still not speaking. She rips out a ten, checks his impassive eyes. Then a five, a one. "That's all I have!" She's on the verge of tears.

I try to reason with the dude. "Look. That's all we have. That's my crazy husband in that picture." I stab the photo with my finger. "I have a restraining order and I want to know if he's got a gun to kill me with, and we know he was here. We both want to find out if he's already shot a guy in Yachts Village." I feel on fire and imagine that my nostrils flare. I can't hold back when I'm talking about Brandon. "Did he or did he not buy a gun?" I'm thinking of threats I could throw at the pawn broker—call the police, violations, whatever.

The man's huge pink fist rests on the counter. At last he steps back and pulls out a laptop from under the counter. "Okay," he says. He scoops up the money and stuffs it in his pocket, then scrolls through the pages. It's a slow computer, whirring. While Lorissa and I wait, I feel nauseated from the reek of mold. "Here it is: 'Pat Narrow.' That's the guy. It's my business to remember these names and faces."

I start to speak. Stop. A shiver creeps up my skin. I've got to get out of here. "Thank you," I say as I grab Lorissa's arm and yank her out of the shop. Once the door shuts behind us, I pull on her hand. "Lorissa! Pat Narrow—that's Brandon's brother-in-law. Brandon looks sort of like him! Brandon bought a gun using his brother-in-law's ID. He bought the gun."

Lorissa grasps the implication right away. "We're so close!" Then her glee shifts and she smashes her palm to her forehead. "We didn't ask what kind of gun he bought. How could we have forgotten that?"

Stupid, stupid, stupid. "Cripes!" I say and open the door once again.

"Having too much fun to leave?" the guy says.

"Too much fun," Lorissa responds. "We need to know what kind of gun he bought."

"It'll cost you extra."

I feel like dissolving onto the floor. "Please. Please." How do I beg without losing every ounce of dignity? "My husband is a maniac. Her son has been accused of something my husband did.

We're both totally stressed."

The man holds up his hand. "I don't want to hear no personal problems."

"Then," Lorissa drops her voice, "please. An act of kindness. Just so on the day you die you remember the generous act you did for two crazy women who were falling apart." He smirks.

"Think of all that good karma." He ignores me but, thankfully, pulls out the laptop again and scrolls through the pages.

"I ain't supposed to." Again, an interminable wait. "A S&W 686. That's a six-inch barrel. . ."

"Thank you!" My shoulders drop with relief. We charge back to the car, give a high five—not that a high five feels natural, but it just seems right. Lorissa drives off from the store as fast as she can and I say, "That was bizarre!"

"No kidding. Did you really get a restraining order?"

"No," I say. "Not yet. I haven't had time." I remind myself that even though this new information from the pawnshop may help Connor, there's still a crazy man on the loose with a gun, and I'm his target.

"Well, we did confirm Brandon's ID and what kind of gun he bought." Lorissa's relief is palpable. "We need to celebrate!"

"And I finally visited Scott." She has a point: don't let the things that still need doing overshadow the progress we're making. "What did you have in mind?"

"How about celebrating at the Pilchuck Tavern? A couple of beers?"

Sounds good to me. When was the last time I went out for a beer?

Lorissa calls Graham to give him a quick rundown—Connor, Scott, the pawnshop, the kind of gun. She asks him to relay it all to Jasmine. "I'm tired of doing it all," she says.

Lorissa pulls into the tavern's lot, driving past a dozen parked cars, when I spot an all-too-familiar black Beamer. My heart starts beating at rocket speed. I can hardly breathe. "Lorissa, park in the back corner," I whisper frantically. "You've got to go check to see if those are Massachusetts plates. Please!"

She finds a spot where we can see the tavern door, anyone coming or going. She runs out, then hops back in. "They are! Massachusetts."

I can barely speak. "That's Brandon. Brandon's here!" I feel that old familiar terror, feeling utterly helpless. There's no escape. I shrink down in my seat. "I've got to think. Think this through." I ponder the possibilities. Leave? Just leave? Or find out what he's up to? Be one step ahead of him, for once. "Would you mind—only if you really don't—seeing if he's in there? What he's doing? Who he's with? Anything?"

"Flirt with him?" She wiggles her eyebrows. She's kidding, but her point is made. This is ridiculous.

"Forget it."

"No, no. I'll spy." She's actually giggling, after all this.

"Glad to do a little extra espionage. It will cost you." Yeah. Cost me, like, my life?

Lorissa pinches her cheeks to give them some pink, undoes her ponytail, and brushes her hair with her fingers. "Here goes." Getting into the part, she sways her hips like she's looking for action.

My back aches as I crouch halfway underneath the glove compartment. I can't let him see me, or I'm dead. I peek above the dashboard, eyes glued to the tavern door. I wait. And wait. And wait some more.

Lorissa's been gone two minutes. Five. There are voices two cars over. I try to hear. Buying some pot. Haggling over the price. Two kids with jean jackets next to their motorcycles.

I check my phone. Ten minutes. Fifteen. What the hell is happening in there? The door flings open, and I'm sure it's him. My veins electrify, currents running up and down from my head to my toes. I plunge back down, certain he can't see me. Terror is alive within me, like a beast roaring to life.

I wait a minute. Two. Hear a car pass. Peek. See the car driving out of the lot. No, it wasn't him. Just some kid in a white Ford. Lorissa, come back here. I can't stand this one more minute.

What's happened to her? Now I panic again. Is she okay? Will Brandon recognize her? Has he been spying on me all along? Should I call Graham? I check my phone. Dead. Dead? It can't be! I shake it, like that will do any good.

A car with a bad muffler parks next to us. I try to hide deeper under the dashboard. If only I had a blanket. Something to cover me. I reach for a jacket in the backseat and pull it over my head.

Finally, finally Lorissa jumps in the car, and neither of us says a word as she races out of the lot. Then, three miles up the road, she turns into an industrial park and stops behind a health food warehouse, where she flips off the ignition.

I can barely breathe, and I see the same is true for her. "It was Brandon." She's as terrified as I am. "And Meaghan?" She's panting. "He was with Nicole."

"Nicole!"

"That's what took me so long. Figuring out how to leave without them seeing me."

"What happened?" I hear a forklift nearby. We're secluded behind an enormous building with a green metal roof and a dozen closed garage doors. I relax my fists, my clenched fingers.

She lifts her chest, breathing in all the air her lungs can hold. "When I went in, it was so dark I couldn't see till my eyes adjusted. Jimmy Buffet was singing "Cheeseburger in Paradise"; it smelled like dead beer. A few geezers were throwing darts, a man and woman in tight jeans shooting pool—and there's Brandon and Nicole on the far side of the bar, facing me, but they were arguing, fighting. Neither one seemed to notice me. Nicole was flailing her hands, I could almost hear her gold bangles jangling as she pointed her fingers, jabbing them at Brandon's chest. Pissed. I could see that from across the room."

"And him?"

"You know, if I hadn't really studied the photo, I wouldn't have recognized him—except that smug, haughty smile."

I can picture that conceited face, his lips parted, hinting at a grin. He has a way of maintaining eye contact like he's doing you a favor just listening. Oh, yeah. I know what she's talking about. Makes me want to vomit. "They didn't see you?"

"No. I rushed straight into the restroom, which turned out to be convenient because while I couldn't hear the exact words, I could sure hear Nicole screaming. The door to the kitchen is next to the restroom, so I slipped in there and out the back door." She holds out her wobbly hand. "Look. I'm still shaking." But now she laughs. "How's that, Lacey?"

"Not bad, Cagney! Not bad at all!" I never saw that show, and maybe Lorissa hasn't either, but I like the idea of us being a team. Connected. One piece of wisdom I've learned: friendship is more valuable than the crown jewels and more fragile than a porcelain vase. Handle with care, because it can break in an instant, but may take a lifetime to repair.

"What's next?" I ask.

She starts the car. "Let's go home."

Good call.

Kale-broccoli salad, turkey chili, and garlic bread are ready when we get back to Lorissa's. Graham serves dinner to us and Mackenzie while we fill them in on our day. We devour dinner, ravenous after all the excitement.

That night I throw my blankets off my bed, too hot, then a half hour later pull them back up again. I go to the family room and begin to read the newest Mike Lawson, but my eyes blur. I open my laptop. Do a Google search for "bullet in the brain?"

I'm shocked by so many entries. A woman blogging about her experiences before and after a hunting accident. She's in a white gown with a white turban, her two toddler sons climbing on the hospital bed. Entries by doctors describing varying brain extraction procedures. A sister talking about the disability her brother experienced after being shot in Afghanistan.

Conclusion? Scott could live, he could die. He could be disabled for life—physically, mentally, verbally. He could be fine.

What more can I do to help Lorissa? I saw Scott. I learned the truth about his past, about his cheating with Nicole. Sure, it would be nice to talk, yell, ask him what happened, but that's not in the cards, at least not soon. We know Nicole and Brandon are acquainted, and we guess they colluded to shoot Scott. I just don't know if Brandon had to talk Nicole into it, or if it was her idea and he supplied the gun. What else can I do to help not just Lorissa, but all the Orondos? Graham's here, he's on PTO leave, he's the supportive husband Lorissa needs. Maybe it's time for me to go back to Chile. Brandon is just too close, and maybe I've done all I can here for now.

Next time I wake up, my phone reads 6:00 a.m. I drag myself out of bed, pour some coffee, and gaze once again at the gargantuan, snowy mountain. She could blow like Mount St. Helens, her sister in the Cascades mountain range.

A few minutes later, Graham is reading the paper; Mackenzie, putting her books and soccer clothes in her pack; Lorissa, drinking her coffee, not quite awake. A semblance of normalcy that none of us feel.

I return to my room, make the bed, try to read more of my mystery novel, pace. I'm so anxious about Scott's surgery today. Upstairs, I imagine Lorissa and Graham are thinking anxiously about their son, who just might be freed or else the opposite: charged with murder and facing the death penalty. No one has uttered that aloud since we met in Jasmine's office. I enter the kitchen, pour Cheerios in a bowl, add milk, and sit. Lorissa is still in her same spot at the dining room table, looking dazed. She speaks in a fog. "I can't tell you how excited Graham and I were when we found out I was pregnant with Connor," she says. I'm not sure if she's talking to herself or if she's even aware I'm there. She's almost ethereal, a ghost of herself. "He wanted to have kids from the beginning." She lifts her coffee mug, not drinking.

"From the beginning. . .like back in college?"

"Oh, Meaghan. Truly, in college Graham and I were barely friends. When we bumped into each other so unexpectedly in the Berkshires that summer, him taking a break from NYU and me from Juilliard, we got together just for a

coffee, a visit between old acquaintances. Later, though, we had
what I would call one 'real date'—it's always hard to say what's a
date, right?" I nod uncertainly:

I'd never dated that much.

"We picnicked in the grass along the Housatonic River.
French bread, wine, Vermont cheddar—quite romantic,
honestly. By the end of the afternoon, we planned to see a
movie—what was it? *Jerry McGuire* maybe. Anyway, the movie
was perfect, nonintellectual fun, not like a New York 'film.'

"We laughed and afterward, headed to the ice cream
shop. I remember my rocky road cone, a bit of ice cream
dribbling down my chin, which he carefully wiped with his index
finger, and then he held his finger out, as though wondering if
he should lick his finger or if he should have me lick his finger—
but then he just wiped it on a napkin. I laughed. *Coward!* I
thought.

"But, he grinned. One of those giant ones. I've never
known anyone whose smile can truly take over their whole face,
so their cheeks completely disappear, but Graham can. He
beamed, and I wondered, *what does this all mean?* All the time, I
had that joyful feeling in my stomach, like the whole world was
one of those corny round yellow happy faces."

"And that was it? You guys became 'you guys'?"

"No! I didn't see him again that summer. Returned to
Juilliard. I hadn't forgotten him; I actually carried around his
number, daring myself to call, but school really kicked my butt,
so there was always a very good excuse.

"Then around Thanksgiving, three months after I'd last seen him, he phoned out of the blue. We rode the Q into Brooklyn and hiked into Prospect Park, up to Lookout Hill, where the city lights sparkled, so spectacularly alive. He laid down a blanket, opened his backpack. I was curious, of course, especially when he pulled out a small carton of fresh strawberries and a container of Cool Whip.

"'I don't think our summer should have ever ended,' he said. And he dipped a strawberry into Cool Whip and lifted it to my mouth so I could lick it all off."

"'*Our* summer?' I asked him.

"'Well,' and then he blushed like the long, gangly kid he was. 'It *should* have been our summer.' He plucked the stem off another strawberry and dipped it in the Cool Whip. 'We're pretending this is real whip cream, straight from the farm, right?

"'Absolutely,' I told him.

"'So, I was at the tail end of a relationship last time I saw you,' he explained. 'I plain wasn't ready for anything new.'

"'And now?' I'd dipped my finger in the whipped cream. I don't know where he'd found his idea of re-creating the summer, but it was sweet.

"'We'll see,' he'd said.

"I watched him dip another strawberry into the cream and thought, *I like this man. I could love this man.*"

I felt a pang of … what? Envy? Regret? It's what I'd been feeling about Scott just a few weeks ago.

"Then we had months of those cheapo dates that broke New Yorkers love: watching chess at Battery Park played between a private-school kid in her uniform jacket and a homeless-looking guy with weeklong bristles on his chin. We rode the Staten Island ferry, waved to the Statue of Liberty like we were coming to America for the first time.

"And when spring came, crocuses blossomed in the parks, the days lengthened, and we headed to a B and B in Stockbridge, where he pulled out a box and my tummy fluttered."

Lorissa pauses, adding a little drama to her story. "The box had a note. Just a note. Nothing else. I felt myself sinking as if rocks in my pockets were weighing me down, so disappointed.

What kind of tease was this? I opened the paper— 'Will you marry me?' My stomach was having a rollercoaster ride, but before I could ask, he jumped in.

"'I thought we could go to Great Barrington, to the handcraft jeweler there, and he can make our rings together, you know, our own unique rings?' And so, we did."

Now she holds out her hand. "We both have Buddhist mudras—you know, hands in certain prayerful positions? They're different, but they complement each other. They're symbols of our life together, the way it's supposed to be, our life, our marriage, our family. Together, complements of each other."

She takes her coffee cup to the dishwasher. "But in all our years, we've never had to deal with anything like this." We gaze at each other for a few heartbeats, and I nod again. I'm sure

her last sentence is an understatement, but I can't think of
anything to say.

She heads to her bedroom, and I finish cleaning the
kitchen, then dress in my running clothes. Running—my one
salvation. I'm hoping that a longer run, maybe to the bridge and
back, might soothe my mind.

I jog past the old Christmas tree farm with the For Sale
sign. Lorissa is worried they'll sell the thirty acres of forested
land for houses, zoning be damned. Up the hill on Eleventh
Street, my knees are already aching. No way I'm going to make it
all the way to the bridge.

I follow the curve up to the fire station and stop for
water, huffing, realizing I'm too ambitious for my own good.
Then, the Orondos surprise me, braking their car next to me on
the road. "Thorp called Jasmine. He wants us down at the
station again," Graham says.

"Do you know why?"

"No; we'll let you know as soon as we find out."

Mackenzie's still home studying. A late start today.
Every Wednesday, a late start."

"I hope Connor gets out today!" I say with a
cheerfulness I don't feel. Their car speeds off, and I twist the cap
onto my water bottle tightly. How on earth do our simple lives
get so complicated? The problems with loving someone.
Anyone. It just makes life harder.

I glance up as a black car flashes by. For a moment I think it's Brandon's BMW, but I remember how many times my stomach has curdled imagining him. *Stop it*, I say to myself.

Twenty minutes later, I jog up the Orondos' driveway and notice the front door is open. *Odd*, I think. Inside, I go downstairs to my bathroom and rinse off my face, drink a glass of water, then on my way back upstairs I shut the front door before trudging up toward the kitchen.

"Mackenzie," I call. When I reach the top of the stairs and turn toward the kitchen, a movement catches my eyes. I freeze like I've been shot. No. It can't be.

45

Meaghan Farren

"Brandon," I say to the skeletal creature clasping a huge kitchen knife an inch from Mackenzie's throat.

He barely resembles the husband I left eight months ago. No gelled hair. No carnation in the lapel of his gray suit. No polished shoes. Still, a dash of the arrogant air he'd had the morning I'd escaped, when this cocksure man had bragged about his "big deal." That "big deal" that was always within reach, "just" within reach, that deal that would have happened years ago if only he hadn't been screwed by some jerk, if only the other guy wasn't such a double-cross, if only some idiot had done their job. I'd heard every excuse.

But today, in the Orondos' great room, splattered mud covers his wrinkled golf shirt and jeans. There's a scar on his cheek, dried blood staining his filthy shirt. A husk of a man, boiling with rage. Trembling in front of him with quivering knees is my friend's adorable daughter, Mackenzie——with a chef's knife at her throat.

Brandon seethes, foam spewing from his mouth. "Helll-ooo, Meaghan," he sneers. *Play it cool*, I tell myself, ignoring the adrenalin galloping through my veins. This is Lorissa's daughter, and I will fix this. Mackenzie's wet eyes beg—*please save me.* "Brandon, I'm here now." I steady my voice. "Let Mackenzie go, and we can talk." Brandon jeers, words unintelligible. "What do you want, Brandon? Let her go."

His cheeks have a week's worth of stubble, blotchy and ugly. "I want you, babe."

"Okay, I'm here."

"It's not that easy. You left me! How dare you? I own you, woman. I spent eight months tracking you down. You're mine."

I'm beginning to panic. His pupils are pinpricks and his eyes have that crazed look I remember well. Violence runs through every fiber of his being, and now insanity is creeping into the mix. That oh-so-familiar terror throbs in my bones. *No,* I suddenly remind myself. I'm not going there. I'm not going to let him climb inside my head and torture me again. "Let her go!" I command.

Mackenzie whimpers, dread in her eyes.

"She's fifteen!" I yell. "Let her go!"

"I see you're gettin' scared, darlin'. You're a sweet young thing, Mackenzie." He strokes his gleaming knife against her cheek. "That's right, yes? You and me—we could have some fun," he cackles.

Mackenzie whimpers again, and then suddenly, in a single swift movement, he pushes Mackenzie to the couch, yanks my arm back with one hand, and with the other jerks the knife up to my throat. I feel the silver blade against my skin—sharp, cold. I'm afraid I'll faint, there in his arms, slicing my own throat without him even moving.

Get it together, Meaghan, I think frantically. You survived him once; you can survive him again. I wonder what his end game is—or if he even has a plan—and then I spot a flicker in the doorway to Graham's office. Or do I?

Mackenzie shudders on the couch, rolling her shoulders, as if she's trying to make herself as small as possible. Her cries sound like a puppy's squeals. I'm furious I got her into this mess. That anger is exactly what I need to get the upper hand. "Mackenzie," I say, pretending there isn't a knife aimed to carve my throat. "It will be okay." I need to remain still, because a smidgen of a shift will cut my neck.

Screw him. No matter how terrified I am, I'm even more enraged that this sadist has hurt my friends. Lorissa's son is in jail because of him, and now her daughter is in danger, falling apart like a rag doll. I want to throw my arms around Mackenzie and hug her tightly like an auntie should, because that's how I feel—like I am her aunt and I'm going to protect her.

I flash on every mystery book I've ever read, every CSI episode I've watched. How do captives escape? Get the villains talking. That's one way. Another movement from the office catches my eye. Friend of ours? Or friend of Brandon's?

"Brandon," I say. "Did you shoot Scott? If you're going to kill me, there's no problem telling me, right?" He pulls me tighter, his sweaty chest against my back, and I stiffen. He repels me, but I cannot budge.

His voice isn't normal, just a sound like a savage wolf's.

"Now why would you think that?"

That might be as much of a confession as I'm going to get, but I push on. "Why?"

"Hey, woman," his voice bites, and I feel as if cockroaches are crawling up my skin. "You left me. You walked out on me. Any friend of yours is an enemy of mine."

I spasm, the knife edging closer to my larynx. All the time he's speaking, I wonder who's in the office. A friend, I hope. Rhys, maybe? Wouldn't that be ironic. Rhys does seem to keep coming through, the knight in scruffy armor.

"Did you shoot him? Or did Nicole? Did you give her the gun? How did you even meet her?"

He smirks, then begins the story of how he'd met Nicole. "She was there at the bar—you know the Pilchuck Tavern? — picking at her cuticles, listening to Willie Nelson croon.

"I start talking, asking questions, and she tells me all about that Scott Crowley, how they're going to run away together, how they're soulmates. I'm a polished sort of guy who women love to open up to, right, babe?" I grab the corner of the table to keep from falling. I thought I'd remembered how much I hate him, but no—and now I'm ready to explode.

"I've got to sit down," I say. "I'm going to faint." I thought I could take it, hear all about Brandon and Nicole and Scott, but I can't. Not another word. At the same time, I recollect what's in Graham's office: a desk, a computer, a futon with two end tables and small reading lamps. Nothing will work as a weapon.

If only there were a golf club or a baseball bat or a …vacuum.

Does Lorissa have her vacuum in there? A vacuum might be light enough to lift without making noise and strong enough to slam over Brandon's head.

"No way you're sitting. It's your throat if you fall, woman." His smell is putrid. His only goal—to feel his power over us. To terrorize. Then what? He doesn't have a clue. If he already shot Scott, killing isn't idle chatter.

Just then the door to the office opens a little wider and—oh, no! It's not a person at all. The fluffy orange tail flops back and forth, and Chumley approaches me. "No, Chumley. No! Go away!" Then she notices Brandon and hisses. Her hiss reminds me of a rattlesnake ready to attack.

"Your stupid mangy cat!"

I'm crestfallen. So much for being rescued by some hero hiding in the office. "Go away, Chumley!" I'm afraid he'll kill her. He's always hated Chumley. He lifts his foot and smacks it into Chumley's belly. "Chumley!" I cry, but she scrambles down the stairs and vanishes in seconds.

"Oww!" When he kicked my cat, the knife nicked me and now I feel blood dripping slowly down my neck to my chest. I close my eyes, try to concentrate. I'm gagging from his reek as he pulls my arm tighter, the pain shooting up my shoulders. "Brandon, you're hurting me." He tugs me harder, rougher. I refuse to squeal for him.

"Oh, you don't want to hear all the gory details about that two-timing boyfriend of yours? You forget you're married or something?" If I had the strength, I'd have grabbed the knife at my throat and stabbed him a hundred times. I glance over at Mackenzie, who's now stone-still on the couch—all but her eyes. She's following Brandon's every movement like a cat, stealthy and aware. She hasn't given in to fear. If pouncing would work, she would jump. She's caught up in Brandon's story, which is good.

Less afraid for herself—or even for me, presumably. "Nicole and me, we met at the Pilchuck. Kept running into each other. She poured out her sob story," he sneers. "I learned all about you and that pussy Scott. Didn't take much to think, *Okay, two with one blow.* Gave her a gun. Now that was a wild twist of fate, right? Seeing that boy, that Connor kid, at the pawnshop?" Brandon laughs like he's pulled something over on the whole world. "When Scott tried to break up with Nicole, she got so crazy green with jealousy, more jealous than I've ever seen. There was no way she was going to let him be with you. Perfect for me. Two problems—hers and mine—solved with one bullet. Told her to report the Roxies missing. Set up Scott. Didn't know exactly what day she was going to pull the trigger, but I knew she would."

"I wasn't even in the country!" He tightens his grip on me. My back is soaked with perspiration now, and I feel his thick, nauseating breath on my neck. How did I forget he's a psychopath?

I'm beginning to lose my mask of indifference when Guru howls across the street, barking as if he's protecting his human, yapping more viciously, louder and more ferocious than ever. Brandon turns ever so slightly toward the sound outside the window, and in that moment Rhys—yes, it *was* Rhys in there the whole time—Rhys races from the office. I lift Brandon's arm that's holding the knife and duck down, twisting away from the arm that's holding me, while Rhys grabs the wrought-iron fire poker, leaps past the couch, and lands on Brandon, smashing the poker over his head again and again and again.

"Don't you dare threaten my girl," Rhys screams, pummeling Brandon. "Don't you ever, *ever* get near Mackenzie again!"

"Stop!" I yell. "Rhys, stop! You're going to kill him."

Faint sirens sound from down the street, louder and louder until at last three police cars screech to a stop in front of the house and that policewoman who's Thorp's partner—Janine, it turns out, is her name—sprints up the steps. "I kept dialing and dialing," Rhys tells me, poker still in hand, Brandon lying on the carpet with his hands over his head, blood everywhere. "But I couldn't talk or that dude would hear me. I guess they finally figured out that it was an emergency."

Mackenzie runs from the couch and collapses into Rhys's arms. Her hero. *Love*, I think. *Young love.*

But it's true. Rhys is the hero once again. Another officer, tall like a star basketball player, handcuffs Brandon, whose bludgeoned face looks like he has a flesh-eating disease. "I'll get you yet, Meaghan," he spits.

"Don't answer him," Janine says. "Don't respond. Don't give him that."

"He confessed," I say. "He confessed to meeting Nicole and giving her his gun. He told us everything."

"We heard it, too," Mackenzie and Rhys say in unison, entwined on the couch.

"He met her at a bar." I start relaying his story, and Mackenzie and Rhys fill in details.

"We'll check out the bartender, see if her story corroborates this."

"Is this enough to keep him in jail? For a long, long time?"

"I'm thinking so," Janine says.

"He's the man I ran away from," I say. "My husband."

"This guy is your husband?" She sounds so appalled that I smile.

"I can't believe I married such a sicko. I'm sure he would have killed me if I hadn't gotten him bragging." Mackenzie and Rhys nod in agreement.

"And if Rhys hadn't saved us both." Mackenzie glows, eyeing her Superman.

"I think we have enough evidence to keep him locked away for a long, long while," the officer says. I can't believe what I'm hearing. I am free? Truly free?

"And Connor?" I ask. "Does this mean he'll be released as well?"

Janine, a small woman in her blue uniform with a belt tight around her waist, puts her hands on her hips. "I'm sorry, but it's not my place to say." She turns to Mackenzie. "Where are your parents?"

Just then a car barrels up the driveway, car doors open, footsteps bound up the stairs. Lorissa and Graham both hurl their arms around Mackenzie. "Mom! Dad!" When they release her, she says with pride, "Rhys saved me. Saved my and Aunt Meaghan's lives!"

Lorissa's face is blank, like she has no idea how to respond. After a moment, she throws her arms around Rhys. "Rhys, thank you so much. I'm afraid I..." Okay, here it comes. The long overdue apology. "I'm afraid I. . ." (it's never easy to admit when you're wrong) ". . .misjudged you."

That's all Rhys needs. "Cool," he says. "Hey, I gotta get home." There's a flush on his cheeks, like the whole scene embarrasses him. He seems like the kind of boy who's more comfortable with his bad-boy image than with being a hero.

The police ask hundreds of questions before they leave, and then I shower for twenty minutes. I'll give the Orondos extra money for the water bill. I want to feel fresh and clean, but it's hard to wash off the scum of Brandon. I check my throat in the mirror. There's a nick, a tiny one that doesn't hurt, but I cover it with a pale pink scarf.

"Any word about Scott?" I ask Lorissa after my shower.

"Sorry, Meaghan. We told Thorp everything you and I learned, but we didn't find out anything about Scott's surgery. I think it may still be going on."

Extracting a bullet from the brain. I imagine that's a mighty long surgery. I need some space, and the Orondo family needs some time together. The coffee shop jumps to mind—a place for reflection, good coffee, warm surroundings, friendly people. "See you all later," I say, and drive into Yachts Village.

I open the refurbished old door and recall my conversation with Scott, right here, when we both remarked on the authentic barn siding and rock fireplace. That day counts as our first date, when I thought my heart would bounce out of my chest, the first time I considered that this guy might be "the one" as we sat on the high stools at the bistro table, drinking mochas, laughing. That warm spring day was an eon ago.

As I scan the room, I notice the corner where Scott had sat that first day. There, today, is the same man Scott had met with back then, in the same chair, with the same briefcase. This time he's meeting a slovenly fellow with uncombed hair and a torn tee shirt, such a contrast to Scott's friend, who's dressed in an ironed shirt with a buttoned-down collar. When Scott had introduced me back then, what had he said his friend's name was? For the life of me, I can't remember.

Minutes later, both men shake hands and begin to leave. As briefcase man passes, I stop him. "Excuse me. I'm Meaghan Farren, and you're...aren't you a friend of Scott Crowley's?" Suddenly I remember. "Mitch, isn't it?" He surveys me, from my now light streaked hair down to my purple sneakers, as though he's debating whether to admit he knows Scott.

"Of course, you are. You were sitting with him in that same chair last spring." I'm insistent. I need to know everything, and I won't let this guy pretend he hadn't been meeting with Scott.

With a small bulge in his stomach and a receding hairline, Mitch's the kind of guy you wouldn't notice in a crowd. Who is he? He's clutching his briefcase as if his life depends on it. At least his welfare. He's dressed neatly, but not in a showy manner like a realtor, nor is he over the top with a ten-thousand-dollar watch like a stock broker. State? He's a state or county employee. Now it hits me. I glance at the scruffy man who just met with him, making his way to the door.

"Excuse me. Were you. . .did you work with Scott Crowley in some way?" I lower my voice. "Like his case manager or something?" He shifts his weight, debating whether to answer. "Parole officer?" His mouth twitches just a speck. "May I buy you a coffee?" I ask. What happened to the days when a woman could just bat her eyelashes and a man would be at her beck and call? Surely, he knows how much this means to me.

"No. Sorry, Meaghan. I need to get back to work."

"You know me! Scott talked to you about me! Please. Please have a seat."

His eyes are kind, compassionate. "No, you just introduced yourself, that's all. I'm sorry. I need to get back to the office." He checks the time on his phone. "I have an appointment in a half hour."

"But tell me—you believe him, don't you? You believe he didn't do drugs? Didn't steal drugs?"

"I can only say that he seems like a good guy, and I was surprised by those claims."

"You are his parole office, aren't you? That's who you are, right?" I'm putting the pieces together. "When he got out of jail for being a gigolo, you were assigned to see he stayed on track. That's it, right?" He's not giving anything away, but I know I'm right. "Scott is a good man, I'm sure of it! Nicole is the one who said he stole those Roxies, but she's the *real* addict. And then she pinned it all on my friend's son! Scott didn't do anything wrong, I'm sure of it." Except have an affair and two-time me—but I don't say that. "Anything illegal, I mean. I'm sure of it!"

Mitch's eyes drop, forlorn, as if he wishes he could help. "I'm so sorry. I'm not allowed to comment on a client." He picks up his briefcase to leave.

"But you didn't think he was strung out or anything, right? You'd know, right? Hey, did he have to take drug tests? That would prove it!"

Mitch inches toward the door, then spins around. "I can't comment professionally, and probably shouldn't personally, but here goes. Scott Crowley was a good man who got himself wound up with the wrong woman. Women have always been his downfall. But drugs? Using or selling? I don't believe it." He opens the door and scuttles down the sidewalk.

I feel my shoulders drop, so relieved, so glad I made him say it. He thinks Scott is innocent too. I head back to the Orondos' feeling like a weight has been lifted.

Brandon confessed, he's been arrested, I'm safer from him than I've ever been. We've collected the evidence to prove Connor's innocence, whether the shooter was Nicole, Brandon, or both in collusion. I've visited Scott. I wonder if there's any reason to stay. Lorissa could fill me in about any new developments over Skype. And in Chile, I could recharge, let go of Scott, the man who deceived me so. Get my feet back on the ground.

The phone vibrates while I'm stopped at a red light. "Meaghan!" Lorissa sounds so excited I imagine Connor will be released this afternoon. "You'll never believe it!"

"What?"

"They did the surgery on Scott."

"And he's alive?"

"Yes, Meaghan. Alive, but not conscious. Still in an induced coma. His vitals are doing well, though."

"Oh, Lorissa. I'm so relieved."

The light turns green and I proceed past the arts and crafts fair. "He'll be okay?"

"Well, actually, they can't say until he wakes up. It's possible he'll be okay; he'll probably be disabled, in some form or another." I'm not sure how to take this. "But he'll live, Meaghan. The doctors can't know one hundred percent, but they're pretty confident. He's going to live."

I sigh, inhaling all the air in the car. "Thanks."

"But that's not the only news. Ready?"

"Okay," I say, but what more could there be?

"The bullet they removed from his brain doesn't match the gun lying on the ground next to him."

I nearly slam on the brakes. "*What?*" I flip on the blinker and pull over to a parking lot. "Doesn't match?"

"No!"

"So. . ." I'm slow to understand the magnitude of this discovery. "So, it doesn't matter if Connor's DNA is on the gun they found at the scene? It doesn't matter because that's not the gun that was used to shoot Scott? What about the gun Brandon bought at the pawnshop?" I'm so confused.

"It's likely, or at least possible, the gun lying next to Scott's body was the one Brandon bought. But it's not the gun that was used to shoot Scott. They don't even need to do a ballistics test, they're so different. One has a shell, one doesn't. That simple."

"A second gun?" This changes everything. "Now there's no reason to hold Connor? The DNA is on the wrong gun?"

"Exactly."

"But what about Damian's statement, and Nicole's? Don't they matter?"

"Not enough," says Lorissa. My hazard light ticks while cars pass, and I ponder. "Could they let Brandon out?"

"They'll hold Brandon for a long while—no question, what with him taking you and Mackenzie hostage and threatening to kill you. As for Scott's shooting, Thorp said he's going to reopen the investigation. They're going back to the pharmacy to check for evidence they might have overlooked. And Brandon—he hasn't confessed anything to the police, according to Jasmine. But they're working on him."

"What do they think happened?"

"The police? They think Connor was telling the truth." Dozens of cars zoom by as I listen, my fingers threading through my hair.

"After all this, they think Connor's telling the truth?" I repeat.

Lorissa's voice lifts with excitement. "Yes! They believe him. Just what Connor said. Nicole was going to kill herself, but Connor talked her out of it and then, when he heard the bell ring over the pharmacy door—that was me—he panicked and chucked the gun."

"Couldn't ballistics or whoever tell whether that gun had been fired?"

"Oh, it had been fired all right. Just not into Scott's brain. Or any other part of him."

I'm puzzled. "Do you think it was Nicole or Brandon?"

"Well, Brandon admitted giving the gun to Nicole."

"Right."

"And Nicole was there, and both of them had motive—jealousy—and opportunity, I suppose. But. . ."

A green pickup truck slogs past, discharging black smoke. "There really isn't evidence, certainly not against Nicole.

Thorp said he may question her again, but for now it's an unsolved crime. Nicole claims she was in shock when she said Connor shot Scott. That it was all a mistake. Detective Thorp believes her, and they're letting her go ahead and move, as long as she stays in state. Meaghan, the Whyrrls are all moving out of town—to Aberdeen."

"Really?" I'm stymied. "But the gun? Where's the gun that shot Scott?"

"I don't know. No one knows." Even though I'm baffled and, actually, disturbed—I want Scott's shooter found—Lorissa is thrilled. "But Connor is getting out. Don't you see? He's cleared! He's getting out and will be free."

"Oh, Lorissa. I'm so, so happy for you. For us. For all of us."

Lorissa says that she, Graham, and Mackenzie are driving down to the police station to see exactly what they need to do for Connor's release.

We say our good-byes and I click off my phone, and I continue my drive to the Orondos'. I realize I'm having a tough time letting go. *Did Brandon shoot Scott? Or did Nicole have a second gun she's hiding somewhere? Maybe she shot him, then immediately regretted it.*

And why the second gun?

46

Nicole Whyrrl

Nicole regards her dead hydrangeas one last time, frail, like dust. Ugly. Begging to be pruned. She grasps her Harvard Street Pharmacy mug in one hand, the other hand on her hip. A deer lopes by the window, its hooves marking the dewy grass. It all smells so green, so fresh. The deer glances up at her, then trots away. Nicole slips her hand in her pocket, throws her head back, and tosses a pill in her mouth. She'd come so close to getting everything she wanted. Scott, passion, a new life.

So close.

"Hey," Joel says, sweeping in behind her, pulling her waist into him, kissing her neck. "We're all set. Torrie wants to say goodbye to Lorissa before we go."

Nicole brushes his hand off her and spins around. "Crap."

"It'll only be a minute. Lorissa is Torrie's godmother and all that," Joel says.

Nicole throws her cup in the trash can. It doesn't break in the plastic bin like she'd hoped. She wanted to smash it in a million pieces. Just like her heart.

47

Meaghan Farren

With the Orondos headed to the police station, I have their house to myself., I look forward to hanging out on the deck with Chumley, reading the paper, and drinking a cup of tea. I see no one's picked up the newspaper, so I cross the street to the Orondos' mailbox. Guru prances down the street, wagging his tail, proud, as if he's won Best in Show, carrying a rag in his mouth with a bit of a swagger in his hips. "Guru, did you get out of your invisible fence again? You rascal, you." He trots over to me, his head high, and drops the rag by my feet. Whatever's wrapped inside lands with a thud on the ground.

I halt mid-step. A flock of crows squawk annoyingly overhead. I stare down incredulously. Peeking out under the rag is black steel. I bend down to see more closely. *A gun.* A gun with caked-on dirt, like it had been buried before Guru got hold of it.

I gingerly re-wrap the gun with the rag, careful not to touch it, then pull out my cell phone and dial Officer Thorp. "This is Meaghan Farren. You know? The Orondos' friend?" I explain about Guru, his barking and digging and hoarding. "You'll never believe what I have in my hand." I describe what happened with Guru, our resident digger.

"I'll drive right over and get it. Don't touch it!"

My first thought is that the gun must be related to
Scott's shooting, though actually everyone seems to have guns
these days. But do they? Who would bury a gun?

Minutes later, the Whyrll's car pulls into the Orondos'
driveway. The last people I want to see—Nicole and Joel Whyrll.
She can go to hell as far as I'm concerned. Nicole had an affair
with the man I had stupidly thought was the love of my life;
she's the one who put my best friend's son in jail. An addict, liar,
and thief. How dare she come here!

Nicole doesn't get out of the car. Instead, she leans over
Joel in the driver's seat and says, "Torrie wants to say good-bye
to her godmother. Is Lorissa here?"

I put one hand on my hip and with the other continue
to hold the rag with the gun wrapped inside. I'm so mad I can't
speak.

"We're moving to Aberdeen," Nicole says.

Finally, I choke out words. "I heard."

"I'll be the Rite Aid pharmacist." So that's what Nicole's
going to do about her failing family pharmacy. The end has
come.

I ignore her—I am practiced at ignoring people in a
hard, ruthless way, as Lorissa can attest from way back in
college. I don't want to see Nicole. I bend over to reach Torrie's
hand in the backseat. "I'm sorry, honey, but Lorissa's not here.
The whole family is in town trying to bring Connor home," I say
in a catty voice, thinking, bring Connor home from that jail your

mom put him in. I can think of a few more choice words, but it wouldn't be fair for Torrie to have to listen to my scathing rebuke of her mom. Torrie will have enough to deal with, growing up with Nicole. "I'll tell her you came by. I'm sure she'll be sad she missed you."

Still pretending Nicole doesn't exist, I ask Joel, "So you're moving just like that?"

"It will be a great change. Closer to the coast."

Connor was accused of attempted murder, Scott is on life support, and they're running away. I clench my fists, even the one holding the gun. This is so wrong. "The house hasn't sold, but Nicole is starting her new job next week."

I'm so pissed. I always will be. But still, my curiosity gets the best of me. "And Joel? You're okay with moving?" Like it's any of my business. I hardly know the guy.

"Sure," he says. Probably mortified by this whole mess. Everyone knows now that his wife was having an affair.

"Of course, he's fine with moving." Nicole speaks with the same haughtiness that Brandon uses. The two make a great pair.

Again, I ignore Nicole, but smile at Torrie one more time. "Bye, Torrie. The whole Orondo family will miss you. I bet you'll love your new house."

"What's that in your hand?" Torrie asks, pointing.

I glance at my hand. "Actually, that's a gun. A very, very dangerous gun."

"Where did it come from?" asks Joel, speaking for the first time.

"Guru had it. I don't know where he dug it up."

"Weird," Joel says. "Well, sorry Graham and Lorissa aren't here to say adios. We're headed off." He turns the key, puts the car in gear, then stops. "Hey, may I use their bathroom before we go?"

"Sure." I beckon him in and point straight ahead. "You know where the downstairs bathroom is, right?" Nicole and Torrie are singing "The Wheels on the Bus" in the car. Nicole— what a demon. Such a liar. What is it like to be Nicole's husband? Doesn't Joel see what a manipulator she is? After all these years of marriage?

He turns and faces me. His demeanor completely changes as though one veil has slipped off and a demonic mask—vile, cruel, hateful—has taken its place.

"Joel, what's going on?" The brown in his eyes remind me of an infinite sea of mud, a drained reservoir.

"Why don't you give me that gun, Meaghan?" I cock my head, stunned to hear his growl. Suddenly a flash of images slides through my mind. What did Lorissa say about the day of the shooting? Joel arrived at the pharmacy seconds after the police, saying he'd *already* dropped Torrie off at Jasmine's? And what had Connor said? He'd heard some kind of commotion before he went in and found Scott on the floor. I'd assumed it was Brandon, but Joel? The brilliant one. The smartest of all of them. How had I missed it?

"*You?!* It was you the whole time?" Joel steps toward me. "Poor Joel, who the neighborhood feels sorry for, being with Nicole?"

"I'll always be with Nicole.," he says.

I walk backward as Joel inches closer. "But how? Why?"

"No one's going to screw my wife and get away with it. The same reason Brandon's going to be convicted for assaulting you. Men don't like the people who mess with their wives, let me tell you."

My chest tightens. I don't think I can speak, but I have to. Maybe this is all a mistake.

"But Torrie? Lorissa told me you dropped Torrie off at Jasmine's?"

"Before. Before I shot Scott." I touch the wall behind me. Backing up, step by step, I turn the corner toward the back door, nearly tripping over the shoe basket protruding from the hall closet. "Everything would have been fine if you and your dear friend Lorissa hadn't started nosing around."

"But how?" I stutter.

"I shot Scott and then that dipshit kid Connor came in the front door, so I jetted out the back."

"He said he heard something," I say. "Before he went to the storage room to look for Nicole." I reach the door behind me, one hand still holding the gun in the rag, the other turning the knob. "That was you? Not Brandon?"

"Yeah, me running out the back." He shouts, commanding, as though he's used to having his orders followed.

"Meaghan, give me the gun—now." Then he lowers his voice, like speaking to a child. Nicole and Torrie and I will drive to Aberdeen, and we can forget any of this happened."

I shuffle backward, now outdoors on the damp lawn.

"What? You think I'm going to just let you get away with murder?"

"Attempted murder."

"Maybe. We don't know yet if Scott will live." I wonder how long it will take the police to get here from town. The drive is twenty minutes, and I called Thorp, what? Five minutes ago?

"Give me the gun, or you'll have a terrible accident."

I back out farther into the yard. I'm glad I've been running so much these past few weeks. I wish there were something I could throw in Joel's path to get a good start, but I don't see anything.

"You just buried the gun in your yard? That seems pretty stupid." Joel's face turns six shades of red. "Guru dug it up and brought it over to his own yard," I say. "That electric-fence collar breaks every few weeks, if you hadn't noticed."

I pivot on my heels and start sprinting; I hear Joel running after me a moment later. I run behind the Massey's yard, across an empty lot, down the street—screaming. Joel's gaining on me. Then, like a sign from the stars, sirens blare. It must be Thorp coming for the gun.

"Just drop the gun," Joel calls, right on my heels. "Drop it and this will be all over." I run faster and faster, clutching the rag wrapped around the gun. He's a few feet away. The sirens begin to fade, heading in a different direction. Joel grabs my hair, pulling me toward him.

"No!" I shriek. "*No!*" I push him away, try the kicks I learned in karate back in college, and land back on my feet, springing ahead. I reach the end of the street, where it turns at a right angle, where going straight leads into the forest and over the cliff. He's right behind me.

I fly into the woods, then veer sharply to the right through the trees, holding on to a branch with one hand, the gun in the other. Joel doesn't stop; he keeps running—running through the trees, not able to stop himself, right over the cliff, and before he can break his fall, his scream pierces the air like a deafening whistle.

I cling to the fir, looking over my shoulder to see him rolling, rolling over the cliff, down the embankment into Puget Sound. Then the splash, like a landslide into the sea. Water frothing. Bubbles. Ripples. Waves washing against the cliff.

I turn and see Lorissa rushing toward me. "I heard you yelling down the street when we pulled up to our house," she says.

"I ran after you, but. . ." I collapse in my dear friend's arms.

Minutes later, a siren. A patrol car pulls up. "Jim, over here," calls Lorissa.

I can't speak, I'm so shaken. "Here," says Lorissa to me. "Sit on this log."

"What happened?" asks Jim.

I try to explain everything from the time Guru showed up with the gun until Joel ran off the cliff. "It's over there," I point to the rag and gun. "I never touched it. I'm guessing you'll find Joel Whyrll's DNA on it and that its bullets match the bullet removed in Scott's surgery."

Thorp picks up the rag and gun, takes a look at it, and mutters, "Hmmmm... a Glock." He walks back toward his patrol car to put the rag and gun in an evidence bag.

"Can Meaghan come home?" asks Lorissa. "She's cold and wet and shaking."

"I'll talk to you in the morning. Right now, we need to cordon off this area, do a search and rescue for his body." He keeps talking, but his voice sounds far away—something about I need to make a statement, get fingerprinted. It doesn't sink in. I hang on to Lorissa as we stumble home.

Nicole and Torrie have vanished. Their car is gone. What happened to them? At this moment, I don't even care.

48
Meaghan Farren

Two weeks later, I Skype Lorissa from Corey and Anastasia's spare bedroom in La Serena. I'm sitting on the white bedspread with my laptop on my legs. Lorissa's eyes look ink black on the computer screen, her cheeks no longer gray. I sense serenity, even over the Internet.

"It turns out," she says, "Brandon had given Nicole the Smith and Wesson he'd bought at the pawnshop so she could shoot Scott—so she'd do his dirty work, just like we suspected. If she shot Scott, she'd get rid of the guy who'd dumped her, and Brandon would be rid of the guy who stole his wife."

Yeah, right. As if Scott had "stolen" me.

"Nicole carried the gun in her purse for weeks," Lorissa continues, "but when it came down to the wire, she just couldn't do it. She was truly, madly in love with that cute guy who worked for her, which Joel had figured out." I picture Scott's sweet face, his glistening green eyes and the dimple in his chin all reflecting in the candlelight the night he'd cooked me that tasty fettuccine. The most romantic night of my life, until Brandon showed up.

Lorissa explained that the day of the shooting, Joel dropped Torrie off at Jasmine's, raced in the pharmacy back door, and shot Scott with the Glock, right in front of Nicole, sending her into shock. That's when she'd lifted Brandon's gun out of her purse and raised it to her head. Lorissa told me that Nicole was really going to kill herself.

"She was? It wasn't just a stunt? Your son saved Nicole's life, and in repayment, she was going to send him to jail?"

"Exactly."

I still didn't understand why she made up that story about Scott stealing drugs and dealing drugs to Connor. Why she planted those Roxies in Scott's truck.

"I guess," Lorissa mused, "she was going to accuse Crowley of stealing them, then prove his innocence, 'rescue him,' so to speak, and then he'd like her even more. More than you, anyway."

Weird. From the little Thorp said, Lorissa surmised that Nicole had pilfered so many Roxies off her own shelf, that was one of the reasons her business was failing. She never expected Joel to come in and shoot Scott. She truly did blank out. Didn't know what to think or say. "In the end, I think she just wanted to protect Joel, so she made up the whole story about Connor doing drugs with Scott."

We are both quiet. "I just don't know how to pick friends," Lorissa finally says.

My eyes avert the screen. I want to say, "Lorissa, I'm so, so sorry," but she knows I'm ashamed for how I acted in college— and she also knows I'd do it again to protect my dad. "Between your picking friends and my picking men," I say, "we're a fine pair." We laugh together. Actually laugh.

"What's going to happen with them?" I wonder out loud.

"Well, Joel is in jail, awaiting trial for attempted murder. Little Torrie is living with a cousin for now, while Nicole is in rehab. She'll lose her pharmacist license. I don't know what's going to happen, to tell the truth. We're going to visit Torrie next weekend, see how she's doing."

I'm struck by how the idyllic Whyrrl family with their neighborhood barbecues, their perfect gardens, the envy of people like me, has gone down in flames. Once again, I'm reminded not to judge people by their outside. "What's next for you guys?"

"Oh, Meaghan. For us, amazingly, life is good. Graham and Connor are poring over a map on the dining room table right now, planning for the big Seattle to Portland bike ride." She lowers her voice. "Connor doesn't realize what a great athlete Graham used to be—one of the best cross-country runners on his Ohio Wesleyan team. Remember? He'll get in shape in no time."

I do remember.

Lorissa resumes her regular voice. "And as we speak, Mackenzie's kicking the soccer ball with Rhys on the front lawn."

"Rhys plays soccer? He's always surprising us, isn't he?" I realize I've said "us," like me and Lorissa are an "us." I like that.

"Apparently he learned in juvie. He's actually quite good. A natural out there with Mackenzie."

"In juvie? Juvenile detention?"

"It's a long story, and I think I've heard only bits and pieces. Rhys will have to tell you himself when you're back."

True enough. I cough, a bit reluctant to ask. "So, Brandon—he's nowhere around?"

"Oh, Meaghan. He's around. Around in jail. Awaiting trial. Turns out he has some warrants." I'm taken aback. "After you left him in Northampton, it seems he got in several fights, assaulting one person so badly he lost an eye. Between what he did to you and Mackenzie, and now this other guy, he'll be locked away for a long while."

Okay, that *is* good news. "And what about you, Lorissa? How are you doing?"

She sighs. "I'm good, believe it or not, after all this. Graham promised not to accept a new promotion—at least not in the near future. Every promotion brings money, yes, but always more travel. I'd rather have him home than have more money."

"How does he feel about that?"

"It's his idea. The kids are going to be home for only a few more years before college, and then that crazy 'empty nesting.' He doesn't want to miss out."

I consider these changes. "But what about your work? Your singing? That was such a big deal for you."

"I was just scrolling down a list for singing gigs in Tacoma and Seattle. You know," she says, "I think I'm going to go back to jingles."

"Jingles?"

Lorissa explains to me that back when she and Graham lived in New York, she used to go to jingle houses. I laugh. "No, really! That's what they're called!" She'd get paid to sing little songs for commercials., like 'All State (Insurance) is best'. Songs in advertisements. Now she'd have jingles as a side gig, hook up with her singing friends, and stay in the field, more or less. "And no five-page confidentiality agreements!" she adds. Plus, she could do it in Tacoma and skip the long commute to Seattle.

"Still one toe in your career while Connor and Mackenzie finish high school?" I ask.

"Right." She nods as though satisfied, more content than during the entire time I lived on Wilkes Island.

"Enough about us Orondos. I miss you, Meaghan."

"That means so much to me." I drink in her words. "Being in La Serena, next to the ocean and the mountains, reminds me of Wilkes Island. It feels so right. Tourists are arriving now." My first day back, I had strolled down to the soft white sand beach, which only a few weeks ago I'd had to myself.

I tell her that I'm cleaning houses, for a while anyway; that I've put the word out, so I can start bookkeeping for the expats. I've already begun a Spanish class. "Most important, I'm meditating regularly again. I can't wait to go back to that shaman and have him tell me my auras are bright and I'm no longer depleted."

I can taste the salt air, even from Corey and Anastasia's hillside house. The sky is melding lavender and pink and gray. "I feel like this is where I belong. At least for now."

Neither of us speak. I wipe a tear from the corner of my eye. "You'll keep me posted about Scott?"

"Sure. I believe he'll be leaving the hospital and going to rehab in a few weeks."

It had been a hard decision to leave Wilkes Island, leave the Orondos and leave Scott, but it still felt right. I'd thought I loved Scott so much, but did I even know who he was? No, not at all, it turned out. But he had been kind to me when I needed it, and that I'll always appreciate.

I cry sometimes unexpectedly. It wasn't easy to leave, but I know it was the right decision. I need to start over without dwelling on Scott or Brandon or any man. I need to truly start fresh, and the little dose I'd had of La Serena before I returned to Washington had convinced me: this is the place I need to be.

Lorissa moves her head from the screen for a moment.

"Hey, Meaghan—just a sec."

The face of a teenage boy appears onscreen—bright teeth, a spark in his eyes. "Bye, Meaghan. Thanks again! You rock!"

"Hey, push over, Connor." Moments later a sweaty, red-faced girl, soccer ball in hand, comes into view. "Come back soon, Aunt Meaghan." By now I can't speak. I sniff and nod.

Next a burly guy with a half-shaved face and deep voice. "Hey," Rhys says and is gone.

I focus on the ray of sun lighting up the neon green pillows on the white bedspread, so bright and cheerful in the strong South American sunlight. "Talk to you later, Lorissa." "Soon," she says, and we end the call.

I inhale the beef roasting in the kitchen. "Dinner, Meaghan," Corey calls.

"Coming." Coming home.

The End

Acknowledgements

Writers may spend hours, days, years in solitude tapping on the keyboard, but without the support, encouragement, and the sometimes brutally honest feedback of early readers, we do not have a book. Five years in the making, *An Unfamiliar Guest* couldn't have been written without the initial critiques of Pat Strickland and Nadine Feldman. Many thanks to my loyal, loving, and frank writer's group: Arissa Rench, Julie Gardner, Kristine Forbes, and Ann Hedreen. More gratitude to the readers and experts I relied on over the years: Kevin Bailey, Jana Bourne, Carol Wissmann, Monica Rivituso Comas, Cheryl Ferguson Feeney, Mia Carroll, Sheila Blanchette, Pat Harrison, Heather Lazare, Pat Skiffington, Deborah Hope, Anjali Banerjee, Nick Murray, Police Chief Busey, Mari Nelson, Gwynn Rogers, Joan Steiger, Susan Corcoran, Colleen Hogan Taylor, Garry Squires, Shakti Sarkin, and Kris Fulsaas. Much appreciation extended to Julia Glass at the Southampton Writers Conference and Maria Semple at Hugo House, Seattle.

Thank you to Paul Murray who nudged me through the final stretch.

We hope you enjoyed *An Unfamiliar Guest*. If so, would you consider writing a comment in the review section at the bottom of the Amazon listing https://www.amazon.com/Unfamiliar-Guest-1-C-Murray-ebook/dp/B082QQKXCP ? No matter where you bought or borrowed the book, your comment is helpful and one of the best ways of saying thank you to independent authors.

E.C. (Elizabeth Corcoran) Murray lives on a small island in the Pacific Northwest. She was raised in Massachusetts and traveled to La Serena and Cochiquaz, Chile in 2014 with her husband and daughter. A shaman read their auras and declared them bright and healthy. She and her family love traveling the globe, but she's also content sitting on the couch writing the follow up novel to *An Unfamiliar Guest*.

Murray loves hearing from readers. You may contact her at truwryter@comcast.net or through the Websites www.ecmurray.com and www.writersconnection.org

You can follow her:

Instagram:
https://www.instagram.com/ecmurraywriter/

Twitter: https://twitter.com/WritersConnect3

Facebook:
https://www.facebook.com/elizabethcorcoranmurray

Thank you!